ZORAVAR

ZORAVAR

BOLLYWOOD SAGA 1

MAHARSH SHAH

HarperCollins *Publishers* India

First published in India by
HarperCollins *Publishers* in 2021
A-75, Sector 57, Noida, Uttar Pradesh 201301, India
www.harpercollins.co.in

2 4 6 8 10 9 7 5 3 1

P-ISBN: 978-93-5357-817-6
E-ISBN: 978-93-5357-818-3

Typeset in 11/14.1 Sabon LT Std
Manipal Technology Limited, Manipal

Printed and bound at
Replika Press Pvt. Ltd.

FSC
www.fsc.org
MIX
Paper from
responsible sources
FSC® C016779

This book is produced from independently certified FSC®
paper to ensure responsible forest management.

For my parents, Leena & Sanjiv.

On deathbed: *'I am in the film business, darling – I've already died a thousand times before.'*
– ANON

'There's no business, like show business.'
– Irving Berlin

November 2016
MUMBAI, INDIA

The window panes at the swanky South Bombay hospital were rumoured to be made of strong, soundproof glass, supposedly installed in 1982 after Amitabh Bachchan was admitted there, having been injured on the sets of Manmohan Desai's Coolie. *This was apparently done since so many fans and well-wishers had camped outside the hospital.*

Whether this was true or not, even soundproof glass couldn't keep the noise outside from filtering through today.

The small compound outside was packed with the fancy cars that had driven the who's who of the Mumbai film fraternity to the hospital. The biggest movie stars, producers and directors of Bollywood stood gathered there together, a sea of white clothes, dark glasses and delicate perfumes.

Inside, the room where the body lay felt like a mausoleum. Around the bed stood the cluster of people one generally calls family – siblings and children, their spouses, and a mix of nieces, nephews and extended relatives.

But no tears were being shed. Instead, everyone stood with bated breath, waiting.

A few moments later, the lawyer entered and began to read out the last wishes of the departed. Unbeknownst to them, the radio and TV channels had begun buzzing as the head of the state came on air to make an announcement.

PART I

Opening Credits

1

The silence that enveloped the dark space was broken only by the hurried scrubbing of the floor, accompanied by the periodic splash of a giant broom being plunged into a large bucket of water. Long before the Excel Corp projector had stopped whirring post a rather lengthy end-credit sequence, 'THE END' flashing on the silver screen had been enough for everyone to leave the stalls of Apsara Talkies in Amritsar.

Everyone, but him.

He never vacated his seat till the end credits had finished rolling. He had read that in Europe and America, the audience often stayed behind, to pay respect to every single person who had toiled in the making of the movie. He loved that the firangs had so much tehzeeb when it came to the moving pictures and arts.

Staying back also fed his already comprehensive knowledge of the movies and helped him familiarize himself with the names of people who worked to make them, no matter how obscure their scope of work or designation. It was a private thrill when he recognized the name of a technician who had also worked on another movie he had watched.

It was a month after India gained Independence, and the eighteen-year-old Zoravar had been excited about the prospect of watching this new talkie that the tabloids had been talking about endlessly, especially after he'd read the latest issue of a Bombay tabloid he had stolen from the scrap dealer. 'Famous Films' *Phool*, running to packed houses even after its re- release at Roxy theatre, is a veritable triumph', an article had stated. *Phool* was headlined by the superstar Suraiya, his favourite actress. Her pictures, which he often cut from newspapers and magazines, were responsible for fanning his raging hormones.

Though starring a famous actor, this film had been directed by a relatively new and unknown bloke, a certain K. Asif. The reviews had been rather kind to the man, calling him 'a new director to look out for, despite being one who relies on gimmicks over storytelling'. It helped that the movie had been written by Kamal Amrohi, an established dialogue writer and toast of the season. If the trade news section in *Film India* was to be believed, it seemed like every studio in Bombay wanted to hire Amrohi.

He took out the bulging tin of cigarettes from his trouser pocket and tapped its head before pulling out a filter-less Panama, cursing under his breath as he realized that it was the last one. He struck the Ship matchsticks to light the cigarette, and the flame lit up his face momentarily, accentuating his hazel eyes and light complexion. The cigarette hanging between his lips, he threw the empty tin on the ground.

The sound stopped the old usher who was scrubbing the floor in his tracks. He dropped his broom and looked up, realizing that someone was still in the stalls.

'Ae boy! What are you still doing here? Don't you see the movie has ended?' he called out.

The boy got up slowly; the way he moved made it seem like his every step, every action was deliberate. He made his way towards the exit at a languid, almost dramatic pace, left hand in his trouser pocket, right hand armed with the cigarette. He was wearing a blue bush shirt and ultra-tight grey pants that ended just a bit short of his ankles, clearly intended to resemble the way they were wearing pants in Italy in those days.

'Ae! You are not walking in Hazuri Bagh, you ruffian! Who do you think you are? Get out now!'

The boy stopped and turned around to look at the old man. He drew deeply on the Panama and blew smoke towards the usher, a slight smile on his face. Something about the expression seemed to disturb the usher, and he looked down at the floor again, mumbling to himself.

The boy took another puff and, spitting out some loose tobacco swirling in his mouth, said, 'My name is Zoravar. And I may be a lot of things, but I'm not a ruffian.'

His voice was deep, and without meaning to, the usher looked up again, responding to what was probably the most authoritative baritone he had heard in his life.

'Someday, you will still be bent over the floors, scrubbing them and collecting empty cigarette tins. But when you look up at the screen, it will be me you see there,' continued Zoravar.

There was a moment's silence, and then the usher laughed out loud. 'You? *You* will be an actor?' he mocked. 'Have you even been to Bombay?'

The question pierced Zoravar like a poisonous arrow. With a sharp move, he stubbed the cigarette and threw it on the ground. Then, turning on his heels, he walked out of the cinema hall, exhaling the last of the smoke from his nostrils in the cold night like a dragon.

Zoravar was not the least bit surprised by the usher's reaction to him. The last time he was at this theatre, he had almost been arrested for sneaking into the hall without a ticket. He had been trying to watch a recently re-released *Tadbir* for the fifteenth time. After all, *The Pioneer* had called it the highest grossing film of the year. It starred the child actor Shashiraj, Prithviraj Kapoor's son and the younger brother of the up and coming actor Raj Kapoor, once a child actor himself.

Fortunately, this time Zoravar had been able to pick the wallet of an unassuming movie-goer, and so actually paid for his ticket, as well as bought himself a tin of his favourite cigarettes and a bottle of Coca-Cola. He had hoped to buy some sheng chana as well, but the money had run out.

There was nothing Zoravar loved more in the world than the movies. His father, Sardar Attar Singh Cheema, was barely being able to make ends meet as the cook and owner of a meagre samosa-chholley-tikki stall at the Phagwara Railway Station. Bringing up five children was hard, and his wife was expecting their sixth child, two years after giving birth to a son they had named Amandeep, owing to the fact that he was born on the day the Second World War had officially ended. Amandeep had brought immense happiness to Zoravar, and he doted on him more than on any of his other siblings.

Apart from the movies, Zoravar only really loved his mother, Bibi Benazira. It was often said that she had been the most beautiful girl in all of the North-Western province of Afghanistan, where she was from. Her family had been driven out of their home due to a feud with the most feared family in the Khyber. Her father, Mirwaiz Khan Khattak, had bought his whole family a passage to Lahore, in exchange for his own life. He could have easily escaped with his family and got lost on the streets of Lahore, but he believed that a Pashtun always keeps his word. Legend had it that Mirwaiz Khan was tied to two horses, and the horses were made to gallop in opposite directions till his body split into two. His remains were then left in the desert for the vultures to devour.

Zoravar knew very little about his mother's homeland. He did know that a prominent film writer had once called Afghanistan the Sicily of the East, and that was the description that resonated with Zoravar, even though he had no idea what Sicily was really like. Everything he knew, all the knowledge he had, came entirely from watching movies, and when he was not watching them, he was reading and thinking about them.

The fatherless Bibi Benazira had lived with her mother and three siblings in the Afghan camps in Lahore. It was here that Sardar Attar Singh Cheema met and fell in love with her. It was a whirlwind romance that ended in her pregnancy, and the couple eloped when Benazira's mother found out about her daughter's illicit affair with a turbaned Sikh man.

Nine months later, Zoravar was born.

Bibi Benazira took a month-old Zoravar to her mother, who displayed nothing but scorn towards the newborn.

'Sons are born out of duty. Bastards are born out of sin,' she said.

That was the last time Bibi saw her mother's face. A couple of years later, another son was born to Bibi and Sardar Cheema, and they named him Bir Bahadur. Then came twins in the form of Zohra and Zehra, and finally, fifteen years after Zoravar's birth, Amandeep was born.

As Zoravar walked away from the theatre and towards the bus stop, rubbing his hands furiously against the harsh cold, he hummed a tune from *Phool*. In his head, he was on the screen – the hero, the matinee idol that people would admire and envy.

Zoravar had decided at a very early age that his future lay in the movies. He knew he had some of what was needed already. He knew it from the way women stared at him when he passed them, how even men couldn't help but give him a second, lingering look. He knew he could become a hero like Saigal, and act as well as Ashok Kumar. After all, he had acted in a few plays and had an eidetic memory when it came to remembering lines. English as a language came naturally to him – he loved the subject in school and he was fluent in it, as in Hindi and Urdu, apart from Punjabi.

In Zoravar's mind, his future was already decided. All he needed to do was get to Bombay. And tell his parents about his plan. He knew that they would be far from supportive. He had failed his Matriculation examinations and had never attempted them again, and now did nothing but eat, drink and sleep movies. To his father, he was a nithalla, a good-for-nothing. Zoravar tried to not care, especially after he read an article in *Film Land* about how Motilal, his idol, supposedly doled out advice to all and sundry about the need for artistes to be thick skinned. From that day, Zoravar had made it a point to try and stop himself from caring about what anyone thought of him, even his own father.

2

As Zoravar got off the bus in Phagwara, he thought about how much he hated the place. There were no cinema halls here, and he had to take the bus all the way to Amritsar to devour movies at his favourite Apsara Talkies. He also missed Lahore – its cinema halls, in particular. Over the last few months, the life that his family had lived for so long had changed forever. Merely weeks before the Partition, his father had made the decision to abandon Lahore for Phagwara, a city that was going to be on the Indian side as per the haphazardly divided regions. Sardar Cheema had a distant paternal cousin there, and therefore, it was the only place he could migrate to where he'd have some help. For days before the move, the family had lived in fear, riddled with anxiety because of the stories that they had heard about the violence during the train journeys.

On the day they were to leave, Sardar Attar Singh Cheema had shaved his beard and cut his hair, before letting go of the turban that had been his pride, after hearing about the atrocities that were being committed against Sikhs. The family split themselves up in groups, and Benazira along with their daughters travelled in hijabs while the men travelled as Hindus. His father had told them that depending on the religion of the mob, if they were to encounter one, at least one set of the family would be safe. On reaching Lahore station, they found the compartments overflowing and had to sit on top of the train with countless other people. Halfway through their journey, a mob entered the train. Zoravar saw angry men asking male passengers to drop their trousers and dhotis, to check which faith they belonged to. The compartment had rung with cries and screams, and there was utter pandemonium as some people atop the train even jumped off to try and flee the violence that was beginning to ensue. Zoravar wet himself as he saw the mob douse the bogey right below them with kerosene. But before the man struck a match, the police arrived. There were gunshots fired, and the cops managed to overpower the mob.

Just before it was about to pull into Phagwara, the train was stopped by another group of rioters, albeit a smaller one than before, and Sardar Cheema and his family played dead, along with the other travellers, to outwit them. Zoravar, even in his panicky state, saw it like a role he was enacting and played the character to the hilt, even controlling his breathing. Once again, his family and he were spared a violent end that befell several others.

They finally reached Phagwara shaken but unharmed, and settled down in a small brick house, which came with an adjoining farm. Sardar Cheema had purchased it from a Muslim family that had made the decision to move to Lahore. The deal had been struck on his behalf by his cousin, but in return, the man had taken whatever little ancestral gold Zoravar's father possessed as payment.

Zoravar was appalled by the rank poverty he saw around him in Phagwara, and it hardened his resolve to escape to Bombay – the city of dreams.

The morning after he returned from Amritsar, with the scenes from *Phool* still on his mind, Zoravar spent an eternity studying himself in the only mirror in the house. Then, he set off to get a shave at Aziz's small parlour in the centre of the village. Despite his limited cash flow, Zoravar always managed to look tip-top. He ran a tab with the local barber and just about managed to pay him at the end of every month, mainly by stealing from his father's wallet or selling a household item.

Zoravar was being lathered by Aziz in his favourite Burma-shave cream when he heard a muffled cry from the next room in the barbershop, but when he asked Aziz about it, the man looked nervous and uncomfortable, and quickly changed the subject. Curious, Zoravar requested Aziz to buy him a Panama.

'Please, Aziz. There's no way I can go myself. I can't be seen in public like this,' he said, pointing at his lathered stubble. 'It's okay for commoners, but not for the likes of me.' He grinned to show that he was kidding, and Aziz, despite feeling irked, found himself nodding. Putting down his brush reluctantly, he took the money from Zoravar and left to get the impudent boy his cigarette.

Once Aziz was well out of the shop, Zoravar tiptoed into the adjacent room and saw a middle-aged man sitting there with his back to the door, being attended to by a younger man standing beside him. Even from the back, Zoravar could see that the older man's white kurta was stained with blood. Despite himself, he drew closer to the duo, who heard his footsteps and turned to him, startled. Zoravar noticed that fresh blood was gushing from an open wound on the older man's shoulder, and before him, two bullets lay on a bloody tray, along with other medical instruments.

Before anyone could say anything, Aziz came rushing into the room. 'You scoundrel, how dare you ...' he shouted at Zoravar who, realizing that he'd landed himself in grave danger, instinctively rushed forward and picked up a knife that was lying on the table. He held it up and gestured towards the injured man with it.

'What the hell is going on here, Aziz?' he asked the barber. 'Running a mini- hospital, are you?' But before Aziz could reply, Zoravar was distracted by a cough from the bleeding man; he turned to look at him again. This time, something about the man's face caught his attention. It was familiar, almost like Zoravar had seen it very recently.

'Who are you?' he asked, but the older man sat still, silent. Something clicked inside Zoravar's brain, and he remembered where he'd seen the face before. On a poster, which announced a bounty of five hundred and one rupees on the man's head – enough to get someone to Bombay, should they want to go.

Zoravar couldn't believe that he was standing before the feared brigand Sultana. One of the most feared thuggees in the country, wanted, dead or alive by the authorities. They were prepared to pay for it, and Zoravar realized that the reward could be the kickstart he needed in life. He could barely believe this magnificent stroke of luck.

He cautiously nudged Sultana to a standing position, placing the knife flat against his throat. 'If you both try any tricks,' he said to the two other men in the room, 'I will split open this thug. Remember the bounty for him says dead or alive.' As soon as he uttered those words, the two men laughed. Even Sultana let out a raspy guffaw.

'Money? It is *money* you seek, you nincompoop?' the man with Sultana said.

'If you let me go, I will give you a lot more than the government ever can,' Sultana said. He gave a slight nod to his accomplice, and Zoravar pressed the knife harder against Sultana's neck, growing more anxious by the minute.

After a beat, the accomplice moved forward and put his hands in his pockets. Before Zoravar could shout out a warning to him, the man pulled out a few notes and some gold coins and tossed them on the table before Zoravar. There was enough there to easily be more valuable than the bounty on Sultana's head.

'I can give you a lot more of that. Let me go,' Sultana said with a quiet, menacing authority in his voice. Mesmerized by the riches before him, Zoravar loosened his grip on the knife and moved towards the table. But before he could reach it, he was intercepted by Sultana who, even in his injured state, managed to push the young man aside swiftly, and like a skilled warrior, snatched the knife Zoravar held. He threw it to his accomplice, who moved like lightning and held Zoravar by the neck, rendering him immobile. Zoravar found that the knife was now pressed against his own throat. He felt it press closer, almost cutting his skin, when Sultana shouted.

'No, Pasha! Don't kill him. The boy's a fool, but he's brave. I see passion in his eyes. He will do anything to pursue his dream. I need such people. I have use for them,' he said to his accomplice. 'Though this wretch does deserves a punishment for what he's done.' And then, he gave a slight nod to Pasha, who promptly dragged the knife across Zoravar's face, slitting his cheek open.

'Not my face, not my face!' Zoravar screamed. And them before he could utter another word, Pasha's heavy hand landed like a hammer on his head and everything went black.

3

Zoravar woke up with a start and realized that his hands and legs were tied, and his mouth was gagged. There was complete darkness around him, and he had no idea where he was. What he did know was that his face had been scarred forever by this despicable dacoit. He immediately felt the urge to touch his wound to examine the damage.

Zoravar had never felt this helpless in his entire life. Panic rose within him, and his stomach churned. His legs had been tied to some sort of a contraption. He could smell the faint notes of Jannat Ul Firdaus, which he recognized immediately since it was the ittar that Yakub, one of his favourite actors, supposedly preferred, as per the Hindi movie industry's rumour mills. As soon as Zoravar had read a gossip column that claimed this, he'd gone scouring the streets of Ittar Bazaar till he found the fragrance he was looking for. A small vial had cost him a full fifteen annas, but vicariously feeling like Yakub's character of the bad son in Mehboob Khan's *Aurat* was priceless.

Suddenly, someone switched on a bulb and light flooded the room, blinding Zoravar. Squinting painfully, he waited till the world came back into focus. Standing in front of him was Sultana himself, smiling with a beedi between his lips, his teeth stained and yellow. His accomplice, Pasha, was there too, chopping a large betel nut. Aziz, the barber, was slumped in one corner of the room, staring straight at Zoravar.

Sultana and Pasha came closer, and the older man pulled the gag out of Zoravar's mouth. But just as Zoravar began to speak, the thuggee violently stuffed the cloth back in. 'You will speak only when you are asked to speak. Understood?' he barked. Zoravar nodded in response.

Sultana pulled the gag out again, and just as he did, Zoravar felt a prick on his skin.

'You'll feel much better, now that you have been given the needle,' Pasha said, grinning. 'Sultana has been generous enough to give you a dose of the medicine that is specially administered to him by the firang doctor. It comes from London – this cocaine. A popular medicine,' Pasha continued. 'Sultana has taken a real shine to you. I don't know if it's your handsome face or the shape of your butt, but there is something about you, or you'd definitely be dead.'

Sultana drew back and spoke now. 'Look boy, you can either let me kill you or you can join my troop.' He grinned menacingly. 'Aziz has told me that your family does not have much of an opinion of you. And when they found out that you raided poor Aziz's shop and practically beat up the poor barber to a pulp, *and* are on the run with stolen money to Bombay, your father almost collapsed at the police station. Aziz did his duty as a good citizen by corroborating all this. Your poor mother was horrified.' As Sultana spoke, Zoravar felt the world around him grow dark again. He glanced at Aziz, and noticed now that the man's face was badly bruised, and both his hands looked like they were broken. He was writhing in pain, groaning inaudibly.

Zoravar realized that he had been framed. His life would never be the same again. He stared at the man before him. Sultana was rubbing his hands, and Zoravar observed that his knuckles were wounded and bloody, probably from the beating he had administered to Aziz.

'Look, I am in need, constantly, of people like you,' Sultana said drily. 'Detached and motivated. I promise you all the riches in the world if you join me.' He didn't add it, but his voice implied – *after all, what choice do you have?*

Zoravar heard the unspoken words and knew them to be true. He knew he had no home to go back to, and which studio in Bombay would hire an actor with a scarred face?

There was no reason to think more. He nodded.

Zoravar rode behind Pasha, and Sultana led the way on the black stallion he had fondly named Porus. For the first time in his life, Zoravar saw a different landscape emerge around him. So far, he had never stepped out of Lahore or Phagwara, save for Amritsar, which he'd visited only to go to Darbar Sahib or to watch movies. He had only seen Bombay and other exotic places in the innumerable movies he consumed.

He looked around, spellbound.

They would ride through the better part of the day and find shelter by sunset. Sultana and Pasha were very familiar with the landscape, locating the pit-stops for the night easily, and were adept at finding rivulets to fill their leather pouches with water. They also knew of the best places to hunt deer, blackbuck and rabbit. They'd eat what they hunted, cooked or raw, and fall sleep soundly in their hide-outs. Only Zoravar felt uncomfortable and uneasy, and often lay awake, tossing and turning on the ground.

Pasha, who had the habit of doling out life lessons to the younger man, said to Zoravar, 'If you do anything continuously for a long enough time, you will eventually get used to it.' But Zoravar wasn't used to his hard bed yet.

After riding for hours, they had stopped near a small, dark valley. Looking at the unfamiliar landscape, Zoravar turned to Sultana.

'Where are we headed?' he asked.

Sultana was silent for a moment and then said, 'Home.'

Zoravar felt himself beginning to lose patience.

'Where and how far is home?'

But there was no answer. The men rode on.

The market square was teeming with traders and shoppers. As they walked, Zoravar caught a glimpse of a movie poster and saw the familiar face of Suraiya.

Anmol Ghadi, the poster proclaimed in large letters. The director was Mehboob Khan, and the movie also starred Noor Jehan and the handsome Surendra, the man who had been touted as K.L. Saigal's greatest rival. The story went that Mehboob Khan had been snubbed by Saigal, so he had vowed to handpick an actor and singer he would make more popular than Saigal.

Admirers of these actors were divided into two rival camps, and Zoravar belonged firmly to Saigal's. He made it a point to almost never watch Surendra's films. But despite his loyalty to Saigal, Zoravar made a mental note to watch *Anmol Ghadi*. After all, it starred Suraiya, and his loyalty to her was more important than his support for Saigal.

Zoravar's thoughts were interrupted by the piercing screech of a sharp whistle cutting through the din of the market. He turned his face in the direction of the sound and saw Sultana standing near the newly constructed

Jaisalmer police station. The trio walked towards it after covering their faces with cloth and took a sharp left to a nondescript door that stood right next to it. A uniformed police officer, wearing a rather large turban on his head, smiled and waved at them. When Pasha opened the door, a dark abyss stared back. Sultana went in first, and it looked like he had disappeared, swallowed by the darkness. Pasha then caught Zoravar's hand and directed it in the dark. 'Do you feel the staircase?' Zoravar felt a cold metal object touch his palm. 'Hold it and climb down.' Zoravar felt anxious as he stepped down into the dark. With each step he took, the darkness grew deeper, till he suddenly hear a loud bang.

It seemed like the entrance had been bolted shut.

What he saw when he entered the basement took Zoravar by surprise. Lit with flames contained in small earthen pots, the place was full of several dhoti-clad men, all at work. The place stank of sweat, beedi smoke and roasted betel nut. There was also an odour of some sort of chemicals that hung in the air. Zoravar felt dizzy. The scene around him looked straight out of one Hollywood's World War II movies that had become extremely popular in America. That thought took Zoravar back to his beloved Apsara Talkies and the posh Odeon that played those excessively patriotic and romantic American pictures.

'You seem quite impressed,' Pasha said, amused. Zoravar nodded. 'What is this place?' he asked. Pasha let out an exaggerated laugh.

'This is our fiefdom. It is where we make the weapons. And the funding for it used to come from the British, in exchange for information against the revolutionaries. And now we continue to furnish others with the same needs in exchange for their support.'

'So, what do you think of our little kingdom?' Sultana asked Zoravar.

'Are you an agent and a thug?' Zoravar asked in return.

With a half-smile, Sultana said, 'In war, what is the difference between the two?'

Zoravar looked around him, taking in the revolvers, bullets and other weapons he did not recognize.

'An entrepreneur makes his own goods, Bapu had said. You see, we took him seriously,' Sultana laughed, and Pasha joined him. 'Our operations currently run across the entire northern belt of the country. Some day, we will have conquered the rest of the land, including Bombay.'

The last word hit Zoravar in the chest and his dreams, buried so long, came rushing back.

'When do you think you'll be able to expand to

Bombay?' he asked, hope rising in him in waves.

'Soon' was the only word that came out of Sultana's mouth.

Months passed like days. Zoravar had by now become adept at horse-riding as well as sword-fighting. He had also taken shooting lessons and knew how to dismantle a firearm faster than anyone in the crew. These were things that came naturally to him. He attributed it to the influence of the numerous action pictures he had devoured.

They ransacked the homes of the rich lalas and the firang officers, who hadn't yet left the country. Zoravar had gained the trust and confidence of Sultana during one such operation, where he had saved the older man's life. He was now one of the core members of the band, and commanded respect. Despite now being almost entirely immersed in the life of crime, Zoravar somehow managed to keep in touch with the world of Bombay cinema. He read reviews of films released and kept abreast of all the new and upcoming actors.

The other constant in his life was the yearning he felt for his family, especially his mother. He felt guilty about the fact that he'd let her believe that he was a criminal on the run, though the irony of how he'd ended up becoming exactly that since then didn't escape him. He had tried, multiple times, to get in touch with her and often thought of writing to her, but so far, it had always been too dangerous for him, as well as her.

Fate finally gave him a chance when Pasha had to deliver a consignment of weapons to Delhi. Zoravar begged him to take a handwritten letter to Phagwara to his parents. Pasha completely dismissed the idea at first, but eventually agreed to the detour.

When Pasha returned, it was with the news that his mother's sixth pregnancy had ended in a miscarriage. He did say that he had managed to give her Zoravar's letter. He had even brought back with him her reply. In her letter, Bibi wrote that she miscarried because she'd been unable to handle the embarrassment that had followed Zoravar's disappearance. The letter went on to say that the family was beginning to get used to life in Phagwara and that Zoravar's siblings missed him dearly. Only his father had not enquired about him at all.

Pasha had been in a foul mood ever since his return from Delhi. Zoravar, one day while having lunch with him and Sultana, who was in an even more foul mood, asked them what was bothering them. Pasha revealed to Zoravar that his Delhi trip was to deliver a consignment of European revolvers, but when he had reached the assigned place in Delhi, the people he was supposed to meet never showed up.

Sultana, who was eating silently, finally spoke, 'These no-shows are getting more frequent. I believe we need to focus more on the Italian guns. Maybe even manufacture knock-offs of the Beretta M1934s which I hear are in high demand. We could make our version of it.'

It was a relatively cold day on the last day of January 1948, when the newspaper headline screamed that

Mohandas Karamchand Gandhi had been assassinated. A lot was written about his assassin, but what resonated most with Zoravar was the fact that he had been shot by a Beretta M1934, and that apparently the weapon had been procured from Gwalior. When he passed on the newspaper to Sultana, he merely glanced at the article and grunted before continuing to munch on the chicken leg. Zoravar never broached the topic with him again.

4

It was a muggy evening, and the stars were beginning to dot the vast sky above the infinite Thar desert in Rajasthan. A man in a hooded figure, a lantern in his hand, bent down and put his ears to the tracks. He then looked up and shouted, 'She's coming, the train's here!' A horde of men emerged from the shadows, their faces concealed with cloth. All of them had sickles in their hands. They got to work immediately and started the tedious process of undoing the tracks. The task complete, they disappeared into the shadows as the first whistle was heard. As the train approached the broken part of the track, it derailed and the desert rang with the sound of the accident. The masked men emerged once again and began to ransack the bogies. The initial screams of fear from the passengers were muffled after the first bullet was fired from the Gurkha Rifles the men had stolen from the videshi rifle factory.

Methodically and carefully, they collected the jewels from the women in the first-class bogie and relieved the men of their watches and cash. Outside, the man with the lantern kept watch. After several minutes, the band came rushing out and dumped the loot in a huge drum. Half of them had already started repairing the tracks. A few remained inside the bogie, their guns pointed at the passengers. When the track was fixed, they untied the driver and let the train go, jumping out themselves at the last minute.

Later, on reaching their hide-out and unpacking their loot, they realized that they had made the killing of a lifetime.

'This is going to be recorded as the first major crime in the history of independent India,' their leader Sultana proclaimed. He then turned to the man with the lantern. 'You haven't removed your shawl yet? Come, let us go drink and make merry! The finest whores of the Rajputana await us.' The man put down his lantern and removed the shawl that was masking his body and face. The desert sun had darkened his skin, and made his face even more rugged and charming.

'Yes, let's go,' Zoravar said in a grim baritone as his fingers felt the scar that ran down below his cheeks.

The train robbery successful, Zoravar was back on his horse, which he had named Kundan after K.L. Saigal. Sultana and Pasha rode ahead, leading the men to a place called Balyee Bawar.

'Tonight, the finest whores await us, my dear men!' Sultana shouted as the men cheered him on. He stuffed his hands into one of the sacks filled with the freshly minted Government of India notes and threw them in the air.

Zoravar had heard a lot about this plaza of pleasure that they were headed to. As they drew closer to it, the sound of ghazals and thumris filled the air and Zoravar could smell alcohol fumes, mixed with the finest ittar.

A little before they entered the area, Pasha excused himself and disappeared into a building that had an arched ceiling. The others rode on, and finally stopped in front of a nondescript building called Lutf Mahal.

Zoravar watched as Sultana dismount and walked towards him. 'Don't go by the looks of this place, son. Incredible inner beauty is often found inside the most ordinary of exteriors,' the older man whispered.

Zoravar tied Kundan in the poorly kept horse-stand and walked up to the house with Sultana and the other men. They knocked on the faded wooden door and after a few seconds, the door opened, and he was surprised by the face that greeted them. A pale, clean-shaven man with brightly painted red lips stood before them. He was fairer than the firangs, and even the green veins on his slender neck were visible. He was dressed in a beige kurta and a white pathani.

Zoravar watched with faint amusement as the man threw his arms around Sultana and spoke in accented Hindi.

'My most precious is here,' he said. In the weak light of the evening, Zoravar thought he saw sindoor in the parting of the man's hair. Sultana kissed the man's forehead and turned towards Zoravar. 'What are you staring at? Go on inside with the rest of them and pick whoever and how many ever you want.'

Zoravar nodded and entered the establishment, leaving the lovers to continue their reunion. The others had already disappeared inside, and he found himself alone in a small corridor that led to another door. The brief veranda was dimly lit by small flickering candles. He pushed the small door, and it opened into a huge room, which was in complete contrast to the outside. The flooring was white marble, the walls were mauve and four massive white pillars rose from floor to ceiling. There were green and red dye- papers rolled around the candle stands, giving the room a dim and deeply surreal ambience. The set-up reminded Zoravar of K.L. Saigal's *Devdas*.

His attention was then caught by the attractively dressed ladies in the room. Some were standing around, speaking to each other other as they smoked beedis, others were gyrating to the music, smiling seductively and biting their lips. As he entered, all of them had turned to stare at him, and he felt hot under their gaze.

A tall and handsome woman, older than the others, walked over to Zoravar.

'I am Dilnawaz Aapa. I run this place,' she said. 'Sultana has told me to give you the most special experience.' She gestured to the waiting women and chuckled. 'Take your pick. You can have one, or two, or all of them.' Zoravar felt nervous and unsure. This wasn't his first time at a brother –he'd accompanied the gang to several of them in the last year, but had refrained from indulging himself. And something about this place promised a different experience. There was a kind of magic in the air that was full of promise.

Zoravar found himself remembering the time he had first experienced the touch of a woman. He had held hands with his school sweetheart in the darkness of a cinema hall. They had sneaked out to watch Vijay Bhatt's masterpiece *Ram Rajya*. It was the only film Bapu had ever watched in his life and everybody wanted to watch it after he spoke of it. But their relationship had been limited to holding hands. Zoravar felt young and foolish. He wished that he wasn't so inexperienced.

'Do you want a man? We could arrange that too,' the matriarch asked him seriously. Feeling his cheeks burn, Zoravar shook his head awkwardly and walked up to a group of girls in one corner of the room. As he looked at them shyly, they stared back, their eyes teasing him, and after a pause, he turned to the older woman and, pointing at the girl who caught his eye, said, 'Her.'

'You have chosen well, Janaab. She is going to make you very happy; she even sings very well. Don't you, Naseema?' Dilnawaz Aapa asked as she put the betel nuts in the paan leaf. There was a slight pause before

Naseema nodded. Then she took Zoravar's hand, and he found that her touch thrilled him.

He felt only slightly nervous as Naseema led him out of the large room and towards the staircase, into the dark and exciting unknown.

5

As he followed her up the stairs, Zoravar stared at Naseema – at her hair, hips and the shape of her legs. Her hands were dark with mehndi, and her jhumkas swayed as she walked. He could smell the soft scent of rose on her, some kind of sweet perfume. Her hair was long and luscious, and neatly combed. They reached the end of a long corridor and she stopped at a door. Removing a long key that had been tucked in her waistband, she unlocked it and they stepped inside a dimly lit room, chilly from the mild winter breeze wafting in through frilly white curtains. In one corner of the room, there was a bathtub full of water, with rose petals floating in it. As they entered, Naseema turned and Zoravar smiled, anticipating that she was going to say something. But she simply walked to the door and bolted it. Zoravar grimaced, embarrassed.

Silently, and almost mechanically, she began to remove his clothes, one item at a time. Then, she looked at him and asked him to undo the thin strings of her kurta. He did as instructed, his fingers suddenly clumsy. Slowly, her kurta dropped to her waist. She then guided his hands to the strings that held up her long salwar. He pulled at them and soon, she was completely naked and only inches away from him. She held his hand and led him to the bath. The water was hot and Zoravar let out a small moan of pleasure as he entered it. Naseema giggled and entered the bath herself. Inside, she sat behind him and massaged his shoulders with her soft hands. Slowly, she ran them over his body, cleaning it with fragrant salts. When she reached his penis, she gently took it in her hand and washed it. Although embarrassed, Zoravar felt his erection became stiffer. But nervous and unsure of what to do, he suddenly felt like he could take it no more and stood up, stepping out of the bath. As he dried himself and began to rummage for his clothes, Naseema laughed.

'Are you going to leave me unsatisfied?' she asked.

When he continued wearing his clothes, not responding to her, Naseema got up and walked close to him, holding him tenderly. As she did, he stopped moving. She walked him to the bed. He lay back, and she climbed over him, placing herself on top of him. As he entered her, he saw her face properly for the first time. It was the most beautiful face he had ever seen.

Naseema had big, brown kohl-lined eyes, an aquiline nose with a deep dimple on her chin. Zoravar felt like he was experiencing complete bliss as she began to increase her speed and started to moan, both her hands kneading his chest. He could not take his eyes off her as he came. Mere seconds later, Naseema climbed off him and went to the bathtub to clean off, once again almost mechanical in her movements.

'Water and *beedis* are kept on the table next to you and you can sleep here for a while if you want,' she said and left the room, leaving a naked and stunned Zoravar behind.

He changed and walked out of the room, his heart aching for Naseema. He had never felt like this about anyone before.

As he stepped out of the building and into the darkness of the night, Sultana was already waiting for him next to his horse, smoking a beedi.

'You take that long? Quite a man you must be.' The older man laughed.

'No, nothing like that,' Zoravar said absent-mindedly, Naseema still on his mind. As he prepared to mount his own horse, he missed the pedal and almost slipped. Just then, the air rang with the sound of a gun being fired, a sound Zoravar knew well by now. He watched Sultana fall from his horse and hit the ground. He ran to help the older man and saw that he'd been shot in the eye.

Another bullet whizzed past Zoravar's left ear, grazing the top of it. There was no time for him to even react as another bullet hit his shoulder blade. He shouted in pain and crawled on the ground, his hand instinctively moving to his waistband, where his gun was always holstered. Always, except now. Panic ensued, his mind reaching into the recent memory of the time he had removed his waistband in the room with Naseema. Horror rose within him as he realized that he must have forgotten the gun when he redressed. He would have to go back inside the harem, and just as he tried to stand up to do so, another bullet flew past him, this one missing the target. He figured that his assailant could only fire accurately if he stood up. He calculated that it would take him under a minute to crawl to the door of the kotha. The pain emanating from his ear and shoulder was rendering him almost immobile, but he began to crawl anyway. When he finally reached the door, he pushed it open. But before he could crawl inside, he felt a massive blow to his head. The last thing he saw was Naseema holding his gun, its butt bloody from the blow it had just rained upon Zoravar's head.

6

When he woke up, the sense of déjà vu was palpable. There was a gag stuffed into his mouth and his hands were bound with rope. His shoulder throbbed with pain. He blinked, and his eyes adjusted to the darkness in the room, which was only illuminated by two weak candles. Two faces came into view, and he recognized one of them. It was the same face he had made love to, the same kohl-lined eyes he had looked into just a while ago. Standing next to Naseema was a man who moved forward and splashed a bucket of water into Zoravar's face. The cold from it hit him harder than any slap ever had.

A Few Weeks Ago

The day had started rather badly for Brij Bhushan Rai. He had been summoned by a representative from the Intelligence Bureau, more widely known as the IB. It was an organization created by the British in 1923 and had gained acclaim as India's first reconnoitre group. It was also counted among the few institutions said to have no interference from Prime Minister Nehru.

Rai was one of the few officers who had, under the Raj, circumvented internal politics and switched over successfully to land a mid-level administrative job under free India. He was a Superintendent with the Delhi Police

He had been summoned to an address at 8 a.m. sharp, and the government representative who got in touch with him had refrained from telling him anything more. Rai rode in his private tonga, a horse-drawn carriage that had been assigned to most officials by the new government. As they rode to the designated address, he found himself sneezing constantly. Moving to Delhi had been hard on his health; he had developed an ever-present wheezing in his chest.

The tonga came to a halt in front of a decrepit building that looked like an abandoned colonial bungalow. He was asked to wait in a hallway that smelt of castor oil and cigarette smoke. In his mid-thirties now, Brij Bhushan Rai had dedicated pretty much all of his ten-plus-year career in trying to apprehend Sultana, without any success. It was said that his network of spies was vast, and he had often been very close to apprehending his man. Legend had it that once Rai had gotten so close to making the arrest that Sultana's half, smoked, unextinguished beedi welcomed the ambush party in the room, proving that he had lost out on his target by seconds.

As he waited, Rai played with his closely cropped and perfectly shaped moustache and scratched his chin, which had started sprouting some grey hair. His eyes were red and swollen due to the sneezing and kept watering down his chubby, inflamed cheeks. He always looked like a man nursing the worst hangover in the world.

Finally, he was ushered to a giant staircase, and as he climbed it, he panted and cursed the Delhi weather for making his lungs weak. He was finally brought to a stop in front of a freshly painted white teak door, on which was simply painted a name in black letters: K. SANDIPAN NAIR.

Rai shuddered a bit as an icy chill ran down his spine. This man was the Head of IB and a complete legend in his field. 'What could Nair possibly want with me?' he thought to himself.

Rai knocked a couple of times before a curt voice asked him to come in. As soon as he entered the vast room, he felt a sneezing bout coming on. He fumbled to the desk that was placed in the centre of the room, with Nair sitting in a wooden chair behind it, sorting through papers. Rai was about to put his hand out to Nair for a shake, but before he could, the sound of a roaring sneeze filled the room.

Nair looked at Rai and nodded curtly, asking him to sit down before passing him a box of tissues.

'I have heard a lot about you, Brij Bhushan Rai,' started Nair, his voice brusque as he removed his broad Lund & Blockley spectacles, the ones he had specially ordered from Bombay. 'I need you to undertake a critical job, and it has to be done with absolute urgency. The orders have come directly fr—'

Nair was interrupted by a roaring sneeze from Rai. He waited till the man blew into the tissue and then resumed. 'Like I was saying, the orders have come directly from Teen Murti Bhavan,' he said, referring to Nehru's official residence.

'Okay, Saheb. What can I do and how can I be of help? You know I will do anything.'

'Sultana. I am told you know a lot about him?' Nair asked.

'Saheb, I have been on his trail from the time I was a teenager, from when he committed his first crime, smashing his maternal uncle's head to a pulp with a stone, over some financial feud. The conflict was over less than three rupees and a few naya paisa,' Rai paused before continuing. 'The maternal uncle he bludgeoned to death was my father.'

Nair was listening intently and motioned for Rai to go on.

'We come from the same village, Saheb, and the very reason I joined the force was to bring down that thug.'

'Rai, you do realize that you have dedicated your entire career so far in trying to nab him, and you have only failed so far? Do you know why?'

Rai felt himself wince at that, but was too awed to say a word in retaliation. He waited for Nair to go on, understanding that the question was rhetorical.

'The reason you have failed has nothing to do with your supposed incompetence, the one that has not let you rise through the ranks the way you should have. Sultana has had us all fooled. All these years, he had been a double agent, a spy if you will – for the British as well as the freedom movement, and had been under double protection. It is only post-Independence that he has become more vulnerable.'

Rai absorbed the information and felt the room around him spin. 'A man claiming to be Sultana's top aide has been writing to us for months. It was only last week that these letters actually made their way into my hands. The man has been writing anonymously, of course. But he promises to deliver Sultana to us, now that he knows that the British agents are of no use to the country, and their bosses have long since retired to their English countryside.'

Nair paused for effect as Rai let out another massive sneeze. His face was red, both from the allergies and the frustration of spending years chasing the brigand, only to come across such information now.

'But Sultana looted the British; he made the biggest dent to their treasury,' Rai protested feebly.

'That story was an entirely British creation. Making him look anti-British was the only way the firangs could find out about so many of our operations, so many sleeper cells that were in support of the movement against them. They always tipped him off against you and the others working against him. He had worked out an arrangement where he would hand over most of the British loot back to the treasury, and they turned a blind eye to whatever else he looted. And somewhere towards the last few years, he also quietly supported the Indian freedom struggle and its leaders. To what end, though, remains entirely unknown to us.'

Rai slumped back into the sturdy chair. There was silence for a few seconds. 'So, what do you want me to do next, Saheb?' he finally asked.

'We want you to nab him, and while you are at it, kill him in the act. His damage to you is personal, unlike his crimes against the state. Tell us he was escaping or that he fired at you and you had to kill him in self-defence. We don't need him alive anymore. We also need to make a statement as India's premier security agency. He is about to commit the first heist in independent India. He will be the first criminal we send to his grave in independent India.'

'But saheb, how do we know this is not an ambush or some sort of a twisted plan concocted by Sultana? What is the proof that this anonymous source is authentic?'

Nair got up from his wooden chair and walked to a desk, which was overflowing with a gargantuan pile of papers. Pulling out one heap, he brought it down heavily on his desk, raising some dust in the bargain. Rai's sinuses flared at the act, and another sneezing bout later, Nair explained, 'These are the letters this anonymous man has been writing. See the locations and post office boxes they have been sent from. All the places they come from have either had a crime before or after, that was committed by Sultana and his marauders. This chap, whoever he is, does check out. Why would Sultana want to invite such trouble?'

Restless with all this information, Rai said, 'Where should I begin?'

Nair sighed. 'Rajputana. He is going to be at a whorehouse sometime in the next few weeks, after committing independent India's first heist. The people on the train they will rob will carry fake jewellery and fake currency. After the heist, at the whorehouse, Sultana's guard will be lowered and it'll be easier to apprehend him there.' Nair paused to take a sip of water. 'Be careful about our source though; we need *him* alive; we owe him that much. And you never know how handy he could be to us, maybe even as a trained agent for our ranks. He has said he will identify himself after you have taken Sultana down. He has a funny request though, and I want to abide by it.'

'What is his request, Saheb?'

'He wants full immunity against his complicity in Sultana's crimes, which is expected enough. But he also wants two train tickets to Bombay, five hundred rupees as bounty price, and a letter of recommendation from Nehru to Cawas Jee.'

'Cawas Jee?' Rai looked upwards as his bushy eyebrows rose quizzically.

'Yes. That film studiowallah from Bombay. He produces movies and owns Firdaus Talkies.'

Rai felt quite lost. 'But Saheb, didn't Firdaus Talkies shut down last year?'

'Yes, sadly, they could not move with the times and kept trying to make silent pictures in the era of talkies. I did enjoy some of their movies though, especially the ones that starred Sulochana.'

'So then, what do we do about the source's request? And why two tickets?'

'Does not matter. We will honour it. You make sure of that. Let him find out that the studio has shut down when he gets to Bombay. That's his problem to deal with.'

7

Zoravar was running, faster than he ever had in his entire life. He knew it was a matter of time before Sultana and his men caught up with him. He felt the air going out of his lungs, and even in this moment, probably the last few of his life, he felt like this was a movie scene and he an action hero, like a great climax from one of those American action pictures.

A bullet pierced his lower back. He collapsed and saw Sultana laughing at him. 'You thought you'd be able to get me arrested, you buffoon? I will not finish you off, these birds will.'

He saw Pasha's face, shocked and disappointment at Zoravar's betrayal. He watched another horse pass by, his mother tied to it, crying in pain.

As he lay there, bleeding out, Zoravar felt such rage and helplessness as he'd never felt before. A hawk circled closer to his face, growing bigger and deadlier by the second. Zoravar felt the first sting of its beak as he screamed, and then the very next second, ice-cold water slapped his face and he jerked awake.

He was not dead – not yet. He was still in the room with the dim lamps and the two familiar faces. 'Having nightmares, are you, Mr Anonymous?' said the man with the bushy eyebrows. He was holding a handkerchief in his right hand and kept blowing his nose into it.

Zoravar saw that Naseema still stood beside the man. How long had it been? Was the shootout outside the brothel years ago, or had it just been a few hours? Zoravar had lost all sense of time. His thoughts were shattered by a massive sneeze from the pot-bellied, red-eyed man. He came closer to Zoravar and held his eyes, contempt the only emotion on his swollen face. He ran his chubby finger over the scar on Zoravar's face. 'Those m************ high up in Delhi want you alive,' he spat. Then, he pulled back his hand and slapped Zoravar. 'If it were up to me, I would shoot you down like I did your m*******d boss. I have wasted half my life in pursuit of people like you and now you demand immunity? I am not like that Madrasi IB man in Delhi.'

Naseema was standing behind Rai, mute and expressionless. But Zoravar saw that her hands were trembling. He felt himself begin shaking too as the cold metal of a handmade gun pressed against his forehead.

Suddenly, Naseema spoke up. 'What are you doing, Saheb? He has delivered everything he promised, let him go,' she said, her voice frightened. Rai turned in rage and now pointed the gun at Naseema. 'You whore, you think you can give me orders? I am going to kill you both now.' Naseema drew back, but after a pause, continued despite the fear. 'Saheb, I have done everything you asked me to and I—' Before she could complete, Rai turned towards her and pulling her by the neck to him, kicked her hard in the stomach. Naseema fell to the ground, writhing in pain.

She remembered her first meeting with this man a few days ago, when he had told her that she had no choice but to enlist as a spy or he'd ensure that the Balyee Bawar was shut down.

He began unbuckling his belt and pulled Naseema to her feet.

'I am going to show you what a real man feels like,' he grinned and Naseema quailed, drawing back. She looked at Zoravar, who was slumped on the floor, half-dead as he stared helplessly back at her.

Just as Rai moved towards her, there was a loud explosion and the weak wooden door came crashing down. Smoke and dust filled the air, and a man stood at the doorway, holding another small explosive in his hand. His face was covered with a shawl. Zoravar recognized the eyes and knew instantly that their saviour was none other than Pasha.

Rai was stunned and, before he could react, Pasha ran up to him and the room reverberated with the sound of cracking bones. The next thing Zoravar knew, Rai was lying still on the floor, and Pasha was untying him.

Naseema had rushed to Zoravar's side and now the trio moved together towards the door. But before they could leave it, Zoravar suddenly seemed to remember something and moved towards the unconscious Rai. Bending down, he rummaged in the man's pockets and pulled out two third-class train tickets to Bombay, from Jaipur central station. He also fished out an envelope with the seal of the Indian government. Inside, he found the cash he'd been promised as bounty. He was about to search for the promised note of introduction in another pocket, when he realized that Rai had gained consciousness and was aiming the pistol that had been lying next to him at Zoravar. Before he could shoot, Pasha once again came to Zoravar's rescue and was by his side in an instant, kicking the pistol out of Rai's hand and sending it flying across the room.

'Let's get out of here!' Pasha said to Zoravar, who considered looking for the letter for a second, but then decided to follow Pasha's instruction.

Outside, they scanned the area, looking for Naseema, but there was no sign of her.

8

'Tea, hot tea!' The boy shouted as he went from window to window of the Grand Trunk Express. He was carrying a kettle that looked heavier than him. He was also carrying several clay kulhads. He came to a halt when a man seated in the third-class compartment with a blanket on his face signalled to him. But the man didn't want to buy a cup of tea. Instead, he asked, 'Can you get me boiling water?'

The boy sensed a note of urgency in the man's voice. He peered inside the compartment and saw that there was another figure lying motionless on the opposite berth, also enveloped in a blanket.

Pasha paid the boy an entire rupee to procure hot water from a cooking stall nearby.

The door of their compartment did not have a bolt. Pasha knew he was running out of time before other passengers took their seats in the same compartment. He pulled out a bottle of cheap country liquor and a dagger from his cummerbund. He poured the liquor on the edge of the dagger. He then quickly turned the inert body of Zoravar and poured the boiling water on his left shoulder where the bullet had been lodged. He checked for Zoravar's breath and marvelled at how the man had survived with a bullet inside of him for almost over a day. He then bit his lips, prayed to the almighty – something he did very rarely – and pushed the dagger inside Zoravar's shoulder. Even unconscious, Zoravar moaned in pain. Pasha twisted the dagger and felt its tip hit Zoravar's shoulder bone as blood gushed out. He twisted the dagger once again, inserting its warm tip even deeper and then pulling it out with a jerk. Along with the dagger, out flew the bloody, dented bullet, smearing the ceiling of the compartment with blood.

Pasha dabbed more liquor on Zoravar's shoulder and tore a part of his blanket, pulling out the cotton from inside it. He dressed the wound with cotton and cloth to staunch the flow of blood.

As he was getting done, he heard someone gasp behind him. 'Murder! Murder!' a woman screamed.

Pasha turned to see a middle-aged man, his wife and their two young children staring at him. He realized how the scene must seem to strangers, with Zoravar lying motionless and bloody, and Pasha bent over him with a bloodied knife. He sprang up and, acting on impulse, grabbed one of the two children, pulling him forward and holding his knife against the boy's throat.

'I will slit this boy's throat if you create any more commotion.' The shocked woman started screaming even louder. Pasha stuffed the dagger back in his cummerbund and picked up Zoravar, throwing him over his shoulder, and pushing the family out of his way, he ran out of the compartment.

Pasha could hear the woman still screaming, and he knew that by now, the cops must have been alerted. He wondered at how long it would be before he was caught. He cursed loudly as he realized that he had reached the last bogey, and already, he could hear the sound of police whistles and running foot seps draw closer. He was out of moves.

Hawildar Banwari Lal had been sitting on a bench on the platform, enjoying a greasy pyaaz-kachori and milky, sugary tea – his morning breakfast – when he heard the hullabaloo in the train. He savoured one more bite of that wonderful kachori and cursed aloud, before standing up and blowing the whistle to alert the other hawildars patrolling different sections of the long platform. He trotted towards the bogey and was immediately pointed in the direction of the compartment from which the screaming had originated. He was sure that the other hawildars would also be on their way, and continued to blow the whistle as he ran towards the compartment, as fast as his stocky build and unhealthy lifestyle would allow him. As he neared the end of the bogey, he saw the murderer. The man had a partly torn blanket covering his body and dried blood on his face, mixed with sweat. He was also holding an immobile man on his shoulders. The scene looked like it was out of a gory rendition of one of those *Vikram and Betal* stories his grandmother used to tell him. As Banwari approached the criminal, he suddenly felt dizzy. An excruciating pain rose in his chest. He felt like someone had put a heavy stone on it.

Pasha noticed that the hawildar was panting and struggling to stand up. Sweat lined his forehead, and there was some sort of froth developing on the edges of his mouth. Suddenly, Banwari Lal doubled over and fell to the floor.

This was a godsent opportunity for Pasha, and climbing over the havildar, who was now clutching his chest and convulsing, he ran like a man possessed. Thankfully, there were no other cops around. The travellers stared as they watched this man, a body thrown over his shoulder and his face and hair covered in blood and vomit, running past them. But no one did anything.

As Pasha exited the train, he felt the fresh air and sun on him. Across the platform, there was another train, just pulling out of the station. Without really giving it much thought, he jumped on board. He was just in time, and as he stood at the door of the train and watched the platform, he saw a group of policemen crowded around an officer. He recognized Brij Bhushan Rai. The bastard had a broken and bandaged nose, thanks to Pasha, who now realized the reason no other hawildars had come in his pursuit on the first train. They were busy being given descriptions of Pasha, Zoravar and that girl.

For the first time in what had been an incredible few hours, Pasha heaved a sigh of relief as he slumped down at the edge of the door of the train. The wind was blowing in his face, and he began to feel relaxed as he finally let go of Zoravar.

The clouds thundered, and the first drops of rain were beginning to fall when Pasha stood up again and looked out of the compartment while holding the third- class tickets to Bombay in his hand. What he saw amazed him. He had boarded the train that was taking them to Sarai Rohilla station. If Pasha was not mistaken, this was the name of the main railway station of India's capital, Delhi – in the opposite direction to Bombay.

It was early in the morning when the train pulled into the Sarai station. Thankfully, the journey had been smooth. Pasha had slept like a baby in the tiny space near the edge of the open door, and nobody had come to ask for their tickets. Zoravar had gained consciousness by now, though he was still drained and weak and in pain.

As the passengers started to stream out, Pasha pulled up Zoravar, letting the younger man lean on him for support.

Pasha's mind wandered to the fateful night of Sultana's death. He had realized that night that his letters had finally reached the right hands. The whole thing had been Zoravar's idea. Pasha believed that eliminating Sultana was their only way out, and Zoravar had come up with a plan that would allow them to get to Bombay, where he could pursue a career in the pictures and Pasha could get to the bustling neighbourhood of Dongri, where smugglers sold wares stolen from ships that came from foreign shores. He wanted to be his own boss, and Bombay was the only place in the world that would allow him that. He had a distant relative working in the docks, with whom he was going to reside.

As they were about to exit the station, a posh-looking gentleman passed them and told his companion, 'I cannot wait to get to Bombay.'

Zoravar and Pasha looked at each other and immediately came up with a plan.

It was simple enough to lure the gentleman and his attendant to the toilet – Pasha's dagger came in handy, and within minutes, the man and his companion had exchanged clothes with them. Then, leaving the duo gagged and locked in the small WC stall, Zoravar and Pasha, or Mr Tata and Mr Wadia, boarded the first-class bogie of the train that was going to take them to Bombay. Zoravar silently pledged to himself that this was going to be the last crime he committed. After all, he was finally on his way to a new life, in the city of his dreams.

PART II

Yeh Hai Bombay Meri Jaan ...

1

The first thing Zoravar noticed on alighting at the platform of the Victoria Terminus station was the sheer number of people milling about – passengers of all ages, porters in red uniforms and Gandhi topis, vendors and hawkers shouting at the top of their voices. The platform was alive and bursting with energy.

Zoravar found that he was holding back tears, as he breathed of the city he had dreamt about for as long as he could remember.

As he and Pasha walked out of the Terminus, the first thing Zoravar noticed was the Edward Theatre across from them – the place he had read about in the countless film articles, listings and reviews. There was a massive hand-painted movie poster of the movie *Shaheed*. As Zoravar stared at it, his thoughts were interrupted by Pasha, who tapped him on the shoulder to get his attention. 'This is where you can find me,' Pasha said, passing him the ticket stub on the back of which he'd scrawled an address. 'I still think you should come along with me. There is a lot to be done at the docks.'

Zoravar looked at address and then at his friend. 'I have a different path to forge, Pasha.' He took out two hundred and fifty rupees, Pasha's share of the bounty, and passed it to him. Pasha took the money and said, 'Allah Haafiz, my friend. I wish for you to become the brightest star in the galaxy.'

The two of them embraced awkwardly and Zoravar said, 'I will be indebted to you forever. Thank you for saving my life.'

Pasha replied, 'Well, it was your idea that set us free. It was my debt to pay.' Both men shook hands one last time before Pasha turned around and walked away.

Zoravar stood in front of the Edward Theatre, studying the poster. Filmistan Presents: Kamini Kaushal, Dilip Kumar, Chandramohan, Leela Chitnis in *Shaheed*, it announced. The film had been directed by Ramesh Saigal. A new director on the block, Zoravar thought, and made a mental note of the name. He then turned his attention to the expression on Dilip Kumar's face and thought, I could do that better.

A sharp and loud horn, from a long blue car, interrupted his thoughts. Zoravar looked around him and realized that he was standing in the middle of the road. He cursed and crossed the road, this time being more careful about the vehicles, bullock carts and tongas rushing up and down the road.

At the theatre, he made his way to the box office and asked the wiry man at the counter for a ticket for the next show. His eyes widened at the price. This ticket was more expensive than any Zoravar had ever bought.

Pocketing the stub, he walked to a tobacconist close by and asked for a tin of Panama cigarettes. The seller was reading the newspaper, and the front-page headline announced that there was a strife brewing in Kashmir. Not taking his eyes off the paper, the man reached for a tin of cigarettes and held it out to Zoravar, who put down the money and walked away, wondering why he'd bothered to pay someone who wouldn't have known any better.

As Zoravar entered the auditorium, he eyed the crowd that was leaving the previous show. He caught snatches of their conversation and they seemed to be all praise for Dilip Kumar's performance. Inside the cool, cavernous space, he felt the red carpet beneath his chappals, saw the tall fans that hung from the ceilings and smelt the familiar smell of stale cigarette smoke. He made his way to his seat, restless for the lights to go off so that he could completely immerse himself in the world he loved most. He felt like he had finally come home, after years away.

There had always been an inherent, undeniable romance in the talkie experience for Zoravar. The idea of seeing his beloved actor or actress on the silver screen, a sense of anticipation for the story that was going to be unveiled, and the dark auditorium where, for a while, all his maladies and hardships of life were forgotten. It was a different, magical world of storytelling, and there was nothing Zoravar wanted more than to be part of it.

The lights went off and the screen lit up with the opening credits rolling to patriotic music, accompanied by the visual of a fluttering Indian flag. As the handsome young hero appeared on the screen and uttered the opening dialogues, the hall erupted with hoots and cheers, and Zoravar felt something small and metallic land on his head – a one-anna coin from one of the stalls higher up.

The sun was blazing on the Bombay sky as Zoravar exited the hall. He overheard a distinguished Parsi lady say to her companion, 'Dilip Kumar is the perfect rebel hero. He's going to go far if he keeps up the good work. He has a great future ahead.'

Bitter jealousy rose within Zoravar, the way it did when life refused to deal you a good hand and pitted you against someone who has been gifted the very Koh-i-Noor itself.

2

Outside the theatre, Zoravar hailed a Chevrolet Fleetmaster taxi. As the Sikh taxi driver turned up the meter, he asked Zoravar in Punjabi, 'Where will you go, Sir ji?'

'Firdaus Studios,' Zoravar said.

'Oh ji, Firdaus? It shut down last year!' the Sardar said, turning around in astonishment.

'Shut down? Are you sure?'

The Sardar sat back and put the gear in neutral.

'Haan ji. Financial losses, they say. Nobody goes there anymore. The building has been abandoned.'

Zoravar was flummoxed. How had he not known this? Watching the driver shift restlessly in his seat, he hurriedly said, 'Fine. Take me to Film Lok Studios then.'

The Sardar turned again, manoeuvring his giant frame with great difficulty. 'What are you going to do there? Are you also one of those nithallas who has run away from the pind with idiotic dreams in your head?'

The caustic, mocking tone brought back memories of his father. 'Do as you are told and take me where I want to go,' Zoravar snarled at the driver.

The Sardar's bushy eyebrows rose, and he muttered under his breath as he put the car into gear, something to the effect of how *seenema* had spoilt the youngsters.

'Just the other day, I picked up another bumpkin from here,' the older man said, pointing at the grand Victoria Terminus. 'The lad had come all the way from Ambarsar. Said he wanted to be Dev Anand's duplicate because he looked just like him. I dropped him to Rajkamal Kalamandir, and I had not even begun to pull out before the Pathan at the gate shooed the idiot away like a pie dog!' he laughed.

Zoravar felt himself panicking but knew that he couldn't show it to this man. 'Paa ji, I read a gossip column that said Dev was to marry Suraiya. That cannot be true, right? These journalists write better fiction than screenwriters do!' he said, changing the topic.

The subject seemed to distract the Sardar well enough, and he went back to his congenial self. 'Why will Suraiya marry a supporting actor, good looking or not? He had such a secondary role in *Hum Ek Hain*. I watched it almost twelve times, just for my favourite Durga.'

Zoravar knew that the Sardar was referring to Durga Khote, the foremost leading lady of the 1930s.

For a few minutes, there was silence in the taxi as it rushed past the crowded streets of Bombay. Then the driver spoke again. 'Oye kaake, who is your favourite actor?' he asked Zoravar, who had been staring out the window, admiring the beauty of the Dargah that they were passing, as it stood glimmering in the middle of the sea. He had seen the Haji Ali Dargah in movies, but seeing it in reality before him was something else entirely! And the sea itself ... vast and blue ... Zoravar was mesmerized. Suddenly, he decided that he'd buy a house facing the sea from the money he got after signing his first movie.

'I like Motilal, Saigal and Ashok Kumar, of course,' he said to the driver now, still staring out of the window.

It was almost four in the evening when the taxi swerved left on its way towards Worli Seaface. Outside, Zoravar wondered how far he'd come as he watched the traffic rush past.

Truth really is stranger than fiction, he thought. Who would believe him if he said that he had almost died twice in the last two years and that he had been the henchman of India's most wanted criminal as well as the reason for his downfall?

As the taxi halted in Goregaon finally, he saw a gleaming board that read 'FILM LOK STUDIOS'. A bolt of thrill shot through him. Finally, the bad days are behind me; finally, it is time to be the architect of my destiny, Zoravar thought as he felt the scar on his chin with his right finger. He paid the Sardar what he thought was a rather hefty fee and made his way to the gate of the building. He knew that his life was going to change, and change for the better. He was sure that he had left behind the worst years of his life.

He did not know how wrong he was.

There was an eerie silence as Zoravar walked towards the gate. Seemingly out of nowhere, two guards suddenly came and stood before him, blocking his path. One held a rifle, the other a lathi. The guard with the rifle spoke first. 'Aye, what do you want?' he had a strong Afghani accent.

'I want to meet Saraswath Babu,' Zoravar said, referring to the great director and owner of the studio.

'And I want to meet Devika Rani,' the Pathan said, and followed it up with a loud, guttural laugh. 'Get out, laale di jaan, before we take you to the thaana.'

Zoravar fished out a crisp two-rupee note from his pocket. 'Take this. I will bring you more, but let me in,' he said to the men.

The Pathan looked suspiciously at him. The other guard grabbed the money and put it in his pocket.

'Don't you understand Hindi? I said get out of here, or there will be consequences,' the Pathan said, moving forward threateningly. Zoravar, tired and angry, pushed the man back hard and before he knew what was happening, the other guard had attacked Zoravar with his lathi. Zoravar fell and found himself pinned against the ground with the lathi pressed against his throat. They were now at the edge of the road from atop the hill where the studio was situated. The guards stole the remainder of the money from his pocket as one of them accidentally slammed his fist into Zoravar's nose, when he had meant to aim for his cheek instead. Zoravar cursed himself for moving his face at the wrong time as the pain made him momentarily dizzy. He then staggered back up and, with the intention of fighting back, swung at the guards unsuccessfully and lost his balance, having slipped on a muddy patch at the edge of the bushes, and went tumbling down into the small Goregaon hill that housed the posh studio. He rolled down till he came to the edge of a small lake. A solo hut came into view. Zoaravar was now staring at the full moon, and the only thought in his head even in that condition was that of the coins hitting the floor every time Dilip Kumar mouthed a punchy dialogue. The pain of envy is harder to endure than physical pain, and envy was getting the better of him, despite being broken, bruised and now bankrupt.

3

Saraswath Mukherjee was in a state of dilemma. Manto, his favourite screenwriter, had abandoned Bombay and moved to Pakistan after the partition, convinced he would be better off there. Mukherjee remembered the day Manto had made up his mind.

He'd driven to the writer's house, and upon reaching, had said to the man, 'So many Muslims are staying back!' Manto had been drunk following his customary ritual of guzzling beer every evening.

This time around, Mukherjee had also roped in his old friend and reigning superstar Ashok Kumar to cajole Manto into staying back. Mukherjee kept urging Kumar to speak up, but the latter refused to say a word. It was when Mukherjee had given up that Dadamoni, as he was fondly known, finally spoke up.

'If he wants to go, he should! It is his wish, and the least we can do is respect it,' he said.

When they drove out of Mahim in Ashok Kumar's Morris Ambassador car, Saraswath quipped, 'Dada, I had brought you here to convince him to not move, not support his mad decision.'

Ashok Kumar lit a cigarette, taking both his hands off the steering wheel momentarily. Then, the cigarette hanging from his lips, he threw his hands in the air but did not say a word. They continued to drive in silence for the rest of the journey.

Now, as Mukherjee poured over the dismal collections of his latest picture, he was convinced that a screenwriter like Manto could not be replaced. In his desperation, he had also approached Manto's long-time collaborator and friend, Ismat. There had been positive reports of *Ziddi,* a film she had written. Those who had watched it claimed that it would make an overnight sensation out of Dev Anand and take him from supporting actor to main lead. But his meeting with Ismat had not been fruitful. She had begged him off, saying that she did not have the time due to her unending court cases, and the considerable re-writes on *Arzoo*, a film she was writing for Dilip Kumar.

They were irreplaceable. Dadamoni's time was no longer his own since he agreed to do Kamal Amrohi's *Mahal*, a film that was taking forever to complete. Mukherjee had harboured a distaste for Amrohi from the time the director had fired the superstar Suraiya to make way for that new sixteen-year old child artiste called Madhubala. He remembered lamenting to Ashok Kumar about it during one of Dadamoni's famous homoeopathy sessions.

'How can you take the risk of launching that child artiste in a film that was written for Suraiya?' he had asked. Ashok Kumar, once done packing the small pills in a vial, had gone back to reading out astrological charts, another hobby of his besides homoeopathy.

'Bring it up with the director. I liked her screen test though,' Dadamoni had said casually before adding, 'oh, her planets are well-aligned too.'

For a while, Mukherjee sat in his cabin, his mind in a turmoil. Then an idea struck him – what Film Lok needed was to launch new stars too. It would recharge the studio's batteries, and Mukherjee could own and control the talent he launched.

But how was he going to find his new leading boy and girl? He stood up, still thinking, and made his way to the talent room that housed the portfolios of aspiring actors. Mukherjee perused the catalogues and tossed them on the table in disgust. Nothing in there satisfied him. He left the room and came back to his cabin, where he found his studio manager R. Rao waiting for him, along with the two night-shift security guards. They elucidated in great detail their encounter with a dangerous and deranged man who had tried to enter the studio the previous evening, but as always, they had taken care of the situation.

Zoravar had gathered himself with great difficulty after the previous evening after his encounter with the studio guards. At the foot of the hill, he'd found a couple of Koli kids playing near the bank of the lake. They had taken him to their meagre hut, which smelt of dried fish, and their fisherman father fed him a frugal dinner, taking pity on seeing his condition. Zoravar slept on a cot they had placed outside the hut.

He spent a restless night on the hard cot. He needed to find a place to live, and now, with no money and nothing to call his own, he also needed to figure out a plan of action. When he awoke, he bid the family goodbye and walked back to the main road in the heat, he felt the need to shave, bathe and buy new clothes, in that order. But for all that, he would have to reach Bandra first. He asked a passer-by about the nearest railway station, which turned out to be GOREGAON. When he reached it, he saw that it was not remotely as grand as Victoria Terminus, which surprised him. He had expected all railway stations in Bombay to be similar.

Since reaching Bombay, Zoravar had sworn to himself that he would never indulge in another crime, but he found that now, penniless and homeless, he was left with no other option. He had been used to basic pickpocketing to be able to buy movie tickets and Pasha had honed that skill by training him in myriad ways to cut pockets. He secretly thanked Pasha and surveyed the scant number of people waiting at the station, zeroing in on an old but well-dressed man. All Zoravar needed now was a blade. He made his way to a general stall that was selling food items. He casually asked the vendor for a blade, but the man shook his head. As a dejected Zoravar was about to walk away, he heard the vendor whistle for him. When he turned, the man signalled him to wait. Then he bent down for what seemed to be an eternity and fished out a small pocket knife. 'This is what I use,' he said, smirking at Zoravar.

Zoravar accepted the pocket knife. 'I will give this back to you in a few minutes,' he said to the man, and then walked to his prey.

Zoravar figured that the best approach would be to engage the man in conversation.

'When does the fast train to Bandra arrive, sir?' he asked the old man.

'It only comes twice a day. The fast train is fast only because it halts at fewer stations and is due in the next few minutes. I am going to be taking the same one,' the old man replied, more helpful than Zoravar had expected. When the train arrived, Zoravar ensured that he stuck close to the old man, and cut the back pocket of the linen trouser the man was wearing precisely at the time he was fighting the crowds to board the first class compartment. His wallet dropped into Zoravar's waiting hand, and he swiftly scooted from there.

Once Zoravar was out of the station, he examined the wallet that was now safely in his hand.

Inside, he found a bundle of crisp ten-rupee notes. Pulling it out, he chucked the now empty wallet away. What he missed was the name of the wallet's owner printed on the inside: R. Rao, Head of Administration & Talent, Film Lok Studios.

4

Despite the disaster that was his first visit to Film Lok Studios, Zoravar did not let go of the idea of getting a tête-à-tête with Saraswath Mukherjee. In fact, the first thing he did with the money from the stolen wallet was purchase film magazines. He had decided he would visit other studios to try his luck, but his heart was set on Film Lok, and he was not going to give up this easily.

Zoravar had taken the next train to Bandra after stealing the wallet, and found a place called 'Ideal Lodge', which he had read in *Film India* was famous for housing strugglers trying to make it in tinsel town. A popular lyricist had mentioned the place in an interview during an account of his struggling days.

The conditions at the lodge were appalling. A single and grimy bulb flickered sporadically in the foyer, barely illuminating it. An attractive, feisty woman sat behind a wooden desk that acted as the reception, with the quivering flame of a candle for company on the desk, to aid the poor light emitting from the bulb. Encountering the darkness inside, no one would have guessed that it was mid-afternoon. The woman's head was buried in a newspaper. Zoravar knew she owned the place from there being mentions of her in some of the interviews of the technicians and actors he had devoured. As he walked up to her, she sized Zoravar up, and then, in a strong Sindhi accent and a brash tone, said, 'Two rupees a night. In the morning, you will get a toast and a cup of tea with rationed sugar. If you want to add more sugar, you can buy your own.'

Zoravar nodded.

'You cannot bring girls here, and you will be sharing your room with two other men.' The woman paused for effect like a stage actor. 'You can come and go whenever you like. Alcohol is not permitted. How many days do you intend to stay?'

'I will stay for ten days for the time being and extend my stay if necessary,' Zoravar said, and the woman seemed to make a mental calculation.

'That will be ten rupees now and the remaining ten at check out,' she said.

Reluctantly, Zoravar paid up the money, and she nodded at him, slipping it into the cash register. Then, as he waited for the key, she suddenly glanced at her paper and looked up at him.

'What is a seven-letter word for daytime performance?' she asked.

'Matinee', Zoravar said without missing a beat. Nodding as if he'd passed some sort of test, she passed him a rusty key and gave him the direction to his room.

Turning around to walk to his room, Zoravar wondered how he would manage to groom himself in a shared bathroom. He also needed to get some clothes and toiletries, including pomade, shaving cream and a bar of Yardley sandalwood soap, the one that his favourite film stars often mentioned in their interviews. It was hard, having to look good all the time, and much harder when life was already difficult.

'If you want to get your portfolio done, let me know. The lodgers here get a discount at Maruti Alankar's photo studio,' the woman said to Zoravar's back, and he turned around to look at her.

'How did you know I am an actor?'

'This is Bombay. Half the city is in the film business, and the other half is trying to get into the film business. You don't seem to have the tenacity of a director, and writers are almost always holed up in cheap bars or at the tit of their beloved whore. And well, you are tall, fair and good looking. I think you will make for a good villain,' she said, her voice nonchalant. Then she went back to the crossword.

As Zoravar climbed up the narrow staircase to his room, the image he saw on the lady's desk remained firmly etched in his mind. It was the framed photograph of her with a handsome young man. At the bottom of the frame was an inscription scrawled in broad strokes that said, 'To My favourite Ms Ramani – With Love, Dev.'

On reaching his room, he found the creaky door ajar. He entered and saw a pot-bellied, balding man sitting in a blue, chequered lungi, smoking a cigarette. Opposite him sat a criminally thin, scrawny man. Zoravar was reminded instantly of the Laurel and Hardy movies he adored. The men were engaged in a game of chess. As Zoravar entered, the pot-bellied chap looked up.

'Come, friend. I was just about to eliminate his rook,' he said to Zoravar, as if picking up an existing thread of conversation with an old friend.

Zoravar smiled at the greeting and then looked at the other man, who was wearing a creased kurta and pyjama that had seen better days. He was still focusing on the chessboard, and Zoravar observed his hand was shaking as it drummed the table endlessly.

The bigger man introduced himself. 'Myself Roshan,' he said. 'And this here,' he added, pointing to his opponent who had still not taken his eyes off the chessboard, 'is Khayyam.'

'I am Zoravar. I am here to meet with Saraswath Mukherjee.'

At this, Khayyam finally looked up. 'Oh! You already have an appointment, is it?' he asked with genuine curiosity, and Zoravar could almost smell the desperation in the man. In this city, even a red herring tasted like caviar.

'Oh no! I haven't. In fact, the guards beat me up and threw me out when I tried to get in,' he said hurriedly, not wanting to give the man any more hope than he already had. 'Though I am sure it is a matter of time before I get my big break,' he added confidently, and the other two men looked at each other, their eyes dancing with mirth.

'How long have you been in Bombay?' Roshan asked.

'A couple of days,' replied Zoravar. The men exchanged glances once again, and this time, they laughed openly.

Jogi and Jagat were the guards who manned the day shift at Film Lok Studios, and the former had developed a peculiar habit. After his frugal lunch, he liked to walk down to the local paan shop and buy a loose beedi, the only vice his meagre salary afforded him. But of late, he had also gotten addicted to paan filled with raw tobacco and betel nuts. It was like no other intoxication he'd experienced before. His senses numbed only seconds after putting the paan in his mouth and helped him pass in bliss the languid hours spent manning the gate. Once Jogi returned, it would be his compatriot Jagat's turn to head off to the same shop to enjoy his beedi in peace.

Zoravar knew this because for the past week, he had camped near an abandoned cottage close to the studio, noting the guards' schedule. So far, he'd noticed that at no point was the gate left completely unmanned. He had followed the first guard, Jogi, and watched him buy the paan. He had then followed the other guard, Jagat, and watched him smoke his beedi before leaving.

A plan was beginning to brew in Zoravar's mind as he timed both their routines.

Sundar Lal, the paan vendor, had migrated to Bombay from Benares in search of better career prospects. Back home, his paan stall was one among many, but in Bombay, his brand of Banarasi Saada was deemed exotic. Since moving to Bombay, the volume of business had grown exponentially, but his earning was exhausted paying the exorbitant rent he doled out for the tiny room he lived in.

Today, as he manned his shop, a tall man came up to him, a khadi bag hanging from his shoulder. He spoke in an accent that reminded Sundar Lal of the banks of the Ganges.

'Bhai saheb, I have just come from Benares. I come bearing the freshest of paan leaves for you. Please help me out in this venture,' the stranger said.

Sunder Lal had already purchased his stock for the month, but he felt like he couldn't turn away a man from his hometown.

What the shopkeeper didn't know was that Zoravar stood there feeling thrilled about being able to deceive this man from Benaras and successfully fooling, with an accent he'd picked up from the movies. He was selling

Sundar Lal's own leaves back to him, now laced with the opium powder that Zoravar had bought from an illegally run opium bar near the Bombay Central station – the last bastion of the famous opium dens of Bombay. Zoravar had paid a street urchin to buy Benarasi paan leaves from Sundar Lal.

Zoravar had tried the opium on himself and paid a servant at the lodge to record the exact amount of time and quantity needed to knock Zoravar out.

When Sundar Lal heard the price Zoravar was quoting for the leaves, he was taken aback. He felt sad for this young man from Benaras, who was too naïve to know that he'd have gotten two times more than what he was quoting. But business, after all, was business, and the boy would have to learn the hard way, just like Sundar had.

By the time Sundar had placed the fresh leaves on top of his stall, Jogi was making his way for his daily dose. Zoravar had calculated that it took Jogi five minutes to walk back to the gates, and that within another ten minutes of sitting there, he would pass out, leaving Zoravar with exactly two to three minutes before Jagat Ram returned and found Jogi in a comatose state. He heard Jogi call out his customary greeting to Sundar Lal and the vendor tell him about how he had just procured fresh leaves.

Zoravar dashed back to his stake-out, from where he could observe the guards. As he had calculated, Jogi walked back and sat on the wooden chair. Zoravar felt his heartrate quicken as he saw Jagat leave. Each second passed as if it were an hour. After about seven minutes, he saw Jogi getting up, walking in circles as if uneasy. After taking a sip of water from the clay matka, he sat down once again. It seemed to Zoravar that his plan was going to fail when suddenly, he saw the guard slump forward, his eyes closed. Zoravar knew it was a matter of mere seconds before the second guard would be back, and he ran towards the large iron gates of the studio where dreams were manufactured and sold to the three hundred million people of India.

He thought his heart was going to explode as he lifted the bolt. It swung free and Zoravar stepped inside the studio. Almost subconsciously, the first thing he did on entering was bow down and touch his forehead to the ground in reverence. Once inside, he sprinted towards the first set of offices he saw and as soon as he entered, what he saw made him stop suddenly. There was a man standing down the corridor from him, instructing some people. Zoravar had seen this man before. It was, unmistakably, the face of the man whose wallet he had stolen. He almost cursed aloud as the realization dawned on him. R. Rao worked at Film Lok Studios.

5

Zoravar was not sure if Rao would remember their brief rendezvous. As he walked on, he tried to act like he belonged, hoping to blend in. He passed Rao, who was too busy to bother looking at him.

Once inside the building, he walked the long corridors looking for Saraswath Mukherjee's office. In his hand, he held a large envelope of his portfolio, the one he had gotten done at Alankar Photo Studio. Despite the discount, it had meant using up most of the money he had, and with the remainder, he had had some shirts stitched for himself, along with matching trousers. He was now wearing a new blue bush-shirt and new, sharply creased pants. He hoped that he looked good enough to make an impression on Mukherjee.

The smell of gelatine emulsion and crystals infused the air, and Zoravar gleaned that they were the result of the film stock and reels that were processed and stored in the studio.

At the end of the corridor, he stepped out of a door and found himself facing five giant cottages with thatched roofs. These had to be the film studios, or the floors where the sets were built and shootings took place. He began walking towards one of the cottages, hoping to find Saraswath Mukherjee there, when he heard someone shout from behind him. He turned around to see a red-faced, angry man approaching him.

'Aye rascal! Where have you been?' The man, barely five feet tall, had a pugnacious expression on his fat nose. Before Zoravar could respond, the man was upon him, grabbing Zoravar by the shoulder and dragging him towards the cottage with 'Floor No. 4' written on its door.

'I will make sure you don't receive your payment on time, coming late like this!' Zoravar was still too tongue-tied to react and stared mutely at the man. Had he been caught? His throat dried up as he got ready for a disaster.

Instead, inside the cottage, Zoravar found himself standing before three well-dressed middle-aged men, all of whom were smoking cigarettes. They seemed to be in the middle of an intense discussion.

'Saheb, here is the idiot! You know how these people are. I promise you there will be no delay the next time,' the angry man who had dragged Zoravar to the building now pushed him forward.

Zoravar looked at the man standing closest to him, and the first thing he observed was that his remarkably dark face was glistening with sweat. He was drawing deeply on an expensive looking cigarette. After a few seconds of awkward silence, it dawned on Zoravar that he was looking at Kishore Sahu. Devoid of his trademark expression that entertained so many people, it had taken Zoravar a few seconds to place him, but this was unmistakably one of the most prolific supporting actors in the film industry today, and was now also a successful director. Zoravar felt butterflies in his stomach and tried to control his excitement as he stood there mutely.

After giving Zoravar a quick once over, Sahu simply nodded and turned to the squat man who had brought Zoravar there. 'Majumdar, get him in costume immediately.'

On hearing this, Majumdar once again dragged Zoravar away. After they had walked a few paces, he turned to the younger man and said, in an entirely polite tone now, 'Bhai, I am sorry! Sahu Da has a very bad temper. He had put me in charge of getting the actor, and like a fool, I got drunk last night and completely forgot. I saw you holding your portfolio and looking a bit lost, and I knew why you were here. And you have a great personality, despite that scar on your face. So I decided to save my ass by making you look bad. Rule of life, what to do!'

'What is this shooting?' he asked inquisitively.

'We are doing some patchwork, bhai,' was all Majumdar said.

'Patchwork?' Zoravar asked.

'Oh ho, you have done acting before or no? Don't you now tell me you have never been in front of the camera.' Majumdar looked worried.

'Of course I have acted before. A lot,' Zoravar lied.

'Oh, good, good. But then you should know that patchwork is a bit of shooting we do after the picture is complete. Sometimes, when the director and other crew watch the first cut of the movie, they may feel that there has to be some drama that needs to be added, or there is a producer demand or some actor demand that has to be accommodated.'

'Drama?'

'Haan dada, drama has to be there, else picture does not hold. See, in other businesses, a faulty product can be rectified by recalling it from the market. But in our business, once we have dispatched the product, it cannot be recalled. There is no way it can be rectified. Best is to repair it all while you still can.'

'Majumdar ji, what exactly do you do here?' Zoravar asked, curious about this portly man who was so willingly sharing his knowledge.

Majumdar wiped sweat from his brow and replied,

'I am an assistant director, in charge of costumes and junior artistes.'

Majumdar led Zoravar to a dank room. The door outside read 'COSTUMES'. Inside, Zoravar saw endless rows of clothes in all sorts of colours, sizes and styles

– an armour, various headgears for warriors, a frugal shawl akin to what Bapu wore, even gladiator suits like the ones his favourite action stars wore in those historical extravaganzas directed by Sohrab Modi. There were also endless rows of suits. Majumdar belched loudly as he led Zoravar to a section housing ethnic Indian wear. He handed Zoravar a beige-coloured sleeveless kurta, along with a red turban. Majumdar then picked out a white dhoti that was stained with dirt. 'Don't look at it so suspiciously; the dirt on the dhoti is fake. It has been painted to give it that effect,' he said to Zoravar.

'Yes, yes. Of course!' Zoravar couldn't believe that he was about to go in front of the camera. He couldn't wait. 'These will fit just fine. Where is the changing room?' he asked.

When Zoravar had changed into his costume, he realized that the kurta was ill-fitting and so was the turban on his head, which kept slipping down from his forehead. He felt conscious as he entered the studio and was surprised at the severe heat and dust on set. A waterbody barely a few metres wide had been created, which was clearly serving the purpose of a makeshift river, with a small boat on it.

Zoravar felt his heart sink a little as he took in the scene. Everything looked synthetic and bogus.

'Aye! Come here, idiot. I have to brief you on the scene,' Majumdar shouted, interrupting Zoravar's thoughts.

Now that they were back on set, Zoravar noticed that

Mazumdar's attitude had turned rude and caustic again.

'You have to stand behind the boat, on what looks like the bank of the river. And you have to wave when the person sitting in the boat waves to you. Understood?' Majumdar asked and Zoravar nodded. He walked and took position, realizing that the studio was filled with at least over a hundred people. Various technicians milled about, numerous assistants ran around fixing this or that, and set dressers were putting in finishing touches. He looked up at the ceiling and saw what looked like wooden clouds, in garish blue, dangling from the bamboo sticks that held the ceiling and the clouds, along with the lights.

When Zoravar had walked to his mark behind the boat, Majumdar yelled, 'Okay! Now position yourself. Go towards the left. Don't you know how to take light, you idiot?'

Zoravar did know how to 'take light', something he'd read was the first lesson for an actor. It essentially meant knowing how to stand in the exact position at which the light would best accentuate the actor's face as well as make it most accessible to viewers on the screen. He was following instructions when Kishore Sahu entered the studio, along with a handsome man wearing a maroon waistcoat and a very well-stitched and starched white shirt with matching maroon trousers. The man was holding a packet of Craven A cigarettes in his hand. Zoravar remembered how fashionable these had become in Lahore, after it became known that they were Mohammad Ali Jinnah's preferred brand of cigarettes.

And then Zoravar really looked at Sahu's companion and realized that he was looking straight at Dilip Kumar.

Zoravar realized that there was pin-drop silence on the floor. The melee and frenzy from seconds ago had entirely dissipated as everyone stared at the star in their midst.

An assistant procured chairs out of nowhere. Sahu and Dilip both sat on their respective seats. Zoravar watched Kumar stretch out his legs and saw the spotless tan boots the actor was wearing. Zoravar suddenly became conscious of his own bare feet. He watched as Kumar looked around, as if searching for someone, and within seconds, a man came running towards him, holding various things in his hand, including a mirror. He immediately held up the mirror in front of Kumar's face, who practised a few expressions in it with easy swagger. Another make-up person had joined the first one and was now dabbing Kumar's face with cotton and touching up what looked to Zoravar like Kumar's already perfect hair.

Kishore Sahu lit a fresh cigarette. 'Majumdar,' he called out.

'Yes, Dada?' the response was immediate.

'Have you finished blocking that extra? There's no time to waste.'

'Um, yes Dada, of course I have!' Majumdar replied, stuttering just a little.

The term 'blocking' rang a bell in Zoravar's head. His eidetic memory got to work, and he remembered how he'd recently read a Humphrey Bogart interview in the 'International' section of a film magazine. The Hollywood actor had been asked about blocking in one of his interviews and had patiently explained how important it was to rehearse the actual physical movements performed in a scene by the actors before the camera rolled. This helped producers and directors not waste time and costly film stock during the actual shooting by avoiding multiple re-takes. This kind of rehearsal was called blocking.

Majumdar turned to Zoravar, who was standing at the spot like a statue, conscious and stiff. He saw Kishore Sahu walk to the camera, put a single eye on the viewfinder, and then have an animated discussion with the cameraman. Kumar made his way to the boat and sat down in it, which is when Zoravar realized that he was going to be in the scene with the actor.

Kumar looked at Zoravar. 'If you don't wave at the correct time we will miss the shot, as it is a wide shot, not a close-up. Let's wrap this quickly,' he spoke in chaste Urdu. Zoravar managed a faint nod.

After what seemed ages, Sahu was ready to take the shot. 'Rehearsal!' he screamed into the large tin-plated megaphone he was holding. Dilip Kumar started rowing the boat. He passed Zoravar, who stood there frozen and forgot to wave his hand at the star.

'Cut!' screamed the director on his megaphone. He then looked at Zoravar directly and yelled, 'C******, don't you get it? Are you standing there for fun?' Zoravar felt his palms slick with nervous perspiration.

'Sorry, Yusuf. Sorry. Please let's do another rehearsal,' Sahu then addressed Kumar, his tone soft and deferential.

Zoravar realized that Sahu called the actor by his real name, Yusuf Khan.

Once again, Dilip Kumar began rowing the boat and this time, as he waved out, Zoravar waited for a few seconds, and by the time he had waved back, the boat had long crossed the frame of the camera.

'Cut!' the director thundered again. Zoravar felt himself grow red and hot with embarrassment, and prepared himself for more abuses from Sahu. But the director turned to Kumar instead. 'Yusuf, I am so sorry! You know what – f*** the rehearsal. Let's take.' Kumar just shrugged his shoulders. Sahu picked up the megaphone again. 'You better wave that hand properly now!' he screamed at Zoravar, who nodded frantically. He had to get it right this time, or he was sure that they'd get someone else to replace him.

A clapboard appeared as if by magic. It read, 'Nadiya Ke Paar'. Sahu picked up the megaphone. 'Roll Sound!' he shouted into it. 'Rolling!' came the reply. 'Roll camera!'

'Rolling!'

'Action!' Sahu roared.

Dilip Kumar started rowing the boat, and as he waved, Zoravar waved back.

'Cut!' screamed the director abruptly.

Zoravar felt almost ill with fear. He was so sure he'd gotten it right, but Sahu looked livid.

'Kapadia, you idiot! You forgot to rotate the camera when Yusuf waved his hand.' *So it wasn't my fault*, Zoravar thought, and relaxed slightly.

'I am sorry, sir. Let's go for one more. Please,' Kapadia said meekly. The orders were given again as the hundred-odd member crew toiled in the cruel heat and the glaring lights.

After the final take and the last 'cut', Kumar got out of the boat, said Aadab to Sahu and raised his hand in greeting before leaving the room in a puff of smoke from his expensive cigarette. 'Pack up!' was the last thing Zoravar heard as Sahu also made his way out of the floor.

One by one, the lights started going off as the crew began to wrap up. It was time to go home.

6

Outside, Zoravar was taken aback at the size of the car Dilip Kumar was leaving in. The chauffeur was wearing a hat and uniform. As Kumar sped away in the car after signing a couple of autographs for the workers on the floor, Zoravar turned around to see a familiar face.

'Aye man, well done. Sahu Da is happy with you.' Majumdar stood there, a bottle of half-empty dark rum in his hands. He offered the bottle to Zoravar, who shook his head in response. 'Murari Anna is sitting near the gate. He will give you your daily wage and you can leave. Also, don't forget to grab some tea and samosa, the stall is behind the studio floor.'

'Majumdar ji, I actually have to meet Saraswath Mukherjee. That's why I was here.' Majumdar started laughing again. 'I see. Why? What do you want from him?' he asked between chuckles.

'I want to be an actor, a hero ... I wanted to give him these photographs of mine.'

Majumdar looked at Zoravar, his eyes bright and shrewd.

'Buy me alcohol? I'll tell you the best route to
Saraswath Da,' he said.

After collecting his wage – his first honest earning ever – Zoravar exited the gate with Majumdar, calmly passing the guards he had drugged just that morning to get in.

They went to a seedy bar in the vicinity of Andheri West, famous for its quarter-alcohol system, where they served one-fourth of a bottle of alcohol to their customers at an affordable price. The bar, Majumdar told Zoravar, was also famous for being a favourite watering hole for aspiring writers, directors and actors. The older man ordered a quarter bottle of rum, along with a plate of bombil fish fry and deep-fried chicken legs.

'Majumdar ji, how can I meet Saraswath Mukherjee?' Zoravar pressed, afraid to lose Majumdar to a haze of liquor and food.

'I think you will make for a great villain, like Jayant or Pran,' Majumdar said, not answering the question.

'This is the second time someone has told me this in a span of a few days.' The receptionist's words played in Zoravar's mind.

'I have the eye of a director. I am telling you. Abandon all these thoughts of being a star and hero and all. Focus on getting the part of the villain,' Majumdar said.

'But Majumdar ji, how do I begin?'

Majumdar was quiet for a while, chewing on the food and chugging down the last remaining drops from the bottle. Then, after cleaning up his plate, he finally looked at Zoravar.

'See me tomorrow at the studio, or here in the evening. I'll figure something out for you.' He got up and left the bar, rubbing his greasy hands on his shirt and leaving Zoravar to pay the bill out of the wages of his first-ever salary.

Zoravar walked from the bar to the lodge and thought about the scene featuring him and how it would be played all over India to millions of people. And yet, here he was, penniless and unknown.

When he got to the lodge, Ms Ramani was seated behind her desk as usual, the newspaper in her hand.

'Chhokra, sorry. Cannot give you your key today,' she said, a hint of near-regret in her voice.

'Why?'

'Today is the tenth day.' Zoravar cursed under his breath. He had forgotten to keep track of the days in his endeavour to figure out how to get inside the studio. 'I acted for the first time in my life today. I was in a scene with Dilip Kumar. In Kishore Sahu's movie,' he said to her.

'Oh, that's wonderful, baby. Then surely you must have gotten paid,' she said, smiling brightly.

'I'm afraid I had to spend it. But tomorrow, I am meeting Sahu's assistant director, who is going to help me out,' Zoravar said earnestly.

'Then come tomorrow. I don't let anyone stay for free.' Zoravar opened his mouth to protest, to beg, but

before he could, she called for the bellboy.

'Chhotu!' she barked and the young boy came running.

'This guest is not going to be staying with us any longer.

Go fetch his things so he can bid us goodbye.' Ramani buried her face back in the newspaper. 9-across was giving her some trouble today.

Zoravar picked up his things and left the lodge. Outside, he stared at half-moon in the sky and wondered at the day he'd had.

Had he really been in a scene with Dilip Kumar? Had he really been directed by Kishore Sahu? He walked on as if in a dream, unaware of where he was headed. He came upon a bench under a lamppost and sat down on it, hungry and bone-tired.

He remembered his mother, and his life in Lahore and Phagwara. A tear rolled down his face as he curled up on the bench, no longer bothered about spoiling his blue shirt.

PART III

Main Zindagi Ka Saath Nibhaata Chala Gaya ...

1

The docks were eerily empty – well, almost empty. Dayanand Das, the crafty Head of the newly created Goods and Merchandise Export Division, stood in the middle of the large tarmac, surrounded by the sea on three sides. He hated everything about Bombay. The sea, the smell of the sea, and the fish that was found in the sea.

He held a handkerchief to his nose as he stared at the lithe, tall man in front of him. The man sported a close-cropped moustache and wore a heavy cloth on his head that resembled a turban. He was dressed in a loose and flowing white Pathani and an olive-green kurta with the top buttons undone to reveal a white netted vest inside.

Dayanand noticed that the man was smoking a State Express 555, a brand that did not fully fit the image of the lowly dock worker that he apparently was. Dayanand abused this whole idea of democracy in his head. Being a pukka devotee of the Raj, he secretly wished the British had never left. Independent India had brought democracy, which ensured that everybody had a voice, and because of that, agitation had become a way of life. What they didn't realize was that there was nobody to agitate against anymore! Dayanand bristled with hatred as he faced the man across from him. He muttered the name of the elephant lord under his breath as the other man spoke his first words.

'Dayanand bhai, Salam.'

Dayanand Das made a contorted face and folded his hands, 'Ram Ram,' he said. 'I hear you control these dock workers. What is this demand for higher wages? We are not going to yield. Pandit ji too is clear about the matter.' The man stubbed out the cigarette he was smoking.

'Do you swim, Dayanand?' he asked.

'No, I do not. How does that matter?'

The man stared at him. 'Do you know drowning is one of the most torturous ways of dying?' he asked.

'Is that a threat? Do you know that I'm a senior government official?' shrieked Dayanand, fear making his voice high-pitched.

The lithe man unwrapped the cloth that was covering his head. He swung it in the air while holding its edges and then in one smooth motion, wrapped it around Dayanand's neck, dragging him backwards to the edge of the tarmac. Then, with all his might, the man forced Dayanand's face into the water. He held it down for a few seconds as Dayanand's legs and hands thrashed about violently. When he released his hold, Dayanand came up and gasped for air, babbling incoherently. But within seconds, the man had submerged his head back into the sea again, this time with even more force. Dayanand Das felt certain that he was going to die a miserable death in these hated seas, but just then, he felt the hold on his neck loosen, and he came up for air again. His eyes hurt like they had never before, and he couldn't keep them open, so badly affected were they by the saltwater.

'*Now* do you agree to raise the wages of the dock workers?' the man asked.

Dayanand Das nodded vehemently.

Pulling him away from the edge, the man let go of Dayanand, who lay down on the tarmac. The last thing he saw before his eyes closed from exhaustion and pain was the face of the man towering above him.

'Tell whoever needs to be told. Parwaan owns the sea in Bombay. And Parwaan takes care of the labourers. Remember my name. I'm the one who went to Hajj and got my divine name. Haji Parwaan.'

After he had been thrown out of the lodge and realized that a stray bench on the road could not be his home, Zoravar walked to the Gurudwara at Sion, where he was taken in with more kindness than he'd expected, and was allowed to live off the langar and serve as help. The days seemed to be flying, and it had already been a month since he had made this his home.

He had been unable to find Majumdar at Film Lok studios, but after acting in the scene with Dilip Kumar, he had found it easier to enter the premises, and inside, he came across a door that said CASTING. He tried to open it and, to his amazement, found it unlocked. He went and placed his meagre portfolio on top of a stack of files.

Later, he went to the seedy bar in Andheri to look for Majumdar but didn't find him there either.

The last few months had passed for Zoravar without any luck, and now, the monsoons of 1949 were fast approaching.

On a particularly grey morning, he lay in his usual spot in the Gurudwara, leafing through the latest edition of *Film India* when he came across an announcement about the upcoming film *Apna Desh,* by Rajkamal Kalamandir. Patriotic movies were still the order of the day.

The studio was owned and run by V. Shantaram, one of Zoravar's favourite filmmakers and, in his opinion, one of India's greatest. He had acted, produced and directed in several movies, even been appreciated by Charlie Chaplin for *Manoos*. Zoravar remembered watching the Hindi adaptation of the film, *Aadmi*. He had felt slightly confused by it and not really understood why it was considered great. Unwilling to accept that he just didn't like the movie, he had tried to understand it by reading the reviews, one of which claimed that *Aadmi* was the 'true reflection of Bombay and how it became a haven for the avant-garde in the 1930s'.

After some research, Zoravar had pieced together the fact that avant-garde was not the name of a Maharashtrian Brahman and was, in fact, a French term used to describe experiments that were innovative and radical, often exploring unorthodox ideas in the field of arts, music, culture and the pictures.

He was putting the magazine away when he felt a light tap on his shoulder. A Granthi in a flowing white robe, with a white beard and kind eyes, was standing behind Zoravar.

'Puttar, I was watching you. You have a spark in your eyes, a light that seems like it has been bestowed upon you by the Guru himself. Don't worry. All your dreams are going to come true.'

Zoravar stared at the man. He wondered if this was the special one; the one he had heard about since he had come to live at the Gurudwara. Some said he could walk on water. Others said that he had walked all the way from Gurdaspur to Bombay during the partition. He had encountered mobs on the way and no one had dared to touch him.

Zoravar felt an overwhelming urge to embrace the Granthi before him, but the old man had already moved on and was serving langar to other devotees.

2

Zoravar had decided to interview for the job of a correspondence executive at Ranjit Cine-Tone, a mid-level studio. He'd read about the job in the classified section of a discarded newspaper.

On the day of the interview, he borrowed money from one of the members of the devotional troupe that sang regularly in gurudwara.

The studio was in Parel, and when Zoravar reached there, he found that he was let in easily when he told them in English that he had come for a job interview. Once inside, he joined what was a relatively long queue, made up of men mostly his age, a few of them older than him.

After what seemed like hours, his name was called, and he knocked on the wooden door. A voice asked him to enter, and he stepped inside to face Noor Mohammad, an old man with a head full of grey hair that was neatly parted in the middle. Dressed immaculately in a double-breasted suit and wearing an eyepiece, he cut an impressive figure and looked different from the pictures that Zoravar had seen of him in the film magazines.

'Look, young man. I have been looking for an apprentice, and I have liked multiple candidates. I am not even sure if I wanted to interview more people' Mohammad said, getting to the point immediately. 'But now that you're here, let me make it clear, I don't have the luxury of time to groom a candidate from scratch. How much experience do you possess?'

Zoravar replied confidently, 'Sir, I have worked with Kishore Sahu and Dilip Kumar, on their upcoming film *Nadiya Ke Paar*.' Noor seemed pretty intrigued. 'What exactly did you do on the film?' Zoravar replied that he had played a small role. Noor seemed disappointed by the answer, and standing up, began putting together his papers, as if wrapping up for the day. Zoravar could see that the job was slipping through his fingers, and acting on instinct, said, '*Aaina* ... that's the one that broke your heart, isn't it?'

Noor looked up sharply, a question in his eyes.

'These British suits that you wear, you get the affliction for them from the time you left your native Ahmedabad in a boat that took you all the way to London via Bombay,' Zoravar continued. 'You served with Jones & Jones at Savile Row. Didn't you? And that attic you stayed in. That was where *Aaina* was conceived on scraps of paper? The ones you almost lost when you were coming back from Southampton? Also, wasn't *Aaina* partly based on your own life? You haven't directly mentioned it. But anyone who followed your interviews could put together two and two if they wanted to.' Noor was now back in his chair, his eyes alert and interested. Zoravar continued, 'It must have taken a lot of perseverance to mortgage your house to make *Chaar Deewaar*, that too without your father's knowledge. And when it became a raging success, you bought your father two more houses. He died without knowing that he had been living in a house that had been mortgaged behind his back, by his own son. You were so scared of him that you did not speak about this till he had passed away. Remember your interview in the January 1944 edition of *Film India*?'

Noor lit his pipe, his hands trembling very slightly. 'I haven't had the pleasure of smoking a pipe myself, but I know of your love for Virginia tobacco. Your wife and the movies are possibly the only two things you love more. You talk proudly about *Chaar Deewar* and of *Savitri* and even *Oonch Neech* and numerous other successes you have had, but nothing still matters more than *Aaina's* failure. You remember that line you said? "We always like our failed children more than the ones who succeed." That was, what, March 1945? In the next answer you gave, you spoke about how we never move on from our first romance.'

As Zoravar spoke, Noor looked out from the French windows in his cabin, staring with unseeing eyes at the setting sun. Zoravar continued, 'In the radio show you did once, when your studio was at its zenith, you spoke about never being able to make your dream project, on the Taj Mahal. If you'd known that K. Asif is a connoisseur on the subject, you'd have hired him to write it for you. You need to revive that film, and it will revive your passion and interest in the movies, which is beginning to wane after so many years in the industry. And about that other film of yours – *Aakhri Rishta*. Do you know why it failed at the box office? You released it too close to *Dard*. Suraiya had the same romantic angle in the film, and it was still running when your film released in theatres. As an outsider, I always wondered why someone like you would not have the objectivity to postpone the release, considering audiences had just spent their hard-earned money on a similar story and were in no mood for another one. You even had the same music composer. It was bound to fall apart.' Zoravar took a breather before going on. 'Also, I have to tell you, I observed the space adjacent to your cabin when I was waiting outside. That space is a waste of space; you can easily use it as a waiting room for people or for portfolio filing, the way they do in Film Lok. And the awards that have been stuffed there need to be cleaned better. That is your legacy. I understand that you're looking for someone to write your replies to your fan mails and assist you in paperwork, but if you had somebody by your side who could tell you that the case against your film *Gambler*, by its writer Mr Datta, who is in the mood for asking you for money, can be null and void because he himself has copied the story from Cary Grant's *Mr Lucky*, it could save you a lot of money. I have watched *Mr Lucky* and read enough about *Gambler* and the very famous public court case to know that the core subjects are similar. It will take very little to prove the writer wrong and reverse the case. Mr Mukherjee, I have no experience in a job like this, but I know enough about the business to know that if you get an assistant who is street- smart – somebody as passionate as you are about the movies –for the salary of a simple correspondence executive, you should hire him. Right away. I can also correspond in English, and the typist of yours sitting outside can teach me how to type. I promise to learn it quickly.'

For a few minutes, there was utter silence in the room as Noor blew puffs of smoke from his pipe. Then, he finally said, 'You will be paid twenty-five rupees per month, and your remuneration will include a first-class local train pass. Food will be served at the cafeteria at subsidized rates. I will see you on sharp at 8 a.m. on Monday, 15th of July.'

Zoravar could not hide the chuckle as he saw Noor remove a handkerchief to wipe the beads of sweat that had formed on his forehead.

Zoravar walked out feeling like he'd climbed a mountain successfully. He looked at the candidates waiting outside and wondered if they'd now be told to go home.

Just as he was leaving the studio, he heard someone call out his name, and turned to see Roshan, his old roommate at the lodge, waving wildly at him.

Zoravar waved back and then walked to where

Roshan was standing.

'How have you been?' he asked his friend, and then, because he was eager to share the good news with someone, added, 'Ranjit Cinetone is going to be my office, by the way. I just got a job here!'

Roshan stared at him. 'Job? The guys at Film Lok

Studios have been desperately looking for you!' he said.

'Film Lok?' was all Zoravar could manage.

'Kaake, it seems they got their hands on your portfolio, and it caught the eye of the casting team. But the postal address you had given on the back of the photos was that of the lodge. You had left by the time they tried to contact you there, and none of us knew where to find you!'

'So … where's my letter? Where's the letter they sent me?' Zoravar asked impatiently, unable to keep calm.

'It's still with Ms Ramani.'

Barely able to contain his anxiety and impatience, Zoravar bid a hurried farewell to Roshan and made his way to the lodge.

The receptionist smiled as soon as she saw Zoravar. She put her newspaper aside and digging inside the drawer, took out his letter.

'I knew you'd be back, so I kept it safe,' she said simply, handing him the envelope.

The Film Lok Studio's logo stared back at Zoravar, printed in one corner of the envelope. Inside, the letter, typed on buttery soft paper, read:

> Dear Mr Cheema,
>
> I have liked the portfolio you sent to us. I expect you to be free to attend an audition at the Amaltas Floor, in Film Lok Studios, at 9.30 a.m. on Monday, the 15th of July.
>
> It would be advisable for you to bring five minutes of your own material, i.e. extracts from parts that you have played, or would like to play. Do not bring books please, but copy out material you intend to use on to a sheet of foolscap paper. If you have any dialects or accents in which you are particularly good, let this form part of your programme. Also, it is very essential you select material that does not require cueing.
>
> I shall look forward to seeing you there, and of course, wish you every success.
>
> Yours sincerely, R. Rao
Head of Administration & Talent
Film Lok Studios
SV Road, Goregaon

Zoravar could not believe his luck. He had an audition at Film Lok. And it was on the same day that he was to start his first job.

3

Zoravar sat on the same bench near the lodge that he had once spent the night on, the letter in his hand.

Life seemed to always be throwing extremes at him – famine or flood. The last time he'd sat here, he was in the middle of a famine. Now, he was being swept away by a flood.

His heart told him to forget about the job and go for the screen test. But experience and wisdom told him that he couldn't risk losing the only steady source of income he had a shot at.

Hedging his bets seemed like the best option, and he decided to place a call on Sunday evening to Noor Mohammed and tell him that he'd had fallen ill, hoping that the man would let him begin work a day late.

Promptly, when Sunday evening came, he rang the number printed on Noor Mohammad's visiting card, and luckily, the operator put him through immediately. Zoravar wondered if operators were in the habit of eavesdropping on conversations of the people they connected on a daily basis.

When Noor came on, Zoravar delivered the performance of a lifetime, and Noor agreed to let the young man start work a day later than decided.

Hanging up, Zoravar felt relief, but also realised that he had just lied to the only man in the city who had taken a chance on him.

On the morning of his audition, Zoravar entered the familiar gates of Film Lok after showing the letter to the guards. He was cordially directed to the casting area by Jogi, the very man he had once drugged. Zoravar smiled to himself as he walked the halls and finally came upon a door that read 'AMALTAS: CASTING FOR UNTITLED PRODUCTION NO. 15'.

He entered the large, cavernous space and took in the massive pillars that dotted it, adorned with sexually suggestive images carved on them. The images were that of dancers from another era in various poses. As he walked further, he saw men, most of them his age, waiting around. Some were wearing shirt and trousers, but most of them were in the traditional Indian outfit of dhoti and kurta. Zoravar noticed that a couple were even wearing tailored suits, like Sahebs. They were all waiting near a closed door with a sign that said 'KEEP SILENCE' in bold letters. A red bulb glowed above it.

All of Zoravar's illusions, that perhaps he was the only one whose photos had impressed the casting department, were shattered. A short, middle-aged man walked out of the audition room and the bulb temporarily went out. After several auditions, an elaborate lunch break and an even longer high-tea recess, Zoravar was finally summoned inside. As he walked into the room, he saw a rickety Mitchell film camera. Behind it sat its operator. R. Rao himself was seated behind a large wooden desk, and an assistant stood beside him, taking notes. There was another man sitting next to Rao, and he looked up at Zoravar now.

'Mr Zoravar! We are tired and done for the day. Why don't you come back tomorrow morning? The least we can do is ensure that you are the first person we audition. Please be here at 9 a.m.,' he said to Zoravar, flashing him the broad, professional smile of a stranger.

R. Rao stood up to leave, and as if on cue, the crew in the room began to pack up for the day.

Zoravar stood there, watching as people brushed past him and left the room, and he wondered how he was going to get out of the mess he'd landed himself in.

Somehow, Zoravar had managed to buy himself another day from Noor Mohammad, after faking a couple of sneezes and coughs. His new boss had sounded as calm enough, and Zoravar hoped that this delay wouldn't cost him too much. Now, he was ready for another trip to the studio, dressed in a white shirt and khakhi pants.

On reaching Amaltas at 9 a.m., Zoravar saw even more aspirants than had been there the previous day. As he entered, he could feel the eyes of every single person staring at him. Everyone liked checking out the competition. As promised, Zoravar was let in as soon as the first round of auditions began. As he entered, the bored cameraman looked into the viewfinder and the assistant who had been standing next to Rao came scurrying over with a clapboard in his hand. On the clapboard was written in chalk: Zoravar. Take No. 1.

The assistant passed the board to Zoravar and asked him to pose, first facing the camera and then turning sideways to show both his right and left profiles to the camera. The photos done, the men seated behind the desk spoke to Zoravar.

'We want to cast for our upcoming film. It is based on folklore, a classic love story,' Rao said. He then looked at the man next to him. 'This here is the director of the movie, Giridhar Mukhopadhyay. He has been on our payroll and worked as an apprentice to our senior-most directors.'

'Saraswath Da is in the mood to experiment. We want to do a picture with only newcomers,' Mukhopadhyay said. 'We have already finalized the heroine for the picture, as well as most of the supporting cast. It is the leading man that we have not been able to find.' The man took a long hard look at Zoravar. 'Take this sheet. Memorize the lines and perform them. Make sure you don't look into the camera at any time,' he said.

Zoravar had read in a second-hand, dog-eared copy of the legendary Russian theatre practitioner Konstantin Stanislavski's *An Actor Prepares* that it was a must for actors to work around the concept of the invisible fourth wall by never looking directly at the audience. The fourth wall was essentially the invisible barrier that separated the audience from the on-screen action unfolding before them. Much of the work done by the actor depends on maintaining that illusion. If an actor looked directly into the camera, it would essentially be the same as making eye contact with the viewer. And the viewer isn't supposed to be there. No one is supposed to be there. Breaking this fourth wall was a cardinal sin. Zoravar knew this and had made sure to follow the rule even when he had performed in plays back home.

Now, wanting to make an impression, Zoravar said rather effusively, 'Oh yes sir, I know never to break the fourth wall.'

Mukhopadhyay nodded in a way that implied he hadn't really paid attention, and Zoravar went back to the dialogue sheet. He found the lines to be overly exaggerated and dramatic. He was to play a character called Majnu. He quickly scanned the entire page and gave it back to the men seated at the desk.

'I'm ready,' he said to them.

4

The ant-hill had become grander than Pasha had expected. He had been apprehensive about the implementation of the entire plan. After all, it hinged on ants! He had been told that it had worked before and that it would work again.

As he held the mid-sized gunny sack in his hand, he was convinced that it was time to lure the ants into it. Pasha was not a man who scared easily, but the predicament he was in currently was a first. He had been extremely fortunate to find himself in his current position. He had saved the life of an inmate by default. Some members of the Karim Lala gang, the reigning criminal kingpin of Bombay, had been wanting to kill Abdul, a cousin of the upcoming challenger Parwaan. They had been about to slit his throat with weak blades when Pasha had saved his life by creating a hullabaloo and alerting the guards. In the bargain, he had had his own wrist slit by the assailants.

After a day spent unconscious in the hospital, Pasha had awakened to see a tall, lithe man towering over him, smoking a State Express 555 cigarette.

'You have been the bravest of the brave,' the man had said. 'You have saved my most beloved Abdul. You are a true lapis lazuli, and Alhamdullilah I will get you out of jail very soon.'

Pasha did not know whether the man had been an angel or whether that was just his mind playing tricks, but when he had returned to the jail after recovering, it was as if everything had changed. From a minion who had been arrested for trading in bootlegged alcohol and violating the Bombay Prohibition Act, and an inconsequential inmate nobody gave a damn about, Pasha had become somebody to reckon with. Most jailbirds saluted him and even the policemen slipped him cigarettes and other contraband without him even asking. There were nightly visits by Shabbo and Gulaabo from the neighbouring brothel, and most nights they came together. He no longer shared a cell with others, and there was an attendant who cleaned his cell twice a week.

And then Pasha had been paid another visit by the man from the hospital.

It was in the middle of the night that Pasha saw the man arrive to outside his cell in a black Pathani covered with a maze of intricate white embroidery.

'Salaam, Pasha bhai,' he said, smiling, his lips and teeth stained red from the paan he was chewing. 'Inshallah, I will have you out of here before the next Jumma. But you will have to do one thing for me.' Pasha had only nodded, awed by the sheer magnetism of Parwaan's personality.

'Ever heard of ants making a molehill? Especially red ants?' The question had perplexed Pasha. But instead of explaining, Parwaan handed him a small packet that contained crushed sugar. Over the next one week, Pasha had been delivered a packet a day of the same type of sugar, along with instructions. All he had to do was deposit them in the same place he'd been asked to place the first packet of sugar.

After three days, the first swarm of red ants arrived. By now, there were what seemed like millions of them. They had not changed the location of their cluster as long as the sugar kept being deposited in the same place. Earlier in the afternoon, the gunny sack had been given to Pasha and this one had big cubes of sugar mixed with liquid. He would have to lead the ants inside the bag. The visual was scary – there was an entire mountain of ants now. Pasha finally managed to get the job done – it hadn't been as hard as he had assumed it would. The ants operated, he saw, like a tiny and incredibly well organised army.

There was a tap on the metal bars, and a sentry entered the cell. He motioned for Pasha to follow him. Pasha and the sentry walked through a long corridor, the light from the candle the sentry was holding showing them the way. The stench of blood, urine and defecation mingled together in the air. They finally came to a halt outside a cell door. When they entered it, Pasha saw a man lying on the ground with his hands tied. First, the guard with Pasha fished out a small metal tumbler from a bag and poured water on the man who was grunting. He then then bent down on his knees and turned the screaming prisoner over so that Pasha could see his face. It was the man from the Karim Lala mob, the who had slit Pasha's wrists and tried to kill Abdul. He was gagged and his legs and arms were tied. There was nothing but terror in his eyes. The guard then turned to Pasha. 'Put the gunny bag you're carrying around this man's head. Make sure none of its contents fall out. Do it. Now!' Pasha was hesitant the guard beckoned him to carry on. 'Parwaan Bhai has insisted that you be the reason this wretch meets his maker. Do you want to get out of here or not?' Pasha lifted the bag in his hands as the sentry caught hold of the prisoner. 'On the head,' he reminded Pasha, and Pasha opened the bag, put it around the man's head and tied the strings once again, tight enough that ants would have no other place to crawl out of and they would land up biting the man's face till he died. 'How long will he be here?' asked Pasha as they walked towards the exit. 'At least a week! It will be futile to even check before that. Some of these guys keep breathing right till the end. Stubborn bastards.' The last noise that Pasha heard was that of muffled screaming, and he wondered how much pain a man would have to be in to be able to scream loud enough to be heard, despite a gag on his mouth.

5

Zoravar finally made it to Ranjit Cinetone, two days later than he was supposed to report to work. Noor Mohammed received him with warmth and inquired about his health, making Zoravar feel more guilty than he already was. He even had the office boy make Zoravar an Earl Grey black tea infused with ginger. 'One of the best things to have come out of the Raj is this incredible concoction of their tea and our herbs,' he remarked.

On his first day, Zoravar was given a tour of the studio, which he noticed was relatively humble compared to Film Lok, and had on its roster none of the big names that the latter did. Instead, it had a few up and coming actors and actresses, who had delivered mid-size successes, and that was about it. Zoravar had been put in charge of typing correspondence that came from the office of Noor

Mohammed, as well as ensuring that fan mail from all over the nation was responded to with autographs of the artistes they were addressed to.

Soon, he fell into a routine, and the days began to roll by. Zoravar had also taken to stopping by Ideal Lodge every evening after work, hoping to hear from to Film Lok Studios. It had been weeks now since his audition, and there had been no answer.

Zoravar had decided to move out of the gurudwara as soon as he had saved up enough money from his salary. Thankfully, his clothes had been taken care of by Noor Mohammad, who noticed in the first week that Zoravar alternated between two shirts. He had taken the younger man to Charlie, an Anglo-Indian tailor in Juhu who had been trained in Savile Row in London. Noor, on his own tab, had personally selected clothes for Zoravar and, alongside the shopping, had also taught him a great deal about fashion – the difference between a pocket square and a tie, broad lapels and narrow ones, and what colours were appropriate to wear when. He had also told Zoravar about the exact distance there should be between the collar of the shirt and the collar of the coat. And the distance between the sleeves of the shirt and the wrists.

As more and more time passed with no news, Zoravar gave up the hope of being selected for the part of Majnu. His life, he came to believe, was as doomed as the star-crossed lover he had hoped to portray. Sitting at a desk for more than eight hours a day, writing to fans about other actors, had become frustrating. Girls from far-flung towns and villages he had never heard of gushed about how they fantasized about the dashing Jeet. Demure housewives wrote secret letters to the unconventionally handsome Jaiveer. Men of all ages wrote to Suchitra, describing in explicit detail the passion they felt for her. There was even a dying woman from Kanauj who had sent an ancestral gold coin for Srimati, the up and coming star on the roster of the studio, begging the actress's hand in marriage to her son.

Amidst all of this success, Zoravar's own failure seemed to loom large, and the only thing he looked forward to now was his weekly pilgrimage to the theatre every Sunday, where he devoured whatever was playing – everything from Hindi films to American cinema.

On one such Sunday, Zoravar made his way to Opera House to watch *Aag*, starring the ethereal Nargis, after posting a letter to his mother informing her that he was doing well in his job and that he would write again with a new address after he had found a home to live in. A week after its release, the newspaper had called *Aag* 'an emotional upheaval of a masterpiece'. Raj Kapoor had written, directed and produced the film under his newly launched movie banner, R.K. Films. At the age of twenty-three, he was probably the youngest producer in the history of the Hindi film industry.

Inside the hall, Zoravar marvelled at the sheer size of the place. He looked up at the balcony seats from the lower stall, where he was. The theatre was packed, with not a single vacant seat in the entire auditorium. The lights went off, and the censor certificate proclaimed that this movie was meant for everybody. Mohammad had told Zoravar that studios preferred universally rated movies as they allowed for a larger audience.

'In Hindustan, even art has to be righteous,' Mohammed had remarked.

The film began, and the visual dissolved into a shot of a *yagya*, with the Gayatri Mantra being recited in the background of the burning flame. In simple white letters came the announcement 'RK FILMS PRESENTS', followed by the main cast of Raj Kapoor, Nargis, Kamini Kaushal and Nigar. The next instance, the screen filled with the title of the movie written in large letters. The letters were on fire too. Zoravar shifted uneasily in his seat. This was either a brilliant move or complete sacrilege. It was unlike anything he had seen on the screen.

There were gasps when the beautifully lit side profile of Raj Kapoor came into frame, and then gasps of horror as the light revealed the rest of his face, partially burnt and grotesque.

As the story progressed, Zoravar was consumed by it. The lighting, the framing of the shots, the dialogue – everything was new, everything was radical.

Hours later, Zoravar walked out of the cinema hall, stunned and moved by what he had watched. How could a twenty-three-year-old have produced, directed and acted in this masterpiece? The only other time he had ever felt like this was when he had watched in his late teens that glorious picture by Orson Welles, who had, also at a tender age, produced, directed and acted in *Citizen Kane* – considered America's greatest motion picture.

He saw people running back to the box-office counter to purchase tickets for a second viewing. He knew that they'd be turned away disappointed, since the shows were all sold out for the rest of the week.

As Zoravar walked back to his temporary home, he was still thinking about the film. But all thoughts of it flew out of his head when he saw Ms Ramani standing outside the Gurudwara with a letter in her hand. This was the first time in his life that Zoravar had seen her outside the Lodge and without a newspaper in her hand. He watched her walk towards him, holding out the letter, and he knew that his life was about to change forever.

6

As he waited outside Noor Mohammed's pristine oak crafted cabin, Zoravar felt himself perspire with nervousness. He was going to tell the only man who had given him a chance in this city that he had to now abandon him; that he was going to now be on the roster of Film Lok Studios, on a much higher salary and with sponsored boarding. That he was going to be Majnu, the doyen of unrequited romance. He felt a frisson of excitement, despite the difficult task that lay ahead.

When he had opened the envelope from Film Lok, it held inside it a single page contract. The terms on it were restrictive but simple. He was to not act in another picture for any other studio or producer. He was to not say no to any project or role the studio deemed fit for him. He would be paid a monthly salary for one year, and based on the success of his movies, the salary would be upgraded by the studio to what they deemed appropriate. The studio could terminate this contract at any time without reason, but if Zoravar wished to move to another studio or wanted to work independently, he would have to pay back all the money spent on him by the studio plus a 25 per cent interest per annum on the amount.

Zoravar read the thing once, and not bothering to waste any more time, signing it immediately.

He now entered Noor Mohammad's cabin to tell him this.

'Sir. I uh—'

'Here you are, Zoravar! I thought you'd come by. I know you want to quit this job. After all, it's not every day that you get the opportunity to play an Indian Romeo on the big screen. It is sad that we could not offer you a role ourselves. Maybe you will remember us when you become a big star,' Mohammad said. Zoravar looked at him, stunned. He hadn't even needed to tell his boss anything.

Looking at Zoravar's confused face, Mohammad laughed and handed him the *Film India* magazine that was kept on the desk. It was open to a page that proclaimed in large letters, 'Film Lok Presents NIMMO and ZORAVAR in Giridhar Mukhopadhyay's romantic extravaganza, *LAILA-MAJNU*.'

Taking in Zoravar's shocked face, Mohammed smiled reassuringly. 'Like I said, remember us when you become a star. Especially if we are still around.'

'Still around?' Zoravar asked.

'The studio system is on a decline. More and more independent producers are breaking out to do their own thing. It was unheard of a few years ago, but now it's becoming all too common. Have you studied the box office returns of that movie, *Aag*? And that's not a studio picture. Times are changing, Zoravar. And we need to change with it.'

PART IV

Star-Crossed

1

The weeks in the run-up to the start of the principal photography of *Laila-Majnu* had gone by in a heartbeat. Zoravar had been assigned a lavish room in the guest house of the studio. The guards that had once beaten up and robbed him now saluted him deferentially. He had also been given a first-class railway pass, and there was certainly no dearth of stylish clothes anymore. A 'boy' had been assigned to him – someone who doubled up as Zoravar's man Friday and secretary. He was called Makkhan and was from Jalandhar. Squat and unattractive, with oiled hair neatly parted on the side, Makkhan exuded natural warmth and possessed an entrepreneurial aptitude.

Every day, Makkhan woke Zoravar up at 5 a.m., for the latter's rigorous exercise regime. The boy then gave his boss a head massage, working in dollops of castor oil into his scalp. Zoravar had been asked to grow out his hair, so that he looked more like the lovelorn Majnu. A barber who lived on the studio premises, would wash his hair and massage it with a lotion that had been ordered from London. This was followed by a body massage from a masseuse who worked at the akhada nearby.

Just after Zoravar finished his lavish breakfast, rounding it off with a tall glass of milk and dry fruits, Mirza Beg, the stage veteran, would arrive. Beg's career had come to an abrupt end when he lost his theatre company and home to the Partition. He now trained the upcoming actors on the studio's roster. Despite being a taskmaster, he had been impressed with Zoravar's training.

Lunch was followed by a stretch of 'beauty sleep', a term that actors from the West had recently made popular.

The one thing Zoravar didn't need to learn was horse riding, having mastered it already in his previous life. So he used the extra time in the evening that was reserved for riding lessons to practise his scenes.

Zoravar first met the luscious Nimmo, his Laila, a few days before filming began. She was petite, with luminous brown eyes and a face that could light up a million candles. Zoravar was instantly attracted to her. He'd have made a move, but Nimmo was always accompanied by her mother. And for some reason, the young woman seemed completely oblivious to his presence. Barring minimal customary greetings, she did not indulge in any other communication with him.

The rehearsals they did together lasted for about two hours every day, and he looked forward to them, mostly as opportunities to get closer to Nimmo, but she had remained cold. When they rehearsed their romantic scenes together, she stared into his eyes with intensity and passion, and as soon as the scene was over, she'd immediately shed her emotions like discarded clothes, leaving Zoravar in a bittersweet frame of mind.

He knew, though, that this distance wouldn't last. They were soon to film a song which required his Majnu to hold Laila by her waist, and they would be locked in an embrace. The thought itself aroused him, and he could not wait to film it.

By the time they were ready to begin shooting, it was the mahurat that Zoravar was most looking forward to. He had been informed that the great Motilal, one of his idols, was going to be giving the mahurat clap, and he counted down the days with fierce excitement.

Finally, the day of the mahurat arrived. Mahurats were lavish affairs, preceded by a puja to appease the gods, followed by shooting the first scene of the film. The auspicious day and time for the event were calculated by astrologers.

The puja for *Laila-Majnu* was conducted by Saraswath Mukherjee himself, along with Mukhopadhyay and R. Rao. Motilal, the guest of honour, presided over the rituals. When Zoravar was introduced to one of his favourite actors, so awed was he that not a single word came out of his mouth. Motilal was dressed in a three-piece suit, and on his head was his usual Stetson hat. Zoravar kept looking at him and refused to let go of his hand when Motilal shook it. He bent down instinctively to touch his feet, post which Motilal embraced him. All the moments Zoravar had spent in the movie halls watching this legend on screen came rushing back – he remembered watching *Do Diwane* with his mother, the first film he ever watched in the hall; he also recollected the opening strands of '*zaalim jawaani, kafir adaayein*' sung by the very star in front of him, in Mehboob Khan's *Taqdeer*, which he had watched countless times. As he gaped at Motilal, the interviews he'd read of the star also came to his mind. Finally, Zorávar was shaken out of his reverie when the Pundit offered him prasad. Motilal, being the thorough gentleman that he was, had not reacted to Zoravar's ogling, and instead gently wished the young man luck before proceeding to greet the crew before leaving the floor.

The shooting was being held on Floor No. 4, ironically, the same floor where Zoravar had shot the patchwork scene with Dilip Kumar. The background of the set had blue and white mountains painted on them. A wooden cottage that was to be Laila's house in the movie stood on the set, surrounded by artificial trees laden with wooden green apples. Zoravar sat on a chair that bore his name. Makkhan stood next to him, alert and ready to do his bidding. He was holding a tin of Panama cigarettes and a lighter from Bhendi Bazaar that Pasha had given Zoravar as a gift. It had come all the way from Egypt, Pasha had told him when they had met just two days ago at a hotel near Juhu beach. This was the only place that served alcohol openly, despite the prohibition. It was rumoured that the place was run by the police and the supply of the booze came from the bottles the cops confiscated from bootleggers. The two friends didn't meet often,but ensured that they stayed updated about each other's' lives.

As the crew prepped the floor and Zoravar waited, he unconsciously emulated Dilip Kumar as sat cross-legged on the chair. He motioned for Makkhan to give him a cigarette. He could feel the eyes of the crew on him and felt his confidence soar. He had been preparing for this moment his entire life.

Then he felt all the eyes turn to someone else. Nimmo, his Laila, had just come out of the green room. Her face was made up heavily, with powders and rouge, and her lips were painted a bright red. A large nose ring hung from her nose, and her white kaftan was golden at the edges, making her shimmer in the light. He could not take his eyes off her.

His infatuation with Nimmo had only grown, and

Zoravar was fixated by her luminous brown eyes, smooth complexion and petite frame. She was beautiful, and the thought of taking her to bed occurred to him almost every day. But it had remained just a thought, for Nimmo was always accompanied by her sharp-eyed and protective mother, and he was thinking of ways to get rid of her and see Nimmo still maintained the icy attitude towards him without her mother around.

The whirr of a huge machine interrupted his thoughts as small flakes of cotton masquerading as snow began to descend on the prop house. Zoravar marvelled at how the set desigers had managed to transform a hot summer day in Bombay into a snowy evening in Kashmir!

In the scene they were shooting, Zoravar was to ride on horseback and pass Laila's home as she stood in the balcony. Nimmo was led to her mark. The clapboard came into view and was placed by an assistant director in front of the camera.

It was taking a long time for the crane to be mounted on a trolley, which had CHAPMAN printed in big, bold letters on its arm.

Zoravar called out to one of the assistant directors passing by. 'That is a great machine,' he said to the man.

'Mukho Da wants to establish how epic this scene is going to be. He wants the whole universe to be in motion when you and Laila meet for the first time,' the assistant director explained, using Zoravar and Nimmo's character names to refer to them.

The visual of the crane jogged Zoravar's memory, and he recalled how, about a week ago, he had been eating lunch at the studio's cafeteria when Saraswath had walked in with the legendary Dadamoni. On seeing Ashok Kumar in person, Zoravar had felt himself grow hot and cold with anticipation. And then, in an even wonderous turn of events, Mukherjee had actually introduced Zoravar to Dadamoni. They'd all sat down to lunch together, and as they dug into the fried fish and rice, Zoravar had found it hard to believe that he was actually dining with Ashok Kumar. He had eaten silently, without interrupting the conversation that Saraswath was having with the maestro.

When a huge truck had driven by the cobbled interior road adjacent to the cafeteria, Saraswath had spoken in Bengali to Dadamoni. 'Dada, we have ordered this new Chapman crane. From Los Angeles.'

'Sir, what exactly will a crane do?' Zoravar had finally interrupted the men, his curiosity getting the best of him.

Mukherjee had gone into a rather long-winded explanation, and when he'd finished, Dadamoni spoke up. 'Son, you are an actor. An actor should not bother himself with such things. There are directors for that. A crane is basically the egotistical director wanting to bleed the studio so that he can take wide shots, purely to suffice their own cinematic ego,' he had said to Zoravar, his mouth twisting in a wry smile.

Rather than be offended, Mukherjee had burst into laughter and then gone back to devouring the fried fish the waiter had set before them.

Now, as Zoravar saw the crane being loaded and observed the expression on the face of his director, he truly understood what Ashok Kumar had meant. Mukhopadhyay's voice finally boomed on the mike. 'We are ready to shoot,' he announced.

Zoravar mounted the horse and led it to the mark himself.

'Roll sound!' screamed Mukhopadhyay. 'Rolling,'

came the prompt reply.

'Camera!'

'Rolling, sir!'

'And, action!' he thundered.

Zoravar looked at Nimmo, and before he could even begin moving, he was interrupted by a booming 'cut!'

Giridhar Mukhopadhyay came running towards the horse on which Zoravar was mounted. 'Start looking at her only after the crane has covered a certain distance. Don't screw my shot up,' he said.

'How much distance exactly?' asked Zoravar.

'I don't know. Just make sure you get it right.'

The trolley on which the crane had been mounted took four workers to roll it back into its original position. After several attempts, Mukho Da was still unhappy when lunch was announced. Zoravar marvelled at the amount of film stock and time that had been wasted without anything to show for it.

At lunch, Zoravar found himself seated next to Nimmo, who had not yet exchanged any words with him off camera. Her mother was seated on Nimmo's right. Mukhopadhyay, Dastoor and the chief assistant director were sitting across the table from Zoravar. Mukhopadhyay was waxing eloquent about the need in independent India for a dictator. He claimed that it was the only way the country could flourish. Zoravar was astounded at his callousness.

Lunch passed without a single word being said about the film or of the scenes to be shot that day. Later, the convoy headed back to the studio floor to resume work.

The day finally came to an end at seven in the evening. Mukhopadhyay had not recorded even one scene on the first day of the shoot. On asking the production manager, Zoravar was told that this wasn't uncommon at all. The progress of a shooting schedule never depended on a particular day, and when the shooting happened across several days, it was quite common for some days to be slow, especially the initial ones, when the crew was still trying to bond as a unit and get into the groove.

That night, pleasantly tired after a long day, Zoravar thought about the business of moviemaking, and how it was largely a people's business. If you could be a people's person and manage egos, you could be a successful filmmaker. It was almost as if being creative and talented was an extended bonus, he thought, as he drifted off.

2

When Zoravar reached the set the next day, he found carpenters and painters hovering around. Neither Nimmo nor Mukhopadhyay were there, and the only senior crew member present was the cameraman, Dastur, who was busy giving lighting instructions to his assistants.

'Aye hero,' he jeered at Zoravar. 'What are you doing here so early?'

'I was told it would be a seven-to-seven shift today,' Zoravar replied.

'Beta, seven-to-seven is for us workers. Not you stars.' Dastur smiled and went back to what he was doing.

Zoravar found a chair and pulled it to a corner, sitting down to observe the set preparations.

The heat and dust did not bother him – he'd experienced worse. He watched everything with a childlike fascination, entirely immersed.

After a few hours, Mukhopadhyay finally arrived. He had bloodshot eyes and reeked of liquor as he shook hands with Zoravar. Nimmo arrived a few minutes later and looked like she had been up all night, crying. Her eyes were puffy, and her mother followed in the studio car, flanked by helpers who carried huge bowls of ice. Nimmo and her mother set up camp on one corner of the set and then the older woman proceeded to instruct Nimmo on how to rub the ice on her face to help assuage the swelling. Makkhan was the next person to arrive, panic written all over his face.

'Have you had breakfast?' he asked Zoravar, who nodded in response. He had eaten at the same buffet that had been laid out for the early morning crew and workers, feasting on the greasy saabu-daana wada, a Bombay favourite, and watery tea.

Zoravar was given the same costumes he had worn the previous day. They had been freshly pressed and subtly perfumed. He wore them as the make-up man worked on his face. He had noticed that the artist didn't cover up the scar on his face with make-up.

The rest of the day followed the pattern of the previous one. Nimmo, in costume and with a face full of make-up, came and stood on the same spot as before. The puffiness on her face had dissipated but the sorrow in her eyes remained. The crane was manoeuvred to exactly the same position as before, and the shoot resumed. But this time, Zoravar was finally allowed to say his dialogues.

It took nine more takes for the director to okay the scene, after which the unit broke for lunch. At lunch, Zoravar found Mukhopadhyay in an exceptionally foul mood. He was discussing politics again while wolfing down lamb chops. Nimmo asked for extra helping and was reprimanded by her mother. As they drove back to the floor, Zoravar observed that the menu for the other unit members was the same as it had been the previous day.

By the end of day two, the director had moved to shooting close-ups of the entire scene from a different angle. Scenes began from wide shots and then cut to closer shots for the scenario to be established first, before engaging in close-ups of the characters on screen. It was the cardinal rule of filmmaking. Zoravar had read about an American film director called Alfred Hitchcock, who had been challenging these norms and was not getting studio support, despite his pictures earning a lot of money.

Zoravar had also read that Regal Cinema in Colaba would soon be playing a Hitchcock film titled *Notorious*, starring Cary Grant and Ingrid Bergman. The film was finally releasing in India, two years after its American release. An article had called *Notorious* 'a watershed moment in the history of film making'. The same article had also talked about Hitchcock's role in making pictures in colour. Zoravar thought this to be impossible. He couldn't imagine watching movies in colour.

Zoravar was finding it considerably hard to sleep that night. He tiptoed out of his room and, while walking towards the staircase, heard strange noises originating from the room he had just passed. He heard the wailing of a woman and noise of things being thrown. He started as the door to the room shook with a sudden loud noise. It was as if someone had been slammed against it. On impulse, he pushed the door open and came face to face with a naked Mukhopadhyay, wearing only a white vest and holding a half-empty bottle of rum. On the floor was a woman in a foetal position, her face hidden in her hands as she continued to weep loudly. Tears ran down the side of her face, mingling with the kajal in her eyes. The white negligee she was wearing was torn, revealing her breasts.

Mukhopadhyay turned to Zoravar 'Aye you! Bastard! Get out of here!' he shouted.

Zoravar walked out, and the director staggered forward to shut the door. As the lead actor of *Laila-Majnu* walked back to his room, he couldn't shake off the image of of what he'd just seen.

The woman on the floor was probably under the impression that she had shielded her face from Zoravar, but he knew immediately who she was. After all, he had been staring at her body for days now and could recognize it anywhere.

Zoravar understood, finally, the reason Nimmo had been so aloof with him.

3

Almost two months had passed, and there was little progress to show for the time. A day spent on a film set can seem like an hour or a year, depending on how one chooses to look at it. After four days of incessant shooting, going over the same scene from every conceivable angle possible, the fifth day of the second schedule had been cancelled due to Mukhopadhyay refusing to shoot, citing script issues. He retired to one corner of the set and re-wrote scenes that were to be shot for the day. The actors and the crew just waited, twiddling their thumbs the whole time. After a few days of re-writing, Mukhopadhyay entered the floor a happy man.

'I am finally satisfied by the material I have conjured,' he said with his hands in the air, like a magician. 'My rendition of this forbidden love story is going to be the best one yet.'

Zoravar mentally counted the number of times this story had been told on the big screen. There had been that version by Nazir just three years ago. It had been an excruciating watch and the film had been quickly forgotten by audiences. Then there had then been the American film, *Romeo and Juliet*, starring the gorgeous Norma Shearer. That had a similar story. Zoravar smiled when he remembered how he had indulged himself in the bathroom of Apsara Talkies after being mesmerized by Norma.

'Let's shoot!' screamed the director. His lanky assistant walked to Zoravar, handing him a sheet. 'Memorize these lines quickly,' he said.

Zoravar took the new sheet of paper. The ink was still fresh. This portion had not been a part of the original script, and he found it to be extraordinarily contrived. He wondered if the changes had been run past the big bosses at the studio. He walked up to Mukhopadhyay, who was talking to his assistants, and interrupted him.

'Sir, this scene was not a part of the original screenplay. Can you give me some context on how you'd like me to play this?'

The director's smile turned into a scowl. 'Ae, just memorize the lines and get ready to take the shot. Do not ask questions, okay?' he barked.

Zoravar felt anger and frustration rise within him, and his expression gave away his feelings, because Mukhopadhyay smirked at him. 'You are getting angry eh? C******, what will you do?' he challenged. Closing the gap between them, he moved forward and stood inches from Zoravar, who could now smell the stale rum breath coming off the director.

He took a few steps back. 'Nothing, sir. I am sorry.'

After a few more days of shooting, Zoravar and the rest of the crew had finally been given a day off.

Getting off the local at Charni Road station, Zoravar made his way to Roxy theatre, where *Ziddi* was playing in theatres, having been re-released on popular demand. Zoravar had been in love with the soundtrack of the movie since he had first heard it. With *Ziddi*, the director had also chosen to launch a new playback singer for Dev Anand – Kishore Kumar. His female playback was an up and coming singer called Lata Mangeshkar.

Zoravar felt a tinge of envy when he found out through Dev's interview that Dadamoni had been instrumental in giving him this big break.

Back in his room, Zoravar found Makkhan waiting for him.

'Praa ji, how was the picture?' he asked.

'Still as good, no matter how many times you see it. I'm telling you, Dev Anand has never looked this handsome before! But you know, I now think that this

Kishore Kumar, Dadamoni's younger brother, he is the real talent. You think he will sing for me too?'

'Oh ho, praa ji, you let this picture release. People will forget this Dev Anand. And of course Kishore will sing for you.'

'You are just biased, Makkhan. No point in asking you for an opinion!' Zoravar joked, though gratified by the flattery.

'Yes, praa ji. That is true,' Makkhan said simply.

On shoot days, the morning tete-a-tete's with the crew was what Zoravar enjoyed most. He also came to realize that they were the most accurate source of news or gossip in the film business. The crew members, right from the spot boy to the technicians, worked on multiple pictures at the same time and had access to everything that was going on and everybody who worked in the movies. All of them had at least one good story to share, if not more.

Just last week, the set designer had told Zoravar about Suraiya's favourite on screen actor, the Hollywood star Gregory Peck. The rumour was that Dev, who had just started working on a picture with Suraiya, kept imitating Peck's mannerisms to impress his paramour. He had imbibed the mimicry to such an extent that the director of the film, Rana Pratap, had had to give the young actor a piece of his mind. But it clearly had no lasting effect on the Dev, because the Peck hangover remained.

It was time to film the song where Majnu embraced Laila. The set had been turned into an orchard. Zoravar had asked for betel nut and *saunf* to be brought, to clear his breath. It had been a long time since he had touched a woman, and the thought of embracing Nimmo excited him.

There were two massive blower fans to simulate wind on the set, but the air from the propellers made the lead pair's hair fly in all the wrong directions and Mukhopadhyay had to call for a cut. Another twenty minutes were spent in getting the position of the fans to be in sync with the camera.

Every time Mukhopadhyay called cut and Zoravar found himself embracing Nimmo again, he felt more and more mesmerized by the feel of her in his arms and the powdery fragrance coming off her body.

After fourteen takes, Mukhopadhyay was happy with what they had achieved and called for a break. Nimmo left immediately, and as Zoravar watched her go, he was already looking forward to shooting their next scene together.

As 1950 drew to a close, the second schedule of *Laila-Majnu* was finally complete. While it had originally been slated to finish in September, the delays due to the

Mukhopadhyay's eccentric nature had prolonged it by months.

On New Years' eve, as the world was ushering in the second year of a new decade, Zoravar was told that Saraswath Mukherjee had watched the rushes of *Laila-Majnu* – strewn together to form an assembly cut. Zoravar knew that an assembly or rough cut was the first stage from which the intended final product begins to come together. The editor would have to physically cut the film stock on which the scenes had been shot and reassemble them in the order of the narrative.

Zoravar heard that the words Saraswath had used after watching one hour of the cut were, 'I am going to get a heart attack.' There was a rumour that he actually had suffered a minor one, and because of it, made up his mind. He would rather shut down the picture than spend a single more paisa on what was the worst movie he had watched in his life. The performances were bizarre, and the framing incoherent. Almost everything had been changed to suit the director's whims, and it seemed like the work of a drunk man. The experiment had backfired.

4

The woman had decided that the first place she'd visit after she set foot in Bombay was the Haji Ali Dargah.

Her teenaged son, Bir Bahadur accompanied her, as well her youngest, who was five now. At the dargah, she offered her prayers and tied a dhaaga, wishing for Zoravar's well-being. She could not wait to give him a surprise. Her heart ached at having deceived her husband. By the time he found out that she'd stolen an entire month's income to buy return tickets to Bombay, she had already been halfway to her destination.

But Bibi couldn't blame herself or feel guilty. After all, she had to see her eldest son. And her husband would have never allowed her to visit if she sought his permission. First, she had written to Sahar Gul, a distant relative who lived in Bombay. They had exchanged addresses before leaving Lahore, and she hoped he still lived at the same place. Thankfully, he had replied confirming that she could live with him on reaching Bombay. He did mention that he had a small house, but it did not matter as he had a big heart.

The trio finally reached Film Lok from Tardeo after having changed two trams. When they introduced themselves at the gates of Film Lok Studios, they were told that no one called Zoravar lived there anymore. Bibi Benazira felt herself grow cold with worry. What had happened of her eldest boy? She stood at the gate of the studio, feeling lost and afraid.

'Where do we go now?' asked Bir, as Amandeep began to cry.

Once *Laila-Majnu* was shut down, Zoravar had been served a notice that asked him to vacate the premises within two weeks.

There was a rumour that Mukhopadhyay had been summoned by Rao to his cabin and was told to do the same, and Mukho Da, in return, had picked up the chair in Rao's cabin and threatened to smash the studio owner's head with it if he wasn't allowed to complete the picture, which in his opinion was an absolute masterpiece. Apparently, the police had been called, and Mukhopadhyay was arrested for obscene and violent behaviour.

Nimmo had simply disappeared from the guest house the day after the production shut down. Apparently, the studio heads wanted nothing to do with anyone attached to the doomed picture. They were a superstitious lot.

Zoravar had gone to meet Saraswath Mukherjee in his lavish cabin at the studio. The owner had been contrite, but firm. 'Son, I like whatever I have seen of you on the screen, but I have sunk a considerable sum of money in *Laila-Majnu*. There is no other option now but to make a grand picture with Ashok Kumar or Dev Anand, one that guarantees I'll make my money back,' Mukherjee had told Zoravar.

'Dada, if you like whatever you have seen of me, then why not give me another picture?' There had been no reply to Zoravar's plaintive question. Instead, Mukherjee had turned away, staring blankly out of the window that overlooked the shooting floors.

Zoravar could not believe this was happening to him. He thanked his stars that at least he had saved practically all of his salary so far, and while it was enough to rent a decent home for a short while, life had taught him to be careful with money. It wouldn't be wise to blow the savings on rent, and so he went back to the Gurudwara, and the people there were happy to have him back. The film magazines had exploded with coverage of how a Film Lok-backed film had to be shelved. Zoravar had made it to the cover of a magazine for the first time in his life, and it was about a film that was never going to be made. The photo featuring him was one that was a part of his portfolio, and he had no clue how it had made its way to the office of the magazine to be published like this. He had just been glad that no one ever asked him about his non-existent film career at the Gurudwara.

After a few days of dilly-dallying, Zoravar went back to the only man who he felt sure would employ him. On entering Noor Mohammad's cabin, he observed nothing had changed since the time he had last been there. Noor looked up, peering from his half-moon spectacles, and then looked back at the newspaper he was reading. The front page contained ran a headline that said that it had been one month since the death of Sardar Patel. After a few minutes, he gestured for Zoravar to sit.

'So, your talkie has been shelved? *Laila-Majnu* is a jinxed story. It either doesn't take off or fails at the box office.'

Zoravar was quiet.

'I assume you have come back to ask for work. While I have, of course, already filled the position you had been employed for, there is a proposition I have for you.' He coughed before resuming. 'We are beginning work on a new picture. Despite having Jaiveer as the main hero and a plot of a romantic triangle like that of *Casablanca*, we have been able to raise only half of what is needed to make the movie.'

Zoravar eyes twinkled at the words he heard. 'Saheb ji, do you promise me the second lead in your movie if I get you the money you require?'

Noor thought about the proposal and nodded in the affirmative as he stood up to shake his hand. 'I was going to offer you a job if you managed to help me, but I'll accept this too. Anyway, no one established is going to want to play second fiddle to the hero and lose the girl at the end. But if it's what you wish, may Allah be with you.'

Zoravar had started the day writing a letter to his mother regarding this new twist of fate in his life. He also wrote about his change of address. After posting the letter at the GPO, he entered the neighbouring Dongri. As he walked on, the words of warning and caution he'd heard from people raced through his mind, reminding him of how dangerous and infamous this neighbourhood was.

But he reached his destination without event. He spotted the building with the blue dome and found two men guarding its entrance – tall, burly men with menacing looks on their faces. He gave them his name, and they nodded. They were expecting him. The bigger of the two frisked him, after which Zoravar was allowed to walk in. The air inside felt stale and smelt of fried food.

He walked up the creaking staircase and on reaching the third floor, knocked on the only door there, and a man he almost did not recognize opened it. Pasha had completely transformed, as if overnight. He was wearing tailored white trousers with matching white leather shoes and a white bush-shirt. His hair was slicked back and smelt of Brylcream pomade. He had long sideburns and was wearing a gold chain. On seeing Zoravar, Pasha smiled widely and enveloped him in a hug.

'You have come, my brother,' he said, waving Zoravar into the plush, large room.

As they sat, Zoravar narrated his story and everything that had happened to him thus far. Pasha listened with with rapt attention, only moving once in a while to swat at the flies that hovered around his greasy head. After Zoravar was done, Pasha went to an adjoining room and brought back two stacks of currency notes. 'This is all yours. I will get more of it, but right now, this is all I have. Take it and begin work on your picture to fulfil your dream.'

'This will not be enough to conduct even six days of shooting.' Zoravar smiled with gratitude, but couldn't keep the truth from his friend. He needed more.

Pasha seemed upset, and a bit insulted. He thought for a while, and then, as if making up his mind, said,

'Fine. Come with me. I know someone who will be able to help.'

The memory had returned to haunt him in a way only memories can. His beloved Abdul had been brutally murdered, that too when he had been flogging his sins away. While he had been scourging himself on that fateful Muharram day, someone had mercilessly stabbed him. It had been a masterstroke, Parwaan marvelled. To stab someone in the back while they were self-flagellating. He had to avenge Abdul's death, no matter what. Adding to his woes was the peace treaty signed at the start of the year between India and the newly formed Pakistan that had ended the war, temporarily. Business had been affected. The smuggled goods market was flourishing, but the prices amplified by the war had come down. Parwaan had just lit a 555 State Express cigarette when he heard a knock on the door and it was opened by Pasha, who entered accompanied by a tall and handsome man. Pasha bowed down and kissed the top of Parwaan's right hand.

'Parwaan Bhai, this is my friend Zoravar. My closest friend in the world.' Parwaan nodded, and Zoravar awkwardly bowed down, kissing Parwaan's right hand as well.

'He is an actor. He was starring in a picture from Film Lok studios. Unfortunately, the film has been shelved,' Pasha continued.

'Well, what can I do about it?' grumbled Parwaan.

'He needs to borrow money, so he can star in his own picture. This would be a good entry for us in the business. You keep saying we need to do more to be looked upon as respected busine—'

Parwaan interrupted, frowning. 'Look, Pasha. I do not have any money to spare, and I am not the least bit interested in these silly films. I do not have time for such frivolities.'

This was pointless, Zoravar thought, and then consoled himself by remembering that he had at least tried. Smiling resignedly, he whispered a thank you to Parwaan, bowed again and made a move to leave the room.

He had just opened the door when he heard Parwaan call him

'Yes, bhai?' he said, turning to face the man again with hope in his heart. Had Parwaan changed his mind?

'I have an assignment for you. Pasha has told me about your natural genius for crime.' Pasha looked sheepish and turned away from Zoravar's inquiring eyes.

'And you'd be perfect for this job, because I need an outsider for it – but it still has to be someone I can trust.'

Zoravar felt trapped. He didn't have a job, and it looked like he was not going to have one any time soon. Did that mean he'd have to return to the world he thought he had escaped forever. Did he even have a choice?

'What do you need me to do?' he asked Parwaan.

'A few weeks ago, my most faithful man, Abdul, was stabbed in the back. That too when he was in the midst of seeking retribution for his sins during Muharram. I turned the city upside down and inside out. I first assumed it was somebody from a rival gang. Later, I got to know that it had been the police. While we have taken care of the m*******d who murdered Abdul, the man who gave the orders is still alive and free. I need you to kidnap him. The rest my men will take care of. If you do this for me, you get the money you need to make your picture.'

Zoravar stood there, absorbing the whole thing. He knew that the only way he could get the amount of money he needed was to say yes to this job, and perhaps more jobs such as these. Perhaps he didn't have a choice after all.

'I'll do it,' he said, his voice cold and resigned, like he was sealing his fate.

Zoravar had been briefed that the policewallah he needed to bring to Parwaan purchased oranges at a stall near the vegetable market, the only place he entered without his assistant hawildars. The cramped space made this Zoravar's best chance to nab him. All he had to do was moonlight as the cop's fruit vendor for the day. When the man came, Zoravar would have to keep him busy on the pretext of selling him oranges, giving time to members of the gang, who'd also be nearby, to ambush the cop, put a mask over his face and leave with him. They told Zoravar that they wouldn't be harming the guy. They needed him alive.

The cop had been pursuing Parwaan and his men since Dayanand Das had been assaulted. He had been put on the case by Dayanand and had been responsible for bumping off Parwaan's men.

This meant that he knew all of them by face, having studied and pursued them for so long. Zoravar understood now why Parwaan needed an outsider on this job.

On the day of the ambush, Zoravar studied his reflection in the stained mirror. He was dressed for the part, his face browned with make-up, a thin moustache on his upper lip and a cloth on his shoulder. This was a role, after all, and he had even practised his accent, mimicking the way the actor Zulfiqar spoke in a film Zoravar had watched years ago.

At the stall, he went about his business, feeling and acting exactly like a fruit vendor. At the expected hour, he looked up to see his victim standing before him in a white vest and khaki pants.

Just as Zoravar greeted the man with a 'Ram Ram', the man sneezed loudly and forcefully, and Zoravar found himself grow cold with recognition.

Of all the people in the world, Zoravar was going to be luring Brij Bhushan Rai into a trap.

5

Bibi Benazira hoped to be able to get living quarters in the predominantly Muslim neighbourhood of Behrampada in East Bandra, where Sahar Gul lived. She knew from his letter that he worked with Karim Lala. Lala had made Bombay his home and his fiefdom since arriving there to look for his brother. Sahar Gul worked as a runner for Lala and delivered Hashish packets to a large clientele.

As Sahar received Bibi and her children and shepherded them through to his little shanty at the heart of the slum, Bibi noticed the dirty stagnant water, clogged open drains and narrow lanes around them. There was a stench in the air that no amount of fragrance could help stave off. They arrived at a small house, and when she entered the place, she was taken aback to see an incredibly tiny room, already occupied by a woman sleeping on a gunny bag that had been spread on the floor, and three children stretched directly on the cold, bare floor.

Sahar took Benazira and her two sons to the back room, this one even tinier than the first. This was the kitchen. He made them sit down before what seemed like a dish of rotten fish, and was about to serve them when Amandeep's face crumpled the way it always did before he burst into tears. Right then, Bibi Benazira made up her mind. She couldn't possibly stay here. Getting to her feet, she bowed quickly and bade her cousin goodbye before leaving the house to look for a way out of the colony.

Zoravar pulled the cloth from his shoulder and covered the lower part of his face with it, before swiftly running towards the exit, only to lose his balance and slip as a shocked Rai looked on. The other gang members came rushing from all sides, having witnessed Zoravar's sudden change of plan, and as they tried to hold Rai, he managed to overpower the hoodlums and created enough of a commotion for the hawildars outside to rush in. Rai was now lunging towards the cloth that covered Zoravar's face as he staggered back to his feet, when another one of Parwaan's men came rushing towards him with a baton and hit him on the head from behind. This made Rai turn around and focus his attention onto the new attacker. Zoravar found his escape and continued towards the exit. He cursed himself for agreeing to Parwaan's offer, but every time his mind tried to make a rational decision, his heart played the image of him on screen, and then nothing else mattered.

When Zoravar informed Pasha about the identity of the policeman, he was stunned.

Parwaan, on the other hand, was seething at the failure of his plan. He knew, now that Rai had successfully escaped his attack, that his security was sure to have been doubled. But Parwaan did not care. He promised himself that he would not rest till he had his revenge.

When Zoravar had gone to visit him, he had refused to give the younger man any money. After all, the job had not been completed, he reasoned. When Zoravar had begged and pleaded, Parwaan, out of curiosity, had asked how much was needed to shoot the picture. When he heard the amount, his eyebrows rose in amazement. He did not have that much money at his disposal, but he smelt a business opportunity, nevertheless.

'If your picture works, how much do I stand to gain?' he asked Zoravar.

'If it works, bhai, the returns could be infinite.'

Parwaan came up with a business plan. He would borrow the required sum from the Marwari and Gujrati lalas who paid him protection money. He was well aware of the way the 'hundi' system worked. It was a financial system for credit transactions through which he could borrow money at the designated interest rate (and he would ensure he got lower rates than the market) from the lalas. He would then loan the money to Zoravar, at a rate of interest that would be higher than what he'd borrowed on himself. If the picture failed, and if Zoravar was not able to repay him, he would simply take a bit of a hit on the goods he sold to those lalas. His income would recede, but just temporarily. If the picture fared well, it would give him a lion's share of profits, and he would have paid back the lenders with interest and earned a percentage higher from Zoravar, over and above everything he had earned.

Barely two weeks had passed since the incident at the fruit market, when a red Ford car came to in a halt in front of the gates of the Gurudwara. Noor Mohammad covered his head with a white handkerchief and entered. He found Zoravar sprawled in one corner of the grounds.

'Get up, you poor sod,' he said. 'The money has reached us. Congratulations. You've got yourself the second- lead.'

Zoravar jumped to his feet, too stunned to speak.

'My employers, the Khadim brothers, don't care where the money comes from, so who am I to object? Come over to the studio tomorrow. We have got a director on board,' Mohammad said.

'I will be there, sir,' Zoravar finally replied.

'Jaiveer will be the main lead, as you know. Along with you, we are launching a new girl in the picture too. The budget does not allow an established female lead as well as Jaiveer. I suppose you are fairly well-acquainted with Nimmo, aren't you?' were Mohammad's parting words.

Seated in the lobby of Ranjit Cinetone, Zoravar was upbeat about his new home. He had written to his mother, informing her of the fortuitous turn of events. He had also been reunited with Makkhan, who had been out of work and only too glad of Zoravar's offer.

The director of the picture was an upcoming talent, who went by the name of E. Ezekiel. When Zoravar had heard the name, he had expected a foreign-looking director, but he was pretty flummoxed to see a very Indian looking middle-aged man who spoke Marathi fluently. When he met the director, he learnt that Ezekiel belonged to the Bene Israeli community of Bombay. Zoravar was aware that this community had gained popularity and relevance due to the number of film actors and filmmakers it had given Bombay. Zoravar's fondest memories of the movies had been of the silent pictures. Ruby Myers, Firoza Begum (who had been originally called Susan Solomon and insisted on being called that off screen), and the wonderful Pramila (whose real name was Esther Victoria Abraham) had been instrumental in making him fall in love with cinema. When he took these names, Ezekiel smiled and told him that the Jews in the Bombay film world were divided into Bene Israelis and Baghdadi Jews. The latter had migrated a century or so ago, owing to the fact that the entire trade between Iraq, Syria and neighbouring countries with India had been completely controlled by the Jews. Most of them had left during the Second World War. And then, the plethora of deaths during the Partition of India had exacerbated the Jewish fears for the future, and most of them left for what was the formation of a new state, Israel.

Over a lunch of steamed fish and thick chicken curry with sticky rice, Ezekiel introduced Zoravar to *Deewana Hoon Main*, the love triangle that he had been hired to direct. In a nutshell, the story was about a couple, played by Jaiveer and Nimmo, who fall in love at first sight. They marry despite societal pressure, and at intermission point comes in Zoravar, who claims to be Nimmo's husband from a past marriage. Tensions ensue and the mystery of her past is revealed, which has to do with the evil custom of child marriage. The story eventually veers towards a social message about women's emancipation. In the end, a broken-hearted Zoravar goes away, leaving Jaiveer and Nimmo to begin their new life together.

During the narration, Zoravar kept count of the number of times he would appear on screen. He featured in barely nine scenes. The only silver lining was the fact that the studio had agreed to let him be present during the shooting, even if he wasn't in the scene. On those days, he even convinced Ezekiel to let him double up as an apprentice on production.

Zoravar was sitting behind a small wooden desk. It was 7.30 in the morning. The shooting was not scheduled to begin before 9 a.m., but Zoravar wanted to make sure that he was the first person to get to the location and the last to leave. The months had flown by, and he'd gotten a real insight into the business of filmmaking. So far, he had not only shot his own scenes but also doubled as a driver, spot boy and clapboard boy. Towards the end of filming, he had also been given charge of managing the production when the production controller had died after a huge studio light fell on his head.

Zoravar had picked up the ropes quickly and become the natural choice to lead and supervise the production in the absence of the original production controller. It was better for the movie if someone familiar with the process helmed the production, rather than getting a brand-new crew member, who would naturally take time to acclimatize himself, thereby wasting time.

Zoravar was also impressed with the way Ezekiel had handled the picture. And he learnt that to be a good producer, one needed an amiable director in charge. But the set itself was not a warm place. Nimmo had remained cold and removed, and barring formal niceties, she had largely kept to herself. The colossal failure of Jaiveer's recent release had permanently put him in a foul mood, and he too kept to himself.

Noor Mohammad was extremely worried, since their picture was dependant entirely on Jaiveer's box-office dependability, as the rest of the cast was unknown. This was Zoravar's second brush with the volatility and fickle nature of the business. He saw hands-on the fortune of their leading man changing drastically from the time the film was budgeted to the time it neared completion.

'You are as good or as bad as your last film,' Noor had once boomed to Zoravar.

Now, as Zoravar watched the set filled with people, he thought of how long the journey had been to get here. He felt a certain thrill to be right there, in the very centre of a set.

'Murugan, the dancing girls need to be here for the song we are shooting today. They need to be powdered, rehearsed and ready before dance master Dilshad Begum shows up,' he told a sleepy Murugan, one of the crew members.

'Seth, three girls live in Chembur. The remaining are divided between Kamathipura, Sewri and Versova creek. They have other businesses in the night. It has become a nightmare to go all over the city chasing these girls,' Murugan replied.

'You say this every day. I hear it every day. Now go quickly. I have a song to shoot.'

On hearing this, Murugan stretched out his hand, and Zoravar handed over a crisp five-rupee note. He then looked at the second man standing there, 'Patil, you need to collect the playback equipment. The director called me late last night and has requested for a rain machine sprinkler to be brought in. He feels a rain sequence will add drama to the proceedings.'

Patil, also sleepy, replied, 'Sir, you were here till eleven last night. If the director called you late, and you are here already, have you even slept?'

Zoravar lit a cigarette. 'Don't you know production is the most thankless job in the world?' He then turned to the only woman present on set. 'Shirley, please ensure all the lights are in place. Cameraman Ghosh will be extremely livid if all the things he has demanded do not show up. I am already running up a debt on his account, but there is no time to calculate right now.'

After Shirley left, four other people assembled in Zoravar's makeshift office, awaiting instructions.

'Mehta Saheb,' Zoravar said, as he rubbed his red eyes furiously and handed over a carton of Lucky Strike cigarettes to him, 'deliver this to all head of departments, and to the actors. Tell them it's with the warm regards of Mr Parwaan.'

An eventful day had come to an end. The water sprinklers had malfunctioned and had to be replaced, resulting in a delay of two hours. The dancers had been on time, but the costumes had all been incorrectly fitted and the tailor had to re-do most of them, especially when they were wet and took a long time to dry. Lata Mangeshkar, who was Nimmo's playback voice in the picture, was still to record two more songs for the movie. She charged a high price, but given her fame and talent, the producers had agreed. The last day of shooting for *Deewana Hoon Main* coincided with the rumours that the twenty-six-year-old Raj Kapoor was looking for a large space to establish his own studio and had been scouting locations across Parel and Chembur for the same. Not far behind was Dev Anand, who had also started his own production company and aptly named it Navketan Films. Everyone seemed to be surging ahead – everyone except Zoravar.

6

As post-production work on *Deewana Hoon Main* began at the start of 1952, Zoravar began to worry. It had been too many days since he last heard from his mother, and he planned to make a trip to Punjab once the picture released.

A couple of months later , Ezekiel finally held a preview screening for the cast and crew. The industry folks at the time were using the word 'trial' for this kind of viewing. A trial screening referred to the act of the complete picture being viewed for the first time. These screenings were usually attended by people involved in the making of the movie, along with friends from the fraternity. At the first screening of *Deewana Hoon Main*, everyone who watched it seemed confident of its outcome. An eager assistant director even compared it to Mehboob Khan's *Andaz*, starring Raj Kapoor, Dilip Kumar and Nargis, which had been hailed as the casting coup of the decade.

Only one person had looked grim, and when asked what he felt about the picture, replied, '*Bilkul nahi chalegi. Bundle hai.*'

That person was Haji Parwaan.

The day of reckoning arrived. *Deewana Hoon Main* was going to hit the theatres. Zoravar featured in the top left-hand corner of the poster and only part of his face was visible. Jaiveer and Nimmo had engulfed the remainder of the poster as mainstays. The studio had managed to get a matinee show at Roxy Theatre. On the Friday that the movie opened, Zoravar wished he could have his parents with him, especially when he was going to actually see himself on the big screen. He had been informed that the movie would open in Amritsar, the closest city to Phagwara, after a few weeks. Hindi movies had staggered releases. They would open in the bigger cities first. After the business had been exhausted, the same reels would move to smaller towns. So typically, a major film would only release in other centres weeks or often months after their initial release date. Zoravar had mailed a copy of the poster of the film to his mother and eagerly awaited her reply.

On the day of the release, accompanied by Makkhan, Zoravar reached the hall. With great trepidation and nervousness, he bought two tickets to the matinee show, and then asked the man at the counter,

'How is the response?'

The teller replied without looking up, '*Picture let gayee hai*. It will be out of cinemas by tomorrow.'

The duo did not take what he said seriously, till they walked in and realized that they were the only two people in the entire balcony section.

After the film ended, they walked all the way to an illicit liquor shop at Kalbadevi and ordered beers and drank till they were thrown out of the establishment. As Zoravar hit the footpath, he saw an urchin tear a poster of *Deewana Hoon Main*. In its place, he stuck the poster of an upcoming film titled *Baiju Bawra,* starring Bharat Bhushan, along with a new heroine called Meena Kumari.

When he awoke the next day, Zoravar found himself near the promenade at Marine Drive. Makkhan was coming to his senses too. They both took the train from Churchgate to Ranjit Cinetone without exchanging a word. There was absolute silence at the studio too. A sense of loneliness had enveloped the surroundings, as if the place was in mourning. A failed film, marvelled Zoravar, was no less than a funeral, especially for the people involved in it. He took a long bath and crashed on his bed, but sleep eluded him. He anticipated that it would be a matter of time before he would be asked to vacate the premises. And then there was also that matter of having to repay the loan to Parwaan.

The reviews had been poor, and the critics scathing as ever. There had been barely any mention of Zoravar, barring one review that referred to his performance as an 'able and confident debut', but ripped apart the movie in general.

Zoravar wondered if it was time to give up on his dream.

Zoravar decided to speak with Noor Mohammad about the future, sure that he'd be asked to leave and wanting to pre-empt that conversation. Finding the owner's office empty, he walked towards the wing that housed the clerical offices and heard excited voices coming from within. In the accounts department, a bunch of men were huddled together in a haze of cigarette smoke. Noor Mohammad was one of them.

Spotting Zoravar, he came running up to him.

'*Deewana Hoon Main* has been accepted very well in parts of North India and the trend is encouraging. We are removing the Bombay prints and sending them to centres across CP and CI.'

Zoravar had become familiar with the terms. CP referred to the large chunk of box office revenue that came from the territory that included theatres from Vidharbha (Maharashtra), South and West Madhya

Pradesh, Central Provinces and the Berar State. CI referred to large chunks of Madhya

Pradesh that were not a part of CP.

'There is a huge demand for *Deewana Hoon Main* in these territories. Rajasthan and Bihar are looking like earning sectors too,' added SP Gaur, the head of distribution and revenue.

'Bombay and the southern centres have rejected the picture. We are moving all the prints from those cinemas and sending them by express rail immediately to the Northern part of the country. Mubarak ho! It seems that overall, the picture will be a superhit in some parts of the country. Also, congratulations – certain sections of the vernacular press are calling you the reason for its success. See this,' Noor showed Zoravar a clipping from a Hindi newspaper.

It read, '*It is the unassuming and roguish-looking debutante, Zoravar, who steals the show in this heart-breaking love triangle. Modern-day Majnus would relate to the struggle and heartbreak of the husband who loses his wife to another man. Jaiveer is side-lined as the sympathies of the audiences lie with the faithful, sacrificial husband!*'

The irony was not lost on Zoravar. A tabloid had used the word Majnu in reference to him! Before he could let the words sink in, another tabloid piece was handed to him. A newspaper from Patna had printed a small piece that said, '*Zoravar is emerging as the hero of lovelorn young boys. They are relating to him as he has become a messiah of unrequited love. They seem to be rooting for him, and there are catcalls against the picture's leading girl, especially from the men. The ladies in the audiences are said to be rooting for Jaiveer and Nimmo, especially the latter, but it is clearly Zoravar who steals the show, even though his scenes are too few.'*

'We have come up with an idea,' said Noor Mohammad. 'We are going to picturize a song with you walking on the Colaba promenade, the same location where the on-screen characters of Jaiveer and Nimmo fall in love, and Kishore Kumar will be your voice for the song. This will compensate for your lack of screen time.' He clapped Zoravar on the back. 'Barkhurdar, we are also going organize cinema visits for you to select towns and cities in CP and CI. The theatre owners are willing to bear all costs. They feel that the additional song and the presence of its leading stars at those cinemas will further boost ticket sales.'

A week before the additional song was shot, Ezekiel summoned Zoravar to the studio where they were recording the song with Kishore Kumar. He wanted him to be present for the recording in order to familiarise himself with the emotions in the song, as there was hardly any time for rehearsal.

When he had entered the recording studio, he found Kishore Kumar there, chewing paan, a spark of mischief in his eyes. And then, when he started singing, his voice was like magic. His rendition was flawless, and the music director had no option but to announce 'pack up' for the day, hours before the estimated time. Zoravar had been quite starstruck by the man.

The newly recorded song, featuring Zoravar on the promenade, had been added for centres where the movie was yet to release. The song had a very positive impact on the collections, and people who had already watched the movie before especially travelled to the nearest theatre where they could watch the additional song.

As the city tours began, Jaiveer refused to show up, claiming that he was down with bronchitis. Nimmo refused to be present too, citing lack of time due to the new pictures she had signed.

'Know the truth, Barkhurdar. Those two are not showing up for the tour because of you. You have stolen the show from them, and remember one thing, two actors can never be friends, unless there is a huge disparity of status between the two,' Noor Mohammad said to Zoravar.

They travelled first-class and traversed through the length and breadth of the country. In Bhagalpur, groups of young men followed him everywhere he went. In Nagpur, theatres had been houseful for days.

After a few weeks of touring, Zoravar returned to Bombay, and the euphoria he had just experienced suddenly died. On the streets of Bombay, nobody asked him to sign autographs, and there were no second looks from people either. He was inconspicuous again and could travel on the local trains freely.

There was one thing that did happen to lift his spirits again. Ranjit Cinetone was back in the green due to the profits that *Deewana Hoon Main* had raked in. The studio offered Zoravar a place on its roster, with a monthly salary.

It took all of Zoravar's resolve to say no to what was a safe and secure job offer. He knew that being bound to the studio meant tying his destiny to theirs. It also meant not being able to work with the top banners and other studios that Zoravar wished to engage with. He also knew that refusing the offer was a risk, because he was still relatively unknown in Bombay, and in a business where perception meant everything, that seemed to be a huge negative. He knew that you could have all the love and affection from a pan-India audience, but what Bombay thought of you mattered most when it came to this business. The decisions of the futures of stars were made here by the dream merchants.

Haji Parwaan was happy with Zoravar. He had received a pretty decent profit from this venture after having paid off the people he had borrowed money from. It had also cemented his goodwill with the traders. He helped Zoravar rent a house in Bandra, a small villa hidden in the bylanes behind the site where construction for Mehboob studios was going on.

Zoravar had finally received a letter from his mother and realized that his mother had actually travelled to Bombay to meet him, but been unable to find her son. Her letters spoke about a desolate Bombay – a place she had found harsh and unkind. Zoravar's heart ached at the thought of missing an opportunity to meet his mother, whom he hadn't seen for almost six years. To think that they had been merely kilometres from each other and had not come face to face was a tragic thought. The only good news the letter brought was the fact that his father had finally smiled when he saw his puttar on the poster that Zoravar had mailed home. He had proudly put it up outside his house for all of Phagwara to look at.

Zoravar now stood in his balcony, wearing a red silk lungi and a perfectly tailored kurta. He puffed his Panama and, in his other hand, held the cuff of the lungi as he stared directly at the entrance of Mehboob Studios. He had decided upon his next move. But first, he was going to have to travel to Phagwara. *Deewana Hoon Main* was due to release in Amritsar the next week, and he was going to watch it with his mother and the rest of his family. He had won, finally, but he also knew that now, he had a lot more to lose.

The train journey to Punjab was a long one, and throughout it, people came up for autographs and some even offered him food. Zoravar had pined for this treatment his entire life. Now he felt himself wanting more and more of it.

He had booked the entire auditorium of Raja Talkies in Amritsar. As they reached Phagwara, he was made to sit in the tiny, dank room that acted as the railway office. The stationmaster had shown up in his freshly pressed uniform. He offered tea and a piping hot samosa to Zoravar, who declined the offer. Zoravar had dark glasses on and did not remove them even while sitting in the dimly lit station office as the officer stared at him in awe.

'Saheb, the entire village has seen your poster. You are the son of Phagwara, after all!' the man exclaimed.

Makkhan came running inside, informing him that the tonga had arrived. As Zoravar got up, brushing ash off his grey trousers, he looked for an ashtray to stub the cigarette he had been smoking, and the stationmaster sprang up. He joined his hands and requested Zoravar to give him the half-smoked cigarette. He gave it to the stationmaster, who took it carefully.

'Thank you, saheb,' he said, as if he had been given prasad.

As the tonga rode on, Zoravar observed the dismal poverty of his hometown. Nothing had changed from the last time he had been there. The streets were littered, and were green fields and farms on one side of the road and houses shrouded in poverty on the other. As the carriage shook due to a sharp left turn, he observed how meek the horse pulling the tonga looked.

He finally took off his glasses and looked down at his charcoal-black silk shirt and grey trousers, and wondered if he should have dressed more simply. The tonga finally came to a halt outside his house. He had expected to see his mother waiting at the gate along with the others to receive him, but there was nobody there.

As he got off and walked in, he could hear the wails of a child, and when he entered the foyer, he saw his family standing around a body that was adorned with large sheaths of flowers. He saw his father sitting next to the body; he looked like he'd aged a decade. His sisters were sitting next to him, with their eyes full of tears and heads drooping as they stared at the lifeless body in front of them. His brother, Bir was trying to pacify the crying Amandeep. Sardar Cheema had still not looked up to see his firstborn walk in. Zoravar neared the body and saw his mother lying there, motionless.

A moist-eyed Bir came up to him. 'Mother was absolutely fine last night. She was so excited about watching your picture on the big screen. She was finally going to meet you.' He could not say more and embraced Zoravar, who stood there like a statue.

After a few seconds, he made himself draw closer to the body of his mother, and the face of Bibi Benazira came into view. Even in death, she was beautiful. His mother was gone forever. It had been many years since they had last met. She had even come to Bombay for him, but fate had a different plan for them!

As he stood silent, trying to make sense of everything, he was suddenly faced by a stranger – a young girl, shrouded in white, weeping silently as she stood next to him. He glanced towards Bir in question, but Sardar Cheema answered instead, speaking for the first time. 'She is your bride, Zoravar. Your mother had chosen her for you.'

PART V

A Star is Born

1

After Bibi was put in her grave, the family mourned her for the designated ten days, immediately after which Zoravar was betrothed to Santosh Kaur in a small ceremony at the local Gurudwara.

Santosh was a demure girl of eighteen, who lived next door to Zoravar's family. She had a sweet, round face which hadn't yet shed the baby-fat. She had a dimpled chin, and her cheeks too broke into dimples every time she smiled.

She had been close to Bibi Benazira, who used to help her do the rangolis during Diwali. In turn, Santosh would help Benazira serve the iftar during the breaking of the fast on Ramzan days. During Baisakhi, the two women would be the first to get up and the last to sleep.

The first time Santosh spoke to her husband, it was about his mother. She told him about how Benazira's left shoulder had been aching, how the day she died, the old woman had asked Santosh to read a review of *Deewana Hoon Main* for the umpteenth time. Santosh had just begun reading the words when Benazira collapsed, never to get up again.

Zoravar also learnt that Santosh was the one who had been writing and replying to all of Zoravar's letters on his mother's behalf.

With the death of Benazira, something within Zoravar changed. He didn't have the words to explain it yet, but he knew that he'd never be the same person again. Perhaps if an emotion can be expressed in words, the emotion is not strong enough, he told himself.

Another week passed, and now Zoravar stood watching his family wave their goodbyes as the train pulled out of the platform. Zoravar had tried to convince his family to move to Bombay with him, but his father had refused. Only his younger brother, Bir Bahadur was accompanying the newlyweds back to Bombay. A scrawny young man with freckles on his face, he took mostly after his father.

Finally settling down into their seats once the train left the platform, Zoravar sat back and ruffled his brother's hair as his bride looked out of the window.

Noor Mohammad was cleaning the tobacco from his pipe as Zoravar entered his cabin, wearing his trademark dark glasses, and with the usual Panama cigarette dangling from his lips. He sat down without being asked, and Mohammad smiled to himself. He had seen success go to the heads of far too many actors in his career. Almost always, the loss of etiquette followed. He got up and embraced Zoravar, who smelt of sandalwood. Noor began, 'Well, it wasn't just you who turned us down, Barkhurdar. We've lost Jaiveer to Rajkamal.'

'What?'

'Yes. He thinks that by increasing your screen time, Ezekiel elevated your role and lowered his in *Deewana Hoon Main*.'

'But that's complete hogwash. He will always be the hero of the picture.'

'I wish he believed that. He has also been instrumental in helping Rajkamal poach other talent from us, including Nimmo.'

'Nimmo's gone too?' Zoravar said, surprised. 'I never thought an established star would be so insecure about me.'

'You're never too big to stop being afraid of becoming small,' Mohammad said. 'What I do want to tell you is that I am retiring. I am too old for all this, and I am done with this entire rigmarole. I have delivered a successful picture for the studio, and I've presented you to the world. This is the best time for my exit.'

Zoravar was silent. The news felt like another punch in the gut. The sharp pang of loss, so soon after Benazira, hit him hard. But he noticed that perhaps it wasn't as difficult to bear this news as it might have been once.

He felt like he'd toughened, having witnessed enough upheavals in his life by now. Perhaps that was the good thing about adversity – you got accustomed to it.

'Sir, I respect your decision, but there is one request I have to make,' he said to Mohammad.

'Go on.'

'Before you leave, could you hire my brother at the studio? I will be forever indebted to you.'

For a few seconds, Noor Mohammad considered Zoravar silently and then nodded. 'Fine. I have another four to six months to get things sorted here. Your brother can work with me till I leave. I hope he is as hard-working as you.'

Zoravar was worried. He was running out of money, and he had not signed a single new movie since *Deewana Hoon Main*. And now, he was also responsible for his wife and brother, along with Makkhan, whom he couldn't bring himself to fire, despite his depleting cash flow.

The villa in Bandra where they lived suddenly seemed too small for all of them. Makkhan and Bir would sleep in the front room on charpoys, while the bedroom was inhabited by Zoravar and his young bride. Some things about this new arrangement pleased Zoravar. He liked that Santosh made heavily buttered paranthas every morning for breakfast, and served them with sugary tea. He relished her cooking and consumed it with great satisfaction.

She was a simple girl and seemed to have no interest in movies. This left little in common between them, and their conversations were usually monosyllabic. The only thing she loved was reading, and Zoravar hardly ever saw her without a book in her hand. She'd brought a large collection with herself, and the books spanned a range of subjects. One day she would be reading about the battle of Saragrahi, and the next day, about the ten principals of the Upanishads. Zoravar would sometimes try and speak to her about the books, but usually, they went about their own lives separately.

One balmy Sunday afternoon, Zoravar decided to try something new.

'Do you want to go watch a movie? There must be something or the other playing in Roxy,' he said to Santosh, awkward and uncertain.

She put her book down, a Gurmukhi translation of the Arabian Nights. 'Ji' was all she said. That would have to be enough.

Zoravar asked Bir, Makkhan and Santosh to get ready and, once they were all downstairs, hailed a taxi that took them to South Bombay.

When they reached Roxy Theatre, Zoravar felt his heart skip a beat as he took in what movie that was playing in the cinema. A large poster of *Nadiya Ke Paar* greeted him, complete with the handsome face of its star, Dilip Kumar. Apparently, the movie had been re-released due to lack of new releases that weekend.

Zoravar didn't want his wife and brother to see him as a lowly extra on the big screen.

'Look, I don't think the tickets will be available. Let's just go to another theatre,' he said to them, but Makkhan just guffawed and jumped out of the taxi. Within minutes, he was back with their tickets, much to Zoravar's chagrin.

During intermission, Zoravar tried once again to get them to leave. He claimed that the picture was boring, but no one else agreed with him. So he braced himself and sat, stiff and uncomfortable in his seat.

Soon after intermission came the moment he had been dreading since the second they had entered the hall.

The scene on the screen showed a close-up of Dilip Kumar and then transitioned to a tight close-up of another man waving. It was unmistakably Zoravar.

To Zoravar, those few seconds of him on-screen felt like days. He waited for questions and exclamations, but none came. Instead, he felt Santosh's hand slide into his, but when he turned to her, he saw that her eyes were still glued to the screen. Bir too looked completely enrapt.

Santosh's hand stayed in Zoravar's for the rest of the movie, and she pulled it away only when the lights came back on. As usual, while the rest of the audience began to leave, Zoravar insisted on staying back till the end credits had finished rolling. After that, they hailed a taxi and went back home.

During the drive, the foursome discussed the picture in great detail, but no one brought up Zoravar's cameo.

2

It seemed like love triangles were the flavour of the season. While the patriotic pictures were still grossing huge numbers, other genres were finally breaking out as well.

It had taken another six months for Zoravar to finally sign a new film. The first one he got was backed by Film Lok. Saraswath Mukherjee had sent his own chauffeur to bring Zoravar to the studio.

As he entered the familiar cabin, he realized how much things had changed. This time, he was greeted warmly by Saraswath, who stood up to welcome him.

'Good morning, Zoravar. *Kemon aachho*?'

'I am good, dada,' Zoravar said, pleased at this warm reception.

'Good, good. I hear your wife is expecting?' Saraswath asked.

'Yes, dada.'

'Good, good. Becoming a family man, eh? Okay listen, I want you to do a picture for me.'

'Of course, dada ... Dada, do you mean you want me for your marquee film?' Zoravar asked hesitatingly.

'Ah! No! After the success of *Sargam*, you may have heard that we have just signed Raj Kapoor. He will be in our lead picture for the year,' he said, and Zoravar swallowed his disappointment. He listened quietly as Saraswath continued. 'But there is another project that I want you for. Dadamoni has personally recommended you for the film. In one line, the story is about a man who is murdered by his family members for money. He then gets re-incarnated and exacts revenge on them a few decades later. This will be the first big supernatural picture since the success of Ashok Kumar's *Mahal*.'

'That's great! I'd love to play a wronged hero. I could bring a lot to the role—'

'Oh no, beta! You are to play the younger brother, the one who conspires to murder the lead,' Saraswath explained.

Zoravar stared at him, shocked for a moment. 'So, I'm the villain, you mean?' he asked.

'Yes, of course. That scar of yours will add to the charm.'

Zoravar wanted to say no, but he knew that he could not afford to do so. He had no new movies, and this was an offer by Film Lok, no less.

He said yes, and resigned himself to playing the villain.

The movie had been titled *Bada Bhai*, and principal photography on it began as 1953 rolled around. Zoravar's own work on it ended with the first quarter of the year.

Working on *Bada Bhai* had taught Zoravar a great deal about acting. He had also learned that actors developed their own method of acting after years of experience – something that he'd noticed previously in Ashok Kumar. Dadamoni could be talking about his travels to America, but as soon as the camera rolled, he would deliver a great performance and even shed tears without using glycerine. He would then get back to cracking jokes and reading charts as soon as the scene ended. Zoravar once asked him, 'Dada how do you do this whole switch on, switch off thing?'

'It is just experience. Nothing else,' came the terse reply. And Zoravar remembered Noor Mohammad's line, 'No two actors can ever be friends.'

The year also brought with it Zoravar's first extra-marital affair. He had been sending signals to Srilatha, a supporting actress who played his sibling in the film, and she reciprocated. They made love almost everywhere they could, including small, dark alleyways between two studio floors. Srilatha's knowledge of sex was so advanced that it would give Vātsyāyana a complex!

Santosh, who was now in her advanced stage of pregnancy, had developed an extremely sensitive sense of smell, and every time she smelt rose powder on her husband, she asked him about it. Zoravar made excuses and everytime he lied to her, he felt guilty, but not enough to stop. That initial reservation about cheating on his spouse had disappeared the moment he'd given in for the first time. After that, there was no looking back and no amount of guilt could make him stop himself from indulging.

Soon after he bagged *Bada Bhai*, Zoravar signed another film –a patriotic saga titled *Mera Desh*, where he was to play a soldier who betrays his country, before realizing his mistake and eventually absolving himself by giving his life for the nation.

Zoravar found himself shooting two movies simultaneously, and he was sure that both of them were destined to be successes and would stabilize his career.

Soon on the tail of both offers, Ezekiel came to Zoravar with his next movie, which was once again a love triangle. This time too, Zoravar would be playing the second lead who loses the girl to the hero.

He found no real difference between this story and *Deewana Hoon Main*, except that it had a new location and setting – that of pre-Partition Bengal. Perhaps what surprised Zoravar most was that he would once again be sharing screen space with Jaiveer and Nimmo – the two people he had not set eyes on since *Deewana Hoon Main*. He had heard that there were no permanent friends or enemies in the film business, and considering how readily Jaiveer and Nimmo had agreed to star with him in a new film, this really did seem to be the case.

Quite without irony, the movie was titled *Deewana Hai Dil*. It was a clear ploy to cash in on the success of its predecessor, and Zoravar's character was from Awadh. Once again, a move clearly designed to exploit Zoravar's popularity in the heartland.

3

Mera Desh went on to become the highest-grossing movie of the year, and on the heels of it, *Bada Bhai* tanked. Yet again, the film pundits had been wrong. Patriotic fervour was still the flavour of the day, give or take a few aberrations. And those did not include *Bada Bhai*. Zoravar did get noticed in both the movies, and critics gave him mostly encouraging reviews.

He was finally beginning to get second looks on the streets of Bombay. People stared when he and a heavily pregnant Santosh went to watch English movies at the Regal or Odeon. But so far, his popularity was restricted to mostly just that – second glances.

Even so, Zoravar enjoyed this newfound recognition, no matter the source. When people did walk up to him, he'd nod and smile humbly before signing autographs.

He had even started keeping a fountain pen with him at all times.

Zoravar and Santosh were attending a screening of *Paapi*, in which Raj Kapoor was essaying the role of an atheist who masquerades as a godman. Zoravar was immersed in the duality of the character when Santosh's water broke.

Zoravar rushed her to the Breach Candy Hospital and after a night-long ordeal, she gave birth to a boy. When Zoravar held the baby for the first time, he saw his mother's face in that of his son. Zoravar felt like his mother had returned to this world as his child.

They named the boy Dilawar, and the week after the birth of their first child, a comedy starring Zoravar, titled *Ande Ke Chhilke*, which had required only six days of work from Zoravar, turned out to be an above-average grosser at the cinema halls. Zoravar's performance was appreciated, and one critic wrote, 'Zoravar is a supporting actor who must be taken more seriously, especially as a comedian.' It made Zoravar wonder whether this had been a compliment or a taunt.

Zoravar spent the rest of 1953 shooting for *Deewana Hai Dil*, and as the year approached its last quarter, the film was finally ready to hit the theatres.

The day of its release dawned with the news that Sir Girija Shankar Bajpai, Bombay's revered first

Governor of State, had breathed his last. First, the news was thought to be a rumour, but then it gained further momentum as thousands lined up the street to pay homage. The city went into mourning after the official announcement of his demise was made, and no member of the public was in any mood to watch a saga about lost love. Despite this, while *Deewana Hai Dil* opened feebly, it managed to pick up momentum as the days passed and did average business at the ticket counter.

He had been reading a review of the film and rocking Dilawar to sleep when Zoravar suddenly heard a loud sound from the living room and rushed to it. When walked in, he saw that Makkhan had Bir in a headlock. The room reeked of liquor, and Bir's eyes were bloodshot as he tried to free himself.

Makkhan had caught Bir stealing a showpiece that Dadamoni had gifted Zoravar after the completion of *Bada Bhai*. Apparently, Bir had been in the habit of stealing money, and when questioned, Santosh admitted that there had been less cash in her purse than usual. Zoravar slapped an inebriated Bir, who continued to laugh at him and ask for more alcohol.

Later, Zoravar asked Noor if there had been such cases in the office too.

'The office? But he quit the job almost two months ago. He said he had taken your permission to leave the position.' Noor Mohammad said, surprised.

Zoravar was aghast at this revelation. 'I had no idea that he wasn't working for you anymore!' he exclaimed. 'What happened?'

'Well, the first time he stole from me, I kept it to myself, out of respect for our relationship. And he is a young lad. The next time it happened, I confronted him, and he lied to my face. I didn't want to pursue the matter further, so I decided to just be more vigilant about him, but he said that he'd been insulted and couldn't work here anymore,' replied Mohammad.

'Sir, I wish you had checked with me,' said Zoravar, his voice disappointed and worried.

'I probably should have, because he even borrowed some money on your behalf from the accounts team.'

'Why on earth would the accounts team entertain this lout?' Zoravar exclaimed.

'Because you are an actor, Zoravar, and one who is relevant right now. No one wants to take panga with you!' Noor said, smiling.

Zoravar sat across from Makkhan and Bir.

'From now on, Bir will work with you,' he said to Makkhan, and lifted a hand to stop Bir, who opened his mouth to protest, from interrupting. 'He will assist you in all the work that you do for me. Let him accompany us to every shoot, let him learn the ropes from you, let him learn how to schedule dates. He is not to be left alone at any time.' Makkhan was about to protest too, but thought the better of it. In any case, he knew he could not say no to his boss.

4

The year 1953 had been a good one for Zoravar, and it was time to take 1954 by its horns. The offers began pouring in, and so did the adulation of people. He had to stop travelling by train and purchased a second-hand Ford Crestliner, one that had apparently originally belonged to the actor Pran, according to what the car dealer claimed.

Makkhan had risen up the ranks, as was the norm with trusted man Fridays of movie stars. He had been managing dates for Zoravar and, by virtue of having hung around him for so long, also made enough contacts in the right places. Zoravar had put Makkhan in charge of putting together film deals for him, and he had managed to bag an offer for Zoravar. This time, it was special as the production house was none other than Dev Anand's

Navketan Films. It was to be directed by an upcoming director called Guru Dutt, who had previously directed the successful noir film *Baazi*. He had followed up his debut film with two other films, which had both bombed at the box office. Even so, Zoravar was excited at the prospect of starring in a Dev Anand production, though he'd have preferred to work with a more established director. He was also not impressed by Guru Dutt's work. In fact, he had watched *Baazi* and marvelled at how it reminded him of Rita Hayworth's *Gilda*. But he was persuaded by Makkhan to visit the director and get a sense of him. After all, he could always listen to the story and reject the offer, the assistant-turned-manager reasoned.

Zoravar drove to the posh suburb of Pali Hill, where the Navketan office was located. There, he was taken to a foyer overlooking a recording studio and introduced to Guru. Zoravar observed the man who stood before him in a dishevelled white Kurta and grey pants. His hair was thick and curly and had been pushed back. Zoravar took an instant dislike to the man, a feeling that might have come from his dislike for not only Guru Dutt's appearance but also his movies.

His thoughts were interrupted when Dutt spoke. 'I have not watched any of your pictures, but I hear you are perfect for the part I am about to narrate to you,' he said.

Zoravar nodded, and Dutt went on to narrate a story about a taxi driver caught between two women. He also made the actor hear two songs they had recorded, one of which was a track sung by Shamshad Begum and the other, '*Babuji dheere chalna*', sung by Dutt's wife, Geeta. Zoravar did not like either, mostly because he noted that they were led by female singers and were sure to be picturized on the leading ladies instead of him.

Zoravar did not think long before saying no to Dutt's offer. He wrote a letter addressed to Dev Anand personally, apologizing and explaining why he did not feel for the script enough to do the movie. The truth was, Zoravar was nervous about working with a director whose last two outings had failed at the box office. No reply came from Navketan Films.

It turned out that Zoravar's worry about Dutt's sinking star was shared by other actors too, and after most of them turned down the movie, the director cast himself as the actor in it and titled it *Aar-Paar*.

Not too long after turning down Dutt's movie, Zoravar finally received an offer that he felt was closest to what he wanted to do. Wadia, an ace director who excelled in larger-than-life action pictures, offered Zoravar a role in a movie about a character who loses the love of his life to a policeman and decides to become a dacoit to fuel the void in his life and avenge his broken heart.

Zoravar was certain that playing a dacoit would come naturally to him. The filming lasted for just under three months and when released, *Daaku* opened to a thunderous box office reception. For the first time in his career, Zoravar received top billing on the poster.

The story was an expensive saga, and the audience was curious. It helped that the tabloids were going wild with articles about the steamy affair Zoravar was having with his heroine, Jayati, something Zoravar had convinced Santosh were rumours intentionally planted to create a buzz around the movie. Santosh had her doubts, but she was too busy with her second pregnancy, which had happened very close to the birth of their firstborn, and she chose to focus on her baby and her pregnancy instead.

When it released, *Daaku* became a bonafide pan-India success, and it established Zoravar as a doyen for the broken-hearted male. The box-office success also brought with it the brunt of the critics, who felt Zoravar's style of loud dialogue delivery was jarring. Despite its massive success, the harsh reviews from the critics angered Zoravar and wounded him deeply. He vowed never again to read reviews of his performances.

On the evening of the party that celebrated the grand success of *Daaku*, Santosh went into labour for the second time in her life, and they were blessed with another son, whom they named Tarsem. On the same day, Guru Dutt's *Aar-Paar* released. Zoravar had been too tied up with his newborn to know at the time that the film had emerged as a runaway success and was being touted as one of the most influential films of the year. It's shadow lighting and noir genre had given birth to a new style of cinema, and critics and audiences alike had hailed Guru Dutt as a filmmaker to watch out for.

Zoravar had put all the money he had earned into the purchase of a sea-facing bungalow, honouring the promise he had made to himself on his first day in Bombay. Nepean Sea Road was the heart of South Bombay, and Zoravar had decided he would live nowhere else. Makkhan had been given a section of the porch that had been converted into a makeshift room, just about enough to house Makkhan and his meagre belongings. Bir Bahadur occupied the room on the ground floor, and Zoravar, Santosh and their two sons lived on the first floor of the house, which was flanked by two parallel and ornamental staircases.

One day, Makkhan entered the garden in the backyard and found Zoravar standing in it and smoking a cigarette, wearing his usual red silk lungi and a matching kurta with four buttons open, revealing a thick gold chain that had been gifted by a fan. He was also wearing his dark shades, despite it being dusk.

'Makkhan, we need to sign a new picture,' he said to his manager.

'I am trying, Praa ji. If you would have said yes to *Aar-Paar*—'

'Don't you dare bring up that movie's name! That picture is a fluke too. His next one is going to be a dud. You watch,' Zoravar thundered.

Makkhan cowered, not used to arguing with his boss.

'Yes, Praa ji. You are probably right.'

'Probably?' Zoravar raised an eyebrow.

'You are right, Sarkar, but that does not solve our current problem.'

Santosh walked into the garden. As usual, she was holding a book in her hand. For a change, Zoravar looked at the book with interest.

'The cover of that book looks intriguing. What is it about?' he asked her.

'It is about twin brothers who fall in love with the same woman,' Santosh said, surprised at his curiosity. He usually never asked her what she was reading.

Zoravar looked at Makkhan, 'This might be our answer! The plot sounds great, and this is the double role film I have been waiting to do.'

He took the gold chain off his neck and put it gently around Santosh's.

'You have just given me my next film. Thank you!'

5

Having sunk his entire fortune into his new residence, Zoravar was convinced he would have to borrow money to continue running the kitchen, and he decided that this time, he wouldn't turn to Pasha or Parwaan. Instead, he went to meet the executives who now ran Ranjit Cinetone and pitched the idea of a double role picture with him, starring as twin brothers who fall in love with the same girl. At the end, one of him would lose the girl (yet again!), and audiences would love the bittersweet feeling that while Zoravar finally got the girl, another Zoravar lost her as always.

The Cinetone executives loved the idea and decided to begin development on it. Zoravar asked them if he would get story credit on the picture and they agreed. 'Excellent!' he said. 'In that case, could I have some money as my signing amount?' The executives looked at each other, 'As the leading man?' they asked. 'No. My fee is for giving you the concept that I could have taken to anyone else.'

'Oh yes!' One of them immediately pulled out a wad of cash from the drawer behind and handed it to Zoravar, sealing the deal right then and there, as a routine gesture. The rest of the deal would be negotiated later.

He was about to leave when he remembered something and turned around.

'By the way, do you have someone in mind to write the screenplay?' he asked.

'There is this young chap. From Madras. He is creating waves. He is not very keen to write films in Bombay, but if we cajole him, he could do a great job with a story like this,' one of the executive said.

'Sounds good. What is his name?'

'Karunanidhi,' replied the executive.

A week passed, and Zoravar did not hear from the executives. Beginning to get anxious, he went to Ranjit Cinetone again, accompanied as usual by Makkhan. He learned that the two executives were just back from Madras and looking pastier than usual. Apparently, the meeting with Karunanidhi had been an absolute disaster.

'The fellow barely spoke to us. And the brief words he did say were all in Tamil,' one of them said.

'Fine, then let's just drop the idea of working with him, in that case. Let's just get somebody from here,' said Zoravar.

'See, that is the thing. We strongly believe that a story like this needs a different sensibility. Something that we have never seen before. Objectivity – that's what will make this story truly compelling.'

Zoravar was beginning to get irritated. 'Then how about getting a new director? Maybe somebody from the heartland? How about a playwright? A playwright will have the required chops need to draw performances and would already possess a great sense of writing. '

The executives looked at each other before one of them said, 'Playwrights won't work. It will be unreasonable to expect a stage director to adapt to screen, and teaching them the technicalities of a film set cannot be done at our cost, especially when a double role picture like this requires tremendous technical knowhow.'

Zoravar sighed, got up and shook hands with them as he lit a fresh cigarette. He had begun to smoke Craven A cigarettes now. He hated them, and they cost too much, but he had a status to maintain. He inhaled deeply and walked out of the studio.

Just as he was getting into the car, Makkhan said something that stopped him in his tracks. 'Praa ji. Why don't you write this picture? You have such a huge library, and you have watched so many films. It shouldn't be that hard,' he winked.

'Makkhan, that is a great idea. Well done!' Zoravar said. Makkhan rubbed his hands earnestly, drunk on the contribution he had just made.

Zoravar had spent sleepless nights trying to draft a synopsis. He had taken inputs from Santosh about the book and referenced various scenes from movies he had watched. Despite the constant wailing and crying of his toddlers, he finally managed to write out a few pages of what he believed was an impressive story.

He wanted Parwaan and Pasha to hear it first and give him what he knew would be an unbiased opinion, before he passed on the material to the Cinetone executives.

When Zoravar walked into Parwaan's office, he hoped to find both Pasha and him their usual congenial selves, but they seemed in a dour mood, and their minds were pre-occupied.

'I have written something that I want both of you to hear it,' Zoravar said, smiling, hoping that whatever was bothering them would not end up costing him.

But to his dismay, Parwaan scowled. 'Yaara, I don't have the bandwidth right now. This f****** Brij Bhushan Rai is creating far too many problems for us. He is the architect of all the pain in our lives. We have just had an entire shipment of opium confiscated at the docks earlier today,' he said, and Pasha nodded. 'Yes, Zoravar, this is not a good time to hear your film stories.'

Zoravar realized that there would be no changing their minds.

'I will be off, then. I will come see you another day. Let me know if there is anything I can do for you,' he said.

On his way back, he passed a paan stall and stopped. Getting out, he purchased his beloved Panama cigarettes. He had taken to smoking these secretly. Only in public did he smoke the fancy Craven A cigarettes. Taking long puffs, he thought of what Parwaan had said. The mention of Brij Bhushan Rai bothered him. It brought forth all the sour memories of his past; the past that now seemed like an old movie, with another actor playing his part.

He knew that the policeman couldn't touch him anymore. He had escaped, and he was free. The man had no proof, and there was nothing he could to do to harm Zoravar. But even then, every once in a while, Zoravar felt a chill run through him when he remembered how Rai had tortured him, what he'd almost done to Nimmo, and the man haunted his dreams. He knew that as he grew more popular, he had much more to lose, and the fear of Rai catching up with him loomed over him, baseless as it was. Hearing his name from Parwaan's lips had brought all that fear back.

Even though he hadn't managed to get his friends to weigh in, Zoravar presented the written material to the executives on his next visit to the studio.

'Who has written this?' one of them asked as he picked up the sheaf of papers.

'Makkhan, of course,' said Zoravar, not wanting to risk embarrassment in case they didn't like the script.

As they read the material, he tried to gauge their expressions, but their faces betrayed nothing.

Finally, they looked up and smiled. 'Well done, Makkhan. You should consider a career in writing. The flow of the story is perfect, especially the first half, and the rest of it is marvellously entertaining. Why don't you write a longer version?'

Makkhan acted his part beautifully. 'Thank You, sir. But I will need some more money to continue,' he said, and turned to Zoravar, who smiled at him and nodded. This had gone off better than he'd imagined.

Zoravar had no idea about writing a long-format story. As his eyes hovered around the room, he looked at Santosh's bookshelf. Zoravar approached it and began pulling out books, flipping through them hungrily. This could be the answer to his problems.

By the end of the week, he had jotted down paragraphs, subplots and characters straight out of the many novels he perused. He had shamelessly plagiarized the language and pilfered ideas. And he knew that what he had as an end result was good.

When the completed screenplay had been read by the men at the studio, they agreed with Zoravar's evaluation. The gimmick of the two leading men played by Zoravar, coupled with the fact that one of him would lose the girl and thereby maintain his image of the doyen of unrequited love, sounded exciting. They were also toying with the idea of getting Kishore Kumar and Mohd. Rafi on board to be playback singers for the respective roles. The upcoming actress Razia, after being screen-tested personally by Zoravar in various hotel rooms, had been signed on to play the heroine. This role had originally been offered to Nargis, who had turned down the picture citing date issues as she was shooting with Raj Kapoor, and Meena Kumari had refused to act in a film with so much focus on the leading man.

Since the studio was saving money by signing a relative newcomer as its leading lady, Makkhan came up with the ingenious idea that Zoravar's salary on the picture should be doubled, because he was playing two characters. In an unprecedented move, the studio agreed to give him double the rate of his market price. The news created a buzz in the trade sections of the movie business as Zoravar's fees that year became the highest charged by any leading man.

The movie, now titled *Sipahi*, found its director in Maqbool, who had been assistant to prolific directors and therefore had the required technical knowhow to approach a complicated project such as this. He had just resigned from a magnum opus titled *Mughal-e-Azam*, starring Dilip Kumar, Prithvi Raj and Madhubala, because the project had taken up over five years of his time. The picture had been unceremoniously stalled due to lack of finances.

Zoravar felt a tinge of happiness when he heard that Dilip Kumar had wasted so much time on a film that would never see the light of day.

The shooting for *Sipahi* was completed in record time, and taking a punt on a new director had paid off. It had been the hardest shoot of Zoravar's career, and yet somehow, the most fulfilling. It had been a nightmare initially, especially in scenes where he had to pull of the double role. Zoravar had to first dress as Ram and accordingly style his hair and modulate his voice. He would look at an imaginary Raghav, who would be a stand-in assistant mouthing Raghav's lines to Ram's dialogues. Zoravar would then have to quickly change into the costume of Raghav, with a different hairstyle, and switch into a different voice intonation before re-doing the entire scene this time as Raghav, who had to react to an imaginary Ram. Instead of shooting the regular shift of twelve hours, there were days where the entire crew ended up shooting in hot, dusty studios for over sixteen hours a day.

The picture was finally ready for release, close on the heels of Raj Kapoor's *Shree 420*, which was still carrying on in theatres. Zoravar had been secretly worried about releasing *Sipahi* this close to *Shree 420*, which was on its way to becoming the most-watched film of all time.

6

Ranjit Cinetone had secured Edward theatre as the main hall for *Sipahi*. Zoravar, Pasha and Makkhan decided to go to the cinema to gauge audience reactions. Pasha and Zoravar exchanged a silent look when they saw the king-size hand-painted poster that featured two Zoravars on it.

For Zoravar, the moment was bittersweet and surreal. He was going to watch his own film in the same hall where he had seen his first movie in Bombay.

He saw the box-office counter with a board propped up against it, proclaiming the theatre HOUSEFUL, and felt a thrill shoot up him.

In the hall, he felt the sighs and gasps of the audiences feed his soul, and when the movie ended and the lights came on, Zoravar heard resounding applause and whistles fill the hall.

Just then, a woman in the audience spotted him and shrieked, and the sound diverted the attention of the rest of the viewers, who then noticed Zoravar too. Within minutes, they had left their seats to charge towards the star they had just spent the last three hours of their lives with.

It was not till he felt the first prick of a nail on his cheekbone that Zoravar realized he would have to run. He thought, *this is what being mobbed feels like.* He made his way towards the exit door and tried to open it as he felt the surge of the entire Dress Circle behind him. He used all his might to open the door and when it still did not budge, he kicked it hard. His toe hurt as he tried once again to push the door, and he felt someone pull his hair from behind. This time, he pulled the door open, and it worked. Zoravar ran down the long stairs looking for Makkhan and Pasha, only to discover that the crowd from the lower stall sections were running up as they had figured from the melee above that the star of *Sipahi* was here.

Zoravar now felt completely trapped as he saw the throngs of crowd from below coming up and the people from the dress circle and balcony running down. Panic was setting in as people from all sides surrounded him and began screaming his name. Some called him Ram, some called him Raghav, some called him Daaku from his previous outing, and some even called him Deewana. Acting on complete impulse, Zoravar jumped from the edge of the wooden railing, free-falling into the food section below. He landed on his knees and heard the sound of bones cracking. He screamed in pain and it cut through the crowd like a gunshot. Realizing that he was hurt, the crowd began dispersing. They fled the hall and clashed with the huge crowd of people who were waiting outside, impatient for their evening show to begin. Pasha and Makkhan found Zoravar lying on the floor, picked him up and took him out via the rear exit.

Pasha was apologetic. 'I am sorry, brother, that we couldn't help you,' he said.

Zoravar nodded, unable to speak, and clenched his teeth in pain.

Sipahi emerged as a raging success at the box office. Noor Mohammad had come to see a recovering Zoravar at the Harkishandas Hospital in Grant Road. The actor had spent the last few weeks there, nursing his broken bones.

'You have finally seen the magic of our business. The three-hour rule. The greatest thing about show business? It takes three hours for lambs to turn into lions, and lions to turn into lambs. Today you are a lion, enjoy it!' Noor said.

Zoravar's life really *had* changed in three hours. *Sipahi* was completing its silver jubilee in most theatres, and Zoravar now seemed to be in the running towards becoming the number one star in the country. He had received bouquets, cards and letters from dignitaries and fans alike during his time in the hospital.

Towards the end of his recovery period, Zoravar was reading one of the many film magazines on his bedside table when he came across a long article about the widespread success of Raj Kapoor's younger brother, Shammi Kapoor's debut film.

When Zoravar saw the title of the movie, the pain in his soul was more than that in his knees. The title of the film was *Laila-Majnu*!

After *Sipahi's* runaway success, Zoravar had signed an astounding twelve movies. A certain Makkhan Lal Narula had been credited as the writer of *Sipahi*, and initially, producers had wondered who this talented writer was and wanted to sign him on. Makkhan was amused by his faux success but sat it out till the buzz died down.

Zoravar expedited the building of the extension of his bungalow. He then sent Makkhan and Bir Bahadur to handle all matters pertaining to his family's migration to Bombay.

This time, when Zoravar had asked for them to move to Bombay, his father had not objected. Zoravar reserved the entire bogey for his family, and after spending two days on the train, Attar Singh Cheema had landed up at his son's house with his daughters and youngest son. He was moist-eyed when he saw the words on the nameplate of the bungalow.

In big, bold, gold-embossed letters, the sign read: BENAZIR, 27, Nepean Sea Road. Santosh came running out and touched her father-in-law's feet, and Zoravar's siblings Zohra, Zehra and Amandeep greeted their nephews excitedly. The only person missing at the reunion was Bir. He had dropped off his family at the bungalow and disappeared into his room on the ground floor.

At the beginning of 1955, *Mughal-e-Azam* had been remounted entirely from scratch. K. Asif had found yet another financier, and Dilip Kumar had readily agreed to shoot for it. The news troubled Zoravar, since he had assumed that the picture had been permanently shelved. In any case, he was certain that it was going to be a huge disaster, keeping in mind all the behind-the-scenes information he had received from a member of the production, whom he had been paying to spy on the proceedings.

The toast of tinsel town was currently a chap called Bimal Roy. He had directed *Parineeta* and *Do Bigha Zameen*, both of which had been released close to each other and were running successfully in theatres.

Zoravar wanted to work with this young director from Calcutta at any cost. He made a mental note to ask Dadamoni, who had been the male lead of *Parineeta*, for an introduction to Roy. Meanwhile, he managed to wrangle another introduction that he was excited about – surprisingly with another young director from Bengal, Kaushik Basu, who was fast becoming known for his intense and moving films. Zoravar had heard that Basu had a big project in mind and wanted to see if he could bag himself the lead in it.

Basu had agreed to meeting Zoravar in the Taj Mahal Hotel in Colaba.

On the day of the meeting, Zoravar asked Makkhan to wait in the car while he went in to meet Basu.

Makkhan realized that this was the first time Zoravar had kept him out of things, but he tried not to let it bother him.

Zoravar was an hour late for his meeting, and found Basu sitting quietly in a sofa near the lobby. He was wearing a starched white shirt that seemed hastily tucked into black linen trousers. He had a receding hairline, and his hair was pushed back from his forehead. He seemed lost in thought. He looked up when he heard a noise – a crowd had gathered around Zoravar, most of them young girls. He watched Zoravar sign autographs for a minute before turning away disinterestedly.

After Zoravar had finished satiating his fans, he walked up to Basu.

'Hello, Kaushik. It's good to meet you. I admire your work,' he said, sticking out his hand for a handshake.

Basu did not shake the offered hand and was terse in his reply. 'You are late by an hour,' he said. 'Unfortunately, I have to leave for another appointment now.'

'I'm sure it can wait,' Zoravar said, confident arrogance in his voice.

'It cannot. My masseuse is a busy man, and he only comes once a week. I cannot miss the appointment.'

Zoravar smiled 'You are a funny man, Mr Basu.'

'I have gone from Kaushik to Mr Basu in a matter of seconds. I must be really affecting you.'

'Look Mr—uh, Kaushik. I was late. I apologize. Let's not start on the wrong foot. Let's begin afresh,' Zoravar said, and this time, his voice was softer, more polite.

He seemed to convince Basu, who nodded. 'Okay, I'll sit for a while longer. Let's continue talking here,' he said, and indicated that Zoravar join him at the sofa.

'I do not know if you are aware, Zoravar, but I have been very vocal about how much I loved *Devdas* with Saigal in it. He is my favourite actor.'

Zoravar gave an all-knowing nod, 'He is my favourite as well.' Zoravar even quoted a dialogue from the film.

Basu did not acknowledge the same and continued, 'Sarat Chandra is my favourite writer. And when I watched *Devdas*, I kept thinking about how I would tell the story, given an opportunity. I felt I would do it differently. Today, I finally have the chance to tell the story, and the time is ripe for me to make my version of—'

'*Devdas*,' Zoravar completed.

Basu nodded. 'My lifetime dream has been to tell the story of *Devdas* on screen. It has been almost two decades since it was last made.'

Zoravar felt goosebumps. While he had not read it, he had watched his favourite Saigal play the lovelorn character multiple times. He wanted this role at any cost. He urged, 'Kaushik, I fit the part.'

'From what I hear, it is your public image that fits the part, not you per se,' Basu quipped.

Zoravar felt the role slipping away from him.

'Have you watched any of my pictures?' he asked urgently.

'I have watched a few. You are the guy who always loses the girl,' he said. 'Look, Zoravar, the truth is, I am not very sure of whom I want to cast. Casting is generally a collaborative decision I make with my team. I have been fortunate that I have a team that remains constant and their contribution to my movies is as important as mine, if not more. Haridas wants me to cast a new fellow, Sourindra wants me to cast Ashok Kumar, Nithwik Ghosh wants me to cast Kishore Kumar, just so that he can have a hero who sings his own songs. And Roshan has no opinion.' Roy stood up, ready to leave. 'Truth be told, I want Dilip Kumar to do the picture.' Shaking Zoravar's hand, he added, 'I have to leave. Like I told you, Sundar must be waiting.'

'Sundar?' Zoravar asked.

'Yes. My masseuse.'

Zoravar lit a Panama as he sat in the car. Makkhan had seen the expression on his boss's face and knew better than to ask about the meeting. As they passed a giant poster of *Singing in The Rain*, Zoravar finally spoke.

'That man is making *Devdas* with Dilip Kumar. How do I get the part?' he said.

For a few minutes, Makkhan was silent as they sped past Café Royal and towards Marine Drive. Then he looked at Zoravar. 'I know he relies on his team, Praa ji. There is his editor and confidante, Haridas; there is the music director, Sourindra, and then there are his writers, Ghosh and Bedi. Also, there is your friend Roshan, who is also part of the unit. If we can get a hold of even one of these men, we get a foot in the door,' he said.

7

Vasant was a street urchin, one among the countless in Bombay who dedicated the first half of the day to scouring for work and the latter half to executing it. That was the only way to survive. Today had been a good day. A middle-aged man with a funny food name had approached him and given him more money than he had seen in a long time. All he had to do was stick posters of various movies on walls that lined the route from Pali Hill in Bandra to Reclamation grounds. It was like he was making a map for someone to follow. The greasy middle-aged man had even provided him with a rather long car that would help him cover the distance. In places where there were no walls, the posters had been glued to trees.

By the time Vasant had finished the job, the only thing he could see in front of his eyes was the face of the actor on the posters. Handsome, with light eyes and a scar on his cheek.

When the prolific screenwriter Nithwik Ghosh left home, he was already in a foul mood. He desperately wanted Meena Kumari to play the role of Parvati, more commonly known as Paro, the character that was the cause of Devdas's maladies. He wanted Nargis to play Chandramukhi, the courtesan who loses her heart to Devdas. Meena Kumari had turned down the picture because of that husband of hers, Kamal Amrohi. He wanted top billing for Meena Kumari and a copy of the screenplay beforehand. He also wanted her to be the highest-paid actor in the picture and had said that she would not do scenes that would require intimacy.

Kaushik Basu had thrown a fit of rage, and Meena Kumari's exit had been rather unceremonious. On the heels of this news came the information that Nargis had refused to play Chandramukhi. She was a top heroine and therefore would only play the role of Paro.

Apart from everything else, there was also the stress of who would play the titular character. Nithwik wondered whether the project was jinxed and star-crossed, like its lead characters. As his car raced towards Reclamation, he saw the streets lined with the poster of *Sipahi*, and took in the good-looking images of Zoravar as two different characters. Further on, he saw a torn poster of the same actor he had seen earlier, this time as a dacoit. When they turned right on Perry Cross Road, he passed a tree that had a poster of a war movie that had starred Zoravar.

By the time he reached the office, Kaushik and the others had already gathered, and they were discussing how to cast the damn project. As Nithwik entered, he suggested

'How would Zoravar be for *Devdas*? He fits the image.' Basu rolled his eyes. 'Ironically, I met Zoravar just a few days ago, and he seemed very keen to play the part. Now you have suggested his name. Just before you entered, Roshan, who seemed to have no opinion on this before, also recommended Zoravar for the part of Devdas.'

When Makkhan had relayed the information to Zoravar that Roshan was being considered to compose the background score for *Devdas*, Zoravar had immediately reached his old roommate's house. They had gotten drunk on beers that Roshan loved, and Zoravar had convinced his friend to suggest his name for the part.

'I still strongly believe that a new actor should be considered for the part,' said a young bespectacled Haridas. He had also moved from Calcutta to make pictures in Bombay and was apprentice and editor to Kaushik Basu.

'I agree with you. And anyway, how is that Punjabi going to speak in a believable Bengali accent?' asked Basu.

Suddenly, their meeting was interrupted by the Gurkha who guarded the gates of the bungalow. He came running into the room, breathing hard.

'Dada, there is a drunk man at the gates. He is desperate to see you and is uncontrollable. I tried my best to throw him out, but he refuses to listen,' he said.

The men stood up and went outside to see what the hullabaloo was. There was a tall, fair man standing downstairs, wearing clothes that belonged to another era. He was dressed in a white dhoti and a tight golden cummerbund was tied around a white satin shirt, in the style of old zamindars. A thin slash of red was dripping down from the edge of his lips as he spoke in a garbled but chaste Bengali accent. He was swaying and could barely stand on his feet. His breath reeked of alcohol, and he was mouthing a monologue that was addressed to Chandramukhi. If it had not been for the scar on his face, Roshan would have never recognized his friend.

'Zoravar! My God! Is it really you?' he ran towards the drunk. The man was hysterical now, and it seemed as if he had memorized, verbatim, the entire novel. He walked towards the rest of the men as his soliloquies now veered towards the unfairness of society and how he was going to drink himself to death rather than endure rejection in love. After a few minutes of the spectacle, Basu finally went to Zoravar and extended his hand to him. Zoravar refused to stop, as if in a trance. Eventually, it took the force of all the men standing there to take Zoravar inside the bungalow and make him lie down. Even in his semiconscious stupor, Zoravar kept mouthing lines from the novel.

Basu had decided it would be best to produce the project himself. With Zoravar playing Devdas, he knew the flutter it would cause.

Zoravar had been pressing him to announce the picture, but Basu had been holding off. He wanted to ensure that the writing, the sets and the songs were ready before he made the grand announcement.

In the first quarter of 1955, there came two announcements. *Filmfare*, a magazine that had been launched specifically to cover news about the Hindi movie industry, announced a nationwide poll. Its readers would send in their votes across different categories, and the winners would be awarded The Clares Trophy, named after the *Times of India* movie critic, Clare Mendonca. The organizers received over twenty thousand votes and the results were unanimous. Bimal Roy won Best Director for *Do Bigha Zameen*, Dilip Kumar won Best Actor for his performance in *Daag*, Meena Kumari won Best Actress and Naushad won Best Composer for their contribution in *Baiju Bawra*.

The awards were held at the Metro Theatre in Kalbadevi, and the who's who of the business attended.

Zoravar was seated next to Dev Anand, and the men barely spoke, barring exchanging basic pleasantries. Gregory Peck was supposed to be the chief guest, but word was that his flight had faced some technical problem and he was stranded in Ceylon. But much to everyone's delight, while he missed the ceremony, he did manage to show up for the dinner scheduled at the Wellington Gymkhana after the awards.

Suraiya had eyes only for Peck, and it seemed Dev was feeling rebuked. Zoravar could not keep his eyes off Suraiya and Peck either. The man exuded charisma and charm, and looked even more handsome than he did on screen. Zoravar was already tipsy when Suraiya introduced herself to him first and then introduced him to Peck as 'Shakespeare's Romeo'.

Peck looked at him and said, 'Well, you got stereotyped, didn't ya?'

Zoravar nodded. 'I am a fan, Mr Peck. I enjoyed watching you in *Duel in The Sun*, but *The Gunfighter* remains my favourite.'

'That's so surprising to hear! Not many know people about *The Gunfighter*. Not here, at least. I'm impressed!' Peck moved on with Suraiya by his side. In all fairness, Dev Anand was not looking any less handsome, Zoravar thought, as he watched them walk away. He turned to Dev and asked him if he wanted to have a drink together, but the actor refused and left the venue a few minutes later, in what seemed like a foul mood. Despite the crowd, Zoravar felt alone and held conversations with most of the film folk present for a few seconds – mostly customary formalities. He had learnt that film parties were the worst places to discuss work opportunities. He headed to the bar all by himself and ordered a large neat whisky. Zoravar had begun to drink regularly, now and he had no memory of how he got home that night. When Santosh questioned him about it the next morning, he convinced her that this habit was only to get in to the skin of Devdas's character and would stop once filming was over.

On the heels of the film awards came an announcement from the Government of India regarding The National Awards for cinema. The ceremony had been conceived by the government to honour films made across India, on a national scale, to further the cause of Indian art and culture. The Ministry of Information and Broadcast would directly send invites to winners to attend the ceremony that would take place at the Vigyan Bhavan in Delhi, and President Rajendra Prasad was to present the awards. It separated itself from the Clare Awards by considering films made in all languages, not just Hindi. Zoravar was certain he would receive an invite. As the date came closer, and he did not receive one, he began to abuse the institutions of awards itself.

'Let my Devdas release,' he would stay in a drunken stupor, 'then these fuckers will award me.'

He had begun to drink in the mornings too. Zoravar's defence was that he was preparing to play the greatest alcoholic Indian art had ever produced. On the day the national awards were to be announced, Zoravar had woken up earlier than usual, mostly because he had barely slept the previous night.

When the newspaper came, he turned quickly to the movies section and saw that a talkie in Marathi language, one he had never heard of, called *Shyamchi Aai* had won the President's Gold medal for the best feature film. As he read further, the article stated that Bimal Roy had won an All India Certificate of Merit for *Do Bigha Zameen*. He was secretly elated that no other Hindi picture had won the top award.

Zoravar had returned signing amounts to half a dozen producers and opted out of films to make way for *Devdas* and clear his schedule. He wanted to ensure that this would be to be the performance of a lifetime.

One morning, on a visit to Basu's office, hungover from the previous night, he was given the news he had been waiting for.

'We are ready to announce the picture. I am ready to begin filming from this week as my sets are ready. In fact, we will release the picture within a few months itself to qualify for the awards next year,' Basu said, and Zoravar smiled broadly.

On his way back from the office, he saw a huge poster of *Azaad*, Dilip Kumar's new film. He slowed down the car, and as he was studying the Poster, he heard the blaring sound of a horn. An oncoming bus was racing towards his car, and collided with it head-on. Zoravar felt himself thrown against the windshield, which shattered on impact. Just as he felt a searing pain shoot through his body, for the third time in his life, everything went black.

PART VI

Sar Pe Laal Topi Rusi ...

1

The distinct Maharajah logo of Air India welcomed Zoravar as he nodded at the air hostesses, who seemed to have permanent smiles fixed on their faces. Outside, fans who had managed to make their way onto the runway through the barbed fence of the Bombay airport stood chanting his name and calling for him. They were loud enough that the sound reverberated inside the plane.

Zoravar was on his way to Moscow. A year had passed since the crash that had almost cost him his life. The shards of the glass from the car's windshield had pierced part of the cornea of his left eye, and left his sight severely impaired. Both his legs had been badly broken, and doctors were unsure if he would be able to walk again. He had defied expectations, thanks to incessant therapy and Santosh's relentless and unwavering support. His legs had healed faster than the doctors had thought they would, but he still needed the support of a stick to walk. To Zoravar, who had been shaken by the accident and was uncertain about his future, simple things like being able to get out of bed and walk to the bathroom, seemed like an achievement. He wondered at the irony of this, especially for a man who, for a living, jumped from rooftops, beat up villains and danced for the cameras.

Now, as he limped with the help of his stick to his designated seat, he remembered how averse to this trip Santosh had been. He'd promised her that he'd call her every chance he got, and she'd given in, also understanding the unsaid. After months away from the limelight, this was Zoravar's chance to return to the public eye. This time away had been jarring for Zoravar, who was scared that the press and the public would forget him.

Initially, when the news of the accident broke, there had been absolute mayhem, and for a while, people could talk about nothing but Zoravar. Fans queued up outside the hospital and left flowers and letters outside his home. Then the buzz died down, and Zoravar had to mislead the press into believing that he was battling for his life, when he was actually getting better. For a few days, this helped him return to the limelight, but then even that chatter faded.

As he settled into his seat, Zoravar observed that the Ministry of Railway and Transport had stuck to their promise of making the journey utmost comfortable for the contingent and modified the smaller seats into bed-like contraptions. He also noted that most people from their group were already on-board.

Prime Minister Nehru had handpicked a dozen-odd artistes and technicians to represent the Indian film business in Russia. Indian movies had created a huge impact in the Soviet states due to their escapist nature, and the song and dance routines were even more popular. Films in the USSR were made based on diktats from the government to promote propaganda and the Communist ideology, making them mostly devoid of entertainment – the complete opposite of their Indian counterparts. The fan following of the triumvirate of Dilip Kumar, Raj Kapoor and Dev Anand, and the frenzy it evoked, was unmatched in the USSR. People watched their movies despite having no comprehension of Hindi. Film songs were loved, and on the streets of Stalingrad or in the by lanes of Sochi, one could often hear the town folk singing Hindi songs on vodka-drenched evenings. Zoravar was part of the delegation being sent to Russia, thanks to *Sipahi,* which had done exceedingly well in Armenia and was in its seventeenth week. Raj Kapoor's *Awara* had released in over eight hundred theatres across the fifteen Soviet republics, and Dev Anand's *Rahi* was going to be released while the delegation was there. They would be attending its premiere at the Arbatskaya in Stalingrad. Nehru, being an old friend of the Soviet, had to be credited for introducing Indian films to the country, and he was expected to join the delegation himself a day after Zoravar's flight landed.

A year ago

When Zoravar regained consciousness, he couldn't move and felt like something really heavy was pinning down his legs. His left eye was swollen shut, and he was in excruciating pain. He realized as the fog of pain cleared a little that he was trapped inside his car, which had turtled, and he could smell rubber burning. He could see feet outside the window of the car, but no one was doing anything, being more interested in watching the spectacle rather than helping. He first thought was that he was probably going to burn to death. Then, he tried to get a hold of himself, but before he could try to force himself to crawl out through the broken windshield, a loud explosion rang through the air. He assumed that a tyre had burst. Then, a sharp burst of pain shot through him, and he shouted, just as the face of a stranger swam into view. The man was young, and he had finally managed to break open the door of the car. He pulled Zoravar out, and just as they were a few metres away from the car, it exploded.

The stranger wheeled Zoravar into the nearest government hospital. A team of doctors began to examine the injured star as he slipped in and out of consciousness. He felt the world around him grow dark and realized that he had no idea who his rescuer was.

When Zoravar awoke a few days later, he found Santosh sitting beside him and his father on the chair a little further away. The old man was chanting from the holy book. As Zoravar looked around the room, he saw that it was crowded with cards and bouquets. Santosh had also meticulously cut out all the news articles and press coverage around his accident from as many newspapers as she had managed to get her hands on at the public relations office at Natraj Studios. He looked at her, and before he could ask her anything, she held his hand tenderly.

'Your legs are broken, your right shoulder is fractured, and you may lose your vision temporarily in one eye, but it will return in good time,' she said, answering his unspoken questions.

'The shooting of *Devdas* begins this week. I can request Kaushik da to …' Zoravar said, his voice trembling. He paused when he saw the expression on Santosh's face. 'Mr Basu had come to enquire about your health. Unfortunately, he had to shelve the film,' she said gently.

Zoravar tried to get up when he heard his father's booming voice, 'Is there a need to discuss this right now? My son has barely gained consciousness, and you are talking about work?' he said to Santosh.

'Papa ji, forgive me, but I know my husband would like to hear bad news immediately,' Santosh said firmly.

She went on to give Zoravar an article from a prominent film magazine that had a picture of a familiar face on the front page. Along with the photograph, there was a headline in big, bold letters – Bimal Roy to make Devdas, Dilip Kumar to play the leading man.

2

Whisky suited Zoravar well. He had turned to it in preparation for *Devdas*, a role he had now lost because of that very drinking. But he could not quit the habit now.

He loved the way alcohol gave him a heady feeling, the way it numbed him – it acted as the perfect antidote to his pain. He had ordered Makkhan to smuggle bottles of Johnny Walker Red Label for him into the hospital.

The haze of alcohol also helped him cope with a new problem. Since the accident, Zoravar had developed a fear of enclosed spaces and crowds. He had briefly discussed the symptoms with the doctor, who had called it an anxiety disorder. It was a new subject and not much was known about it yet. So Zoravar self-medicated with whisky and found that it took care of all his maladies.

He remembered Noor telling him once, 'Life is a condition that requires constant anaesthesia.'

Now

As he took another swig from his hipflask, Zoravar felt his heart rate settle. A few minutes after take-off, Nargis walked up to him, and he was enamoured by her magnetic personality.

'I read about your accident,' she said in a raspy voice, which sounded very different from her onscreen one.

'I am lucky to have survived!' Zoravar quipped.

She nodded, looking solemn. 'Touchwood!' And then, laughing, she added, 'We must do a picture together! I think we'll make a great couple! Though you'll have to lose me at the end.'

'It would be my honour,' Zoravar replied. 'To work with you that is, not lose you!' He asked her the status of an upcoming film she was working on, titled *Mother India*, to which she replied that there were just a few more days of shooting left, and thankfully, all had gone smoothly thus far.

After she left, Zoravar took another sip from the hipflask and fumbled in his pocket for his lighter when Dev Anand, in the seat across the aisle, passed one to him. Zoravar took it, once again marvelling at Dev's eclectic and impeccable dressing. He was wearing a red shirt and a pair of navy-blue trousers. A beige corduroy jacket was draped over his shoulders and a multicoloured satin scarf covered most of his neck. On his feet were cowboy boots, the kinds that were in vogue thanks to the American star, John Wayne. After enquiring about his health, Dev asked, 'Have you been to Russia before?'

'No, I haven't! This is my first time out of the country, in fact,' said Zoravar earnestly.

Dev puckered his eyebrows. 'You haven't been to London yet?' Zoravar was aware that Anand went to London to buy his clothes, and there was a rumour that he got his hair cut only at Savile Row.

Dev took the half-smoked cigarette from Zoravar's hand and took a drag. As he exhaled smoke from his nostrils and kept the cigarette dangling from his lips, he spoke rather quickly even by his standards. 'It wasn't a good move to turn down *Aar-Paar*,' he paused before continuing. 'Let us consider you for something else though. In fact, why don't we do a picture together? I am working on a story with Goldie.'

Zoravar was aware of Dev's brother, Vijay, who was fondly known as Goldie. 'Yes, we must do a film together!' he agreed enthusiastically.

Dev took a final drag before stubbing the cigarette in the ashtray behind the seat. 'I am reading this great book, and my mind is still stuck there. Have you heard of R.K. Narayan?'

'Unfortunately, I do not read much. My wife does, and I am sure she would have read him.'

Dev nodded as he flicked the fringes of his hair covering his forehead. 'You must read it. It is a story about unrequited love – your genre! Love stories hurt the most. Don't they?'

Zoravar thought better than to ask Dev about Suraiya at this point. He had heard about the famous blow-up between Dev and Suraiya's grandmother. He had supposedly presented his beloved with a diamond ring, and her grandmother had been enraged enough to chuck it outside the window from their Marine Drive residence, straight into the sea, drowning it along with any hope of a matrimonial future for the lovers. Dev had gone on to marry his co-star Kalpana Kartik, while Suraiya remained unmarried.

One by one, everyone seated on the plane had walked up to Zoravar and enquired about his health. Finally, Dilip Kumar approached him, and Zoravar congratulated him on winning the National Award as well as Filmfare award for Best Actor for his portrayal of Devdas.

When the awards had been announced a few days prior, the pain in Zoravar's soul had been harder to endure than the one in his body. It was official, *Devdas* had made its leading man the biggest movie star in the country.

By virtue of sitting on the last row of the plane, Zoravar had a view of all those who sat ahead of him. He had observed that Dilip, Dev and Raj had not exchanged any words with each other barring basic niceties. Nargis was fast asleep with her head perched on Raj's shoulders, who was drinking whisky. Balraj Sahni was snoring faintly. Dev was still reading his book, and Dilip Kumar was staring into a small mirror, touching up his hair.

As the plane began to descend Zoravar looked outside his window. He was going to be on foreign soil for the first time in his life. He motioned to Raj Kapoor and made a sign with his thumb pointing to his lips. Raj got up and passed the Black Label bottle to Zoravar, who took a large gulp and then a second one. Raj winked at him and went back to his seat to Nargis, who was now touching up her face. The plane made a turbulent landing at the Vnukovo airport in Moscow, and Zoravar held the armrest tighter than anything he had ever clutched on to as he looked out at the tarmac.

A massive crowd had gathered outside the entrance of Hotel Metropol, nearly blocking the road. Nadine, a squat, pug-nosed woman who had been appointed as Zoravar's aide, was sitting beside him in the bus and pointed to the crowd from the window, informing Zoravar that they were fans who had been waiting for their favourite movie stars to arrive. Since they hadn't known the exact date of the Indian contingent's arrival, they had been camping in the icy weather for more than two days now.

As the bus pulled in front of the hotel, the crowd broke into the song '*Awaara hoon*' from *Awaara*. Raj Kapoor popped his head out of the window of the bus, looking every bit the movie star he was, his dark glasses on, a cigarette dangling from his lips. The roar that followed was louder than anything Zoravar had ever heard before. Kapoor waved out to the crowd and doled out air kisses. He then called Nargis to him, and they both looked out from the window. The crowd was now beginning to chant '*Ghar aaya mera pardesi*' as the bus pulled into the gates of the hotel, which shut behind it.

After shepherding Zoravar to his suite, Nadine informed him that she would be staying in the drawing-room of the very suite, to be able to assist him in any way possible, while the grand bedroom would house him. Zoravar immediately placed a call back home. He knew that Santosh and the rest of his family had calculated the amount of time it would take for him to reach the hotel and would now be waiting near the phone for his call. After updating them, he hung up and went into the lavish bathroom. He looked at his face in the mirror. His eyes were red, and a day-old stubble was beginning to form. He turned on the heavy silver tap and the water that came out was cold. He washed his face, wiped it with the soft monogrammed towel of the hotel, and felt refreshed. He then crashed on the king-sized bed and fell into a dreamless sleep.

The loud banging on the door awakened Zoravar. He limped towards it and saw a woman standing there. There was rouge on her cheeks, and she was dressed in a white dress that was cut off at her knees. The slits on both sides showed off her toned shins and pale thighs. Zoravar had to literally look twice to confirm that it was indeed Nadine, albeit in a completely different avatar as compared to the stiff and dull uniform she had been wearing earlier.

'We go for ... how do I say ... uh ... *vecherinka*,' she said.

Zoravar figured that she was referring to the ball they were scheduled to attend that evening. The itinerary sent by the government officials had said that a prominent band was going to perform for the guests.

Zoravar told Nadine that he'd hurry up and get ready, and offered her a drink while she waited. As she smiled in acceptance, he grabbed her rear and leaned in to kiss her. She pushed him away sternly and motioned for him go into the bathroom to change. Zoravar complied, knowing better than to push his luck. After having a rather long bath, he changed into the white tuxedo with the black bow tie that he had modelled on the suit Humphrey Bogart usually wore. His hair was slicked back and the close shave gave a sheen to his face. Nadine, keeping her distance, directed him to the foyer, where a car was already waiting for them.

A man, also in a white suit, was already in the front seat. As Zoravar drew closer, he saw that it was Dilip Kumar. What were the odds that the two men were designated to be taken to the ball in the same vehicle? Zoravar braced himself for a long and awkward journey as he entered the car. The atmosphere inside seemed to be chillier than the weather outside.

Zoravar finally broke the ice, 'We have never spoken about it, but we starred in a picture together,' he said.

Dilip turned behind to look at Zoravar, but his eyes lingered on Nadine.

'You are referring to the scene by the river?' he asked.

'You remember? What a surprise!'

'How could I forget? You kept screwing the shot up.'

3

The conductor was leading the band through Tchaikovsky's Romance Op. 5 in F Minor. The performers had introduced it as a piece that the great Russian musician composed for an Italian opera singer he had been infatuated with. Raj Kapoor's right hand kept bobbing up and down, as if he were a composer himself, admiring the piece that was moving and sad with heavy romantic overtures. Zoravar then glanced at Balraj Sahni, who was observing the orchestra but his face clearly gave away his disapproval of such excess. He had hoped that a country like Russia would know better than this. Sahni was an active member of IPTA – the Indian People's Theatre Association, which was the cultural wing of the Communist Party of India. Many prominent associates of the film fraternity, including the great Prithvi Raj Kapoor were members of the unit. Off late, Zoravar had been hearing about crackdowns taking place in America, where a senator by the name of Joseph McCarthy had been accusing Communists of sedition and terming them as the 'enemy within', and a bunch of leading movie stars and filmmakers were being targeted by law enforcement agencies. Even members of the military had not been spared the witch-hunt. The word 'Commie' had become a taboo. It wasn't like Zoravar was the least bit interested in these stories, but Santosh insisted in narrating them to him.

Everybody seemed spellbound by the performance; everybody except Zoravar. He had no interest in Western classical music and felt bored beyond belief, He had been drinking constantly and eventually asked for the whole bottle of Stolichnaya to be brought to him, much to the bewilderment of the serving staff. As he drank the vodka straight from the bottle, the orchestra reached its crescendo, finally coming to its conclusion. But it was another few minutes before the performance came to an end. By then, Zoravar had guzzled more than a half bottle. He did not even stand up to give the orchestra an ovation, pointing at his leg as a reason for the same, but did put up the act of clapping enthusiastically, faking his appreciation for the performance. He looked towards his right and discovered that Nadine had fallen asleep.

After what seemed like an eternity, the applause finally ended and dinner was served. Zoravar staggered and regretted having drunk so much on an empty stomach. As he limped towards the buffet and saw silver trays filled with food, he heard Raj Kapoor exclaim, 'Caviar! God's gift to mankind!' Zoravar followed him and heaped up caviar into his own plate. He took a spoonful in his mouth and made a face. He had never tasted anything fouler.

He turned to Kapoor and said, 'Yes! It's fantastic, isn't it?' Kapoor cheered and raised his glass to Zoravar, who smiled back and then limped slowly towards another counter. He saw a dish there that looked and smelt like chicken, and thought, 'Finally, something I can eat!'

As he heaped a portion onto his plate and dug into it, enjoying every bite, Kapoor joined him. 'Yes, great, isn't it?' he asked.

'It is so good!' Zoravar said, serving himself another portion as Nargis came over to the buffet to join them. Raj put his arm around her and fed her a piece from his plate. 'I must ask them if they can pack up some of this bear to take back home,' he said.

Zoravar could not believe his ears. Had Kapoor said *bear*? As in *bhaloo*? Before he could react, there was a sudden flurry of activity in the room. Prime Minister Nehru had walked in with his Russian counterpart, Nikita Khrushchev. The latter was the First Secretary of The Communist Party of The Soviet Union. That made him the head of state of the entire Soviet Union. This was the first time Zoravar was looking at Nehru in person.

He was wearing a dark grey, hip-length tailored coat that had a Mandarin collar, along with a white topi. He had matched it with tight black trousers and black shoes that shone. He was puffing on a cigarette held in a thin black cigarette holder.

When Nehru and Nikita came to the table where Zoravar was seated, Nehru introduced Zoravar. 'Here is our unrequited lover! A character even Dostoevsky would find complex!' Both men laughed and posed for a photograph with Zoravar. Khrushchev then looked at Zoravar's plate. 'Well done, Zoravar! If I had known you are fond of bear meat, I would have arranged a game night for you in the jungles of Siberia. The great thing about eating game meat is that it tastes of the last consumed food by the bears. In Siberia, we feed the bears bred as game on berries and nuts. Good to see you enjoying our special delicacy,' he said, beaming. He shook hands with Zoravar, and the two leaders moved on.

4

Zoravar found it hard to get out of bed the next day, and his head felt heavy from all the vodka he'd drunk the night before. He ended up missing the train to Leningrad, which the rest of the party had taken to attend the premiere of Dev Anand's *Rahi*. Zoravar thanked his stars that his picture had been clicked the previous evening. At least he had gotten his photo-op. He figured the only way to get rid of the hangover was to drink and eat, in that order. After a couple of neat Johnny Reds, he got Nadine to order him some breakfast, which consisted mostly of black bread and beetroot soup. He spent the rest of the day with Nadine, looking at some of the sites of Moscow. After lunch, Nadine asked him if he wanted to see a 'real' Russian party. He nodded, non-committal.

'I take you,' she said.

Back at the Metropol, Nadine quickly changed into a black frock with a black brassiere top that showed off her curves, and enveloped herself in a large fur coat. They then decided to ditch the official state vehicle, and she guided him silently across the road to a bus stop.

After a few minutes, a bus came into view. By now, it was beginning to rain; they got into the bus, finding themselves two empty seats. As time passed and the bus sped on, Zoravar observed the changing landscape. They were passing a sparsely populated suburb.

They reached their stop soon. Nadine took his hand, and they got off on a deserted street lined with flickering lamps. Zoravar followed Nadine into a tiny lane and they stopped outside a house with a small door. Nadine knocked three times in quick succession as Zoravar wondered what he was doing there. The small door opened with a creak and the man standing at the door let them in, closing the door behind them. The hallway was dimly lit, and as they walked on, an elderly man passed them by with a rather voluptuous and much younger lady by his side. Soon they were in front of another door, and once again, Nadine tapped it three times in quick succession. It was opened by another man, and this time, the room they entered was massive and smoky. It looked like one of those great opium dens on Grant Road back home. There were long, posh sofas and there was a three-man band belting out music in a language Zoravar had never heard before. The place was crowded with men and women. Zoravar had never seen more attractive women in his life. Most of them wore expensive looking gowns that showed off their curvy figures. He also saw girls with trays of cigarette packs for sale.

Nadine told him, 'In this country, you can buy a prostitute in exchange for a pack of cigarettes, even in Moscow square. A small box of cheese is considered a generous tip for most services, so bear that in mind. Go have fun now!' He pushed back his hair as Nadine whistled, and an elegantly dressed woman, taller than Zoravar, walked up to them. Nadine said something in Russian and within minutes, the same woman brought a bottle of *Stolichnaya* vodka, post which Zoravar handed her a tip in cash that brought a smile to her face so bright, it could light up a million bulbs!

Nadine had scampered towards the bar where she seemed to have locked eyes with a face that clearly seemed familiar to her, a girl who looked like she was a teenager, and he watched them embrace. As Zoravar took a sip of his vodka, he marvelled at how, like India, this was a country where deep, rooted socialism had entered the soul of the populace. He thought about the common theme of Indian movies, some of them his own, in which it was romantic to be poor and sinful to be rich. Most rich people at the movies were portrayed to be cold-blooded, avaricious and consistently evil businessmen or feudal lords. He thought of how the movie industry had become the ever-dependable home for card-carrying members of the Communist party, and ironically, so many of these artistes came from wealthy, pro-Raj families. In this cold night in Russia, in the middle of a fest, he was beginning to feel the meaning of being a true outsider. He did not come from an affluent background; he neither starred in intellectual pictures nor indulged in meaningful quotes in his interviews, and he definitely did not enjoy bear meat! Santosh kept telling him about the Buddha and the middle-path, and how embracing extremes would only make him unhappy. He wondered if it was the vodka or the loneliness, for he felt rapturously enlightened in the unlikeliest of places. Maybe enlightenment worked like that. One need not have to sit under a tree in silence for years to find themselves. Maybe it was time to change.

His thoughts were interrupted by a laugh and turned to two women standing behind him. Their necklines were plunging, and they both had a drink in their hand. He was staring at identical twins. One of them said a line in broken Hindi, a dialogue from *Sipahi*. His first double-role had clearly resonated with twins so many miles away from home. One of them took his hand and both of them giggled as they escorted him to a small veranda away from the massive hall. One of the sisters expertly unzipped his trouser and Zoravar closed his eyes, ready for the trip of a lifetime.

As he entered the room again, satiated and drained at the same time, he came face to face with a smiling Nadine.

She took his hand and guided him to a dimly lit corner of the room and removed two small vials of plain liquid from her purse. She also held an injection with a long needle. She extracted the liquid from the tiny bottles and filled the injection completely. She then bent down and injected the liquid between her toes. The act of extracting the liquid from the second bottle was repeated, and this time, she injected the liquid into an inebriated Zoravar's ankle. A few minutes passed and then Zoravar sprang up. Everything seemed to be completely in focus, the images sharper. Zoravar saw masks being offered to every guest. As soon as the masks were worn, everybody began to undress, and in the various stages of undress, there was a surge of sexual energy beginning to fill up the room. Zoravar was about to ask Nadine a question when she shushed him and made him wear a mask that had Stalin's image on it. The masks had an assortment of options. There were images of Marilyn Monroe, Audrey Hepburn, Lenin, Tolstoy – at this, Zoravar felt a sharp pang as he remembered Santosh reading a book with the man's photo – and other faces whom Zoravar did not recognize.

With desire surging within him, a naked Zoravar approached a woman wearing a Marilyn Monroe mask. She had a stunning body, and he held her by the waist and drew her close. She pushed him back and gave him a once over before embracing him again. As they moved together, Zoravar felt himself grow more excited, and with a swift and frustrated gesture, removed his mask and then made a move to remove hers, but just then, another masked woman came bursting into the room, followed by a group of uniformed policemen.

As they took in the scene, they met the eyes of the only unmasked person in the room – a buck-naked Zoravar.

5

The state-controlled newspapers were abuzz with the splash that the movie stars from India had made. The delegation had been a huge success, and the contingent was now headed to another part of the Soviet Union.

Only Zoravar would not be part of it.

When the police had entered the house, not one person had taken off their mask. One man had walked up to the policemen. He pulled up his Tolstoy mask, and within seconds, the policemen had ordered everyone to take off their masks and picked the ones they'd send to prison for indecent behaviour, the ones who did not belong to any influential family or the government. The policemen, clearly not a fan of Hindi Movies, had no idea who Zoravar was, and he was hand-cuffed along with other revellers. Just as he was about to be thrown into the rather large police van, Nadine had intervened at the last minute and spoken to them. Whatever she had told them had worked, for the cops had let Zoravar go.

The experience had shaken Zoravar, and he was desperate to return home to India. When they reached Hotel Metropol, he got Nadine to book him a ticket to Bombay. Fortunately, there was a flight scheduled for the same evening. Before he left, he asked Nadine about the magical medicine that she had injected him with. She did not know its English name but said that in Russia they called it Koka.

On the way to the airport, Zoravar thought about the letter he had written to Nehru that he had sent via Nadine. He had apologized and requested to be allowed to go back home owing to his delicate health due to injuries, which he had assumed had healed. By the time the letter would reach Nehru and the delegation, Zoravar would be on the plane.

He sat back and thought about his Russian adventure, and then smiled at the prospect of announcing a new slate of films, letting the world know he was back. Just then, the driver turned up the volume of the radio, and the strains of a popular Dilip Kumar song filled the car. Zoravar grimaced. There was truly no rest for the wicked.

PART VII

Waqt Ne Kiya ... Kya Haseen Sitam

1

The chaos was deafening. There were people on telephones, yelling instructions. A production manager was asking someone for 'two cans of film'. A production boy was running around with tiffin carriers, and the assistants were speaking in loud voices across the large floor. Trucks were driving up with props and setups. And inside the green room stood Zoravar, firm on his feet and fully recovered. Even the vision in his left eye had returned, although there was still some haziness and he couldn't watch movies on the big screen as clearly as before. The studio lights hurt his eye during shooting, and he had taken to wearing dark glasses at all times, removing them only while in front of the camera for a scene.

In the green room, he was having his measurements taken, while an attendant was making him try shoes, and wigs were being placed on his head. The costume designer now ran inside, bringing with him a bejewelled crown, which he placed on Zoravar's head, making him look every bit the part he was playing – King Prithviraj Chauhan.

Zoravar lit a Panama cigarette and smiled at himself in the mirror – the period costume paired with the cigarette dangling from his lips was a funny image. He turned to the journalist seated in a chair on the left.

'Every actor has two personalities, one that you see on the screen and one off it – what he or she really is,' he said to the journalist, before taking a drag and exhaling slowly for effect. 'Most things fail with age. Our bones break, our eyes stop seeing, the brain forgets, even our good looks fade. What remains is the timelessness of the art we create. The great thing about doing great movies is that they become immortal as time passes. Look at Motilal, for example, and Saigal, not to forget Dadamoni, with whom I hope to one day have the fortune of sharing screen space. He gifted me an Impala car as a present when three of my pictures were running in various stages of jubilees at the same time. *Dopahar*, which was running in its seventy- fifth week, *Chanchal* had just completed one year, and *Uski Marzi* was celebrating its twenty-five-week run. Looking back, I wonder how quickly the last three years of my life have gone by, most of them spent on movie sets. But when I see the love of the people and witness how beautifully they talk about these movies,

I believe it is worth sacrificing my time to serve them. And my fondest time spent listening to the radio is when Binaca Geetmala runs my songs. When Ameen Bhai speaks about how my romantic, and often sad songs, are so popular. It is a feeling that remains unparalleled.'

The journalist seemed awed by Zoravar's presence. He was silent, waiting for the actor to go on, when there was a knock on the door. A scrawny man holding up a pile of papers entered the room. 'The director is calling you,' he said to Zoravar.

Zoravar stubbed the cigarette in a glass ashtray kept on the make-up table and nodded before adjusting the crown. He got up and the journalist followed. In the scene being shot, the character of Jaichand arranges for a Swayamvar for his daughter Samyukta, and invites every eligible bachelor for it, except Prithviraj. A grim-looking Samyukta, played by the promising Sushma, garlands a clay statue of Prithviraj in defiance of her father and in rides Prithiviraj on a horse inside the durbar of the palace.

The journalist found the set garish, the dialogue delivery loud and the dramatic exaggeration of a character entering the durbar in a horse too preposterous. He had been part of the business long enough and had seen that on every set he went to, or every pre-release premiere he attended, the filmmakers believed that they had made a successful film. After it failed, they either went into denial or completely forgot that they had made a flop film, often moving on to the next one with the same level of confidence. Acceptance of failure and lack of objectivity seemed to be the trademark virtues of this business.

A revered director from Madras had been selected to helm the picture. It was a loose adaptation of a successful Tamil movie he had made with the legendary MGR in it. The director walked up to Zoravar after he called for a lunch break.

'Sir, there is this girl, sir. You must see her photograph,' he said to Zoravar, who looked completely disinterested as Makkhan stood there fanning him. 'Sir, I tell you. This one can be a big star. Just a matter of two years, sir,' said the director.

Zoravar lit a cigarette and kept staring at Sushma, who was getting her face powdered. She stared back through the mirror, a naughty smile on her lips. 'Sir, even MGR sir liked her picture. You should consider casting her,' the director pressed.

Zoravar finally took the photograph from him and looked at the image of the girl that stared back. She surely had a spark in her eyes. He gave back the photo to Sathyanarayan, the director. 'Too young, Sathya. Let her grow up a bit.'

Sathyanarayan took the picture and passed it on to Makkhan. 'Please keep this. Her mother is a good friend of mine. She has asked me to help her. Girl's name is Jaya – Jayalalitha.'

'I don't like her name. How will it work here in Bombay?' Zoravar got up and followed Sushma into the green room that had been assigned to her.

As they lay in post-coital bliss, Sushma took a drag from Zoravar's cigarette. 'I am getting an offer to star opposite Sunil Dutt.'

He was playing with her hair as she rested her head on his shoulders. 'You should consider it. After all, *Mother India* almost won the Oscar. The boy has it all, including Nargis. I still cannot believe she married him,' Zoravar said.

'Don't talk like that about her,' she said. 'I think it's great to see a heroine who is happily married, and her husband seems to have a great career ahead of him.'

Zoravar got up and began to get dressed in the heavy robes of Prithviraj. 'She played his mother on screen, she is older than him. It is all too convoluted and not good for his public image,' he said.

Sushma got up too. 'Your mother was older than your father. Nothing seems convoluted about you?' she challenged.

Zoravar stopped buttoning his heavy armour and looked at her like he was going to slap her. 'Get out of this room before I have you thrown out of the set,' he said.

She stared back at him, defiant. 'This is my room, mister. You get out. You men! Fragile erections, and even worse egos! Anyway, I have already agreed to do the film with Sunil Dutt. I was just making you feel good about yourself by asking you for an opinion. It is a great role.

Lots of screen time. People will get to see the real actor in me,' she said.

Zoravar turned to stalk out of the room, but just before leaving, he faced her, eyes blazing.

'Your breasts and hips are padded, and you're wearing artificial hair and fake clothes. You think people care about the real actor in you?' he spat.

Usually, it took approximately two minutes by foot from the Bombay Central station to the newly opened cinema hall, Maratha Mandir. It was the first cinema in the country to house one thousand seats. But today, it was taking hours to get there. There was a long line of cars and Zoravar's seemed to be stuck at the far end of the line. He looked at Santosh, who was looking rather attractive with a mogra gajra in her hair and a pristine white saree with a pearl necklace that he had bought for her from Tiffany's from their last visit to New York. It was a city he found boring and survived only thanks to his two best friends: Johnny Red and cocaine injections.

It was several more minutes before they finally made it to the cinema. He took a shot of whisky, and as they both got out of the car, the flashbulbs went completely berserk. As he ushered her inside the new theatre, Santosh gasped at the sight of a giant cutout of Prithvi Raj Kapoor, in the garb of his onscreen character, Emperor Akbar. The entire foyer of the movie hall had been recreated to resemble a Mughal palace. Just when they were getting used to the atmosphere, they turned to see a giant elephant entering the foyer of the cinema hall. The prints of the movie were being transported via the elephant. On walking further inside, they saw that the Sheesh Mahal had been recreated inside the theatre in which a song called '*Pyaar kiya toh darna kya*' had been picturized on Madhubala. It was sung by Lata Mangeshkar, and the music director Naushad had had to re-create the echo that would occur if a song was played inside the Sheesh Mahal. After much difficulty, he had stumbled upon the idea of recording the song in a bathroom, and it had worked.

Zoravar remembered the invite to the premiere. It was designed in the form of a scroll and made to resemble the famed *Akbarnama*. His and Santosh's names had been embossed on it in gold.

For years, Zoravar had heard t from various sources that the picture would never see the light of day. He himself had firmly believed in it, especially after hiring people on the crew to spy for him. Zoravar remembered distantly the cold winter night on which he had gone to watch *Phool* by the same director. It was the last movie he had watched before fate had twisted him in ways from which he would never recover. So much had changed in the last fifteen years. But here was a man, K. Asif, who had done nothing but spend a decade and a half making one film, and it was finally ready to be unveiled to the world.

When *Devdas* had released five years ago and become one of the highest grossing films of the year, apart from winning laurels for its leading man, Zoravar had slipped into some form of depression. For him, this meant that instead of one bottle, he began consuming two bottles of Johnny Red a night.

The only consolation at that time had been the fact that at least Dilip Kumar's *Mughal-e-Azam* would never release. And now here he was, wearing his most expensive tuxedo, attending the premiere of the same picture. There had been immense pressure on K. Asif to re-do the entire movie in colour, now that fewer black-and-white movies were being made. Asif had not given in and only shot the Sheesh Mahal song in colour, letting the rest of the picture remain black-and-white, exactly the way he had intended it to be. The entire movie industry had shown up for the premiere, eagerly wanting to experience this saga. Everyone except its leading man, Dilip Kumar. He had had a tiff with Asif. Some said it was to do with Madhubala, the woman they both loved and professed marriage to. Instead, she'd married Kishore Kumar!

As the first year of a new decade swerved towards completion, *Mughal-e-Azam* went on to become the highest-grossing picture of 1960 and of all time in Indian cinematic history, and Dilip Kumar scaled new benchmarks of superstardom. In the same year, Guru Dutt released a picture called *Kagaaz Ke Phool*, which was hailed as a more refined masterpiece than its predecessor *Pyaasa*. How was it even possible for someone to make two classics in a row?

Jayalalitha had made her Tamil debut, and the picture had been successful, her iconic waterfall sequence so aspirational that the location at which it was shot had become a tourist delight. Now, she had signed a movie opposite MGR. After watching *Mughal-e-Azam,* Zoravar had delayed his own *Prithviraj-Sanyukta*. He needed to up the game on the picture as he made the producers spend more money to enhance the scale of the film. Towards the end of 1961, it finally released to insipid reviews and an even less encouraging response at the box office. It was meant to be the last big release of the year, coming on the heels of a string of successes for Zoravar. Critics ripped apart the historic liberties and called it a poor cousin of *Mughal-e-Azam*. The expensively mounted picture died a quick death at the ticket window.

All the people Zoravar had shunned out of arrogance had become relevant. He figured he could live with other people succeeding as long as he himself was successful. Now, while others bathed in newfound success, his most ambitious project had proved to be a dud. It was time to take matters into his own hand. He sat in his living room and poured himself another drink, looking every bit the heartbroken hero he played in his pictures. He was wearing his usual red silk kurta and a red dhoti, apart from his dark glasses that shielded his eyes. Santosh was looking resplendent in a yellow saree and was doing up her hair, getting dressed up for the night's celebrations.

Lohri was festival Papa ji always insisted on celebrating with the family. On a cold January evening at the start of 1962, the family was getting ready going to light a bonfire in the compound of the bungalow and celebrate the beginning of the harvest season. Zoravar and Santosh were about to leave when they heard the first gunshot. Within seconds, there was another bullet fired, followed by the scream of a woman. Zoravar opened the door of his room and ran towards the ground floor of the bungalow where the sounds were coming from. There was a woman standing near the door of Bir's room. She was screaming and Zoravar's first thought was that her performance looked over the-top and hammy. She was in a dishevelled state, her white saree partly undone and the large red bindi on her forehead smeared. An inebriated Bir walked out of the room, waving a revolver in the air. Everybody else in the house had heard the commotion and had come running out of their respective rooms. Bir pointed the gun in Makkhan's direction, who had been playing with Zoravar's sons. Zoravar panicked.

'Bir, just put the gun away—' he began, but before he could complete, the woman in the saree interrupted.

'Wah! Look at this man. Finally, his younger brother has found a voice, and he tries to drown that out as well,' she said.

He looked at Santosh then back at the woman 'Who are y— Bir! Put the gun down. My children will get hurt. Goddamn it!'

Bir lowered the gun on seeing Dilawar break into sobs. He looked at Zoravar. 'You are an alcoholic. You cheat on your wife. Then why is it that I am the black sheep of the family and you the harbinger of fortune?' he mocked.

He held the revolver against his own head now. Zoravar did not know how to react, and Santosh was shaking. Bir continued, 'You used to be my hero. None of these people, including Papa ji, ever came with you to Bombay. Only I did. Even when you were not famous. You made me an apprentice to that khota Noor, when I wanted to act and be like you. All these years I have stayed in the shadows of the great f****** Zoravar. I am so happy that your last film bombed at the box office. You don't deserve an ounce of happiness. When mother died, you were not there. When you ran away from home, I was the one who had to grow up overnight. You did not even grant me a proper childhood.'

Zoravar looked at the woman and then looked back at Santosh. He remembered she had told him something about a woman in Bir's life. He had not bothered to listen, thinking that it was something that did not deserve his full attention.

Bir threw the gun, and it slid across the marble floor. Makkhan ran and picked up the revolver and emptied the bullet chamber. Bir now started hitting his head with his own palms, rather dramatically. The woman walked up to Sardar Cheema and touched his feet. She then used the saree to cover her head and folded her hands. 'Papa ji, you are the only reasonable man in this house,' she said, shooting Zoravar a caustic glance. 'Bir is vulnerable but not weak. I request you to give him his share, or whatever it is that you want to give him, and let us leave.'

The old man was pained to see everything that was going on. He looked at Bir. 'Puttar, what is all this? Who is this—' he broke off the conversation midway, realizing that it was foolish to expect any coherent reply from Bir at this point.

Bir slumped back on his haunches and wailed away, 'I wanted to be you. You just kept pushing me away.' The tears streamed down his face.

Zoravar looked at the woman in white and then turned his face to Makkhan. 'Do what it takes. Clean him up. Begin his training. I want to see him up and about. I am giving you sixty days.'

'Clean him up? For what?' Makkhan was puzzled.

'I am going to launch our production banner. It's time. And the first picture we produce will launch Bir as the leading man.'

Santosh gasped. He turned to her. 'If the Anand brothers can do it, if the Kapoor brothers can do it, then so can we.' He then walked up to Bir and held him up.

'I am sorry for ignoring you, Bir. I am going to give you the launch of a lifetime.'

Sardar Cheema looked at his sons and thought to himself, 'The way to compensate for emotional guilt is not by offering materialistic excesses. Only if my oldest son knew better!' He sighed and hugged both of them regardless. 'Let's prepare for the bonfire,' he said.

At this point, the woman in white walked up to the men. 'My name is Poornima, and I am pregnant with

Bir's child. Please give me a marriage date.' She folded her hands and walked to the giant white chair in the middle of the drawing-room that was generally reserved for Zoravar and plonked herself down on it, wiping the tears from her eyes.

2

Since that balmy Lohri evening, Makkhan had taken charge of Bir's life. He had ensured that Bir abstained from alcohol and had hired a wrestler from the closest akhada, the one who had also trained Dara Singh. Bir was learning the basics of Kushti. The morning session would be followed by horse-riding classes. Bir was terrible at it and kept giving preposterous excuses to get out of the training sessions. It was déjà vu for Makkhan, who had been privy to Zoravar's sessions from over a decade ago. There was a huge difference between the two, and he realized that while talent is God-given, passion is not. It either came from within or it did not, and that made all the difference between success and failure.

Zoravar had announced his own banner. It was called Apsara Talkies, and the logo was a photograph of his mother, which in his opinion also tied well with the name. He had thrown a grand party to announce the news at La Bella, his favourite among the many jazz and cabaret bars on Churchgate Street.

Zoravar had invited almost every single member of the fraternity. Nargis and Sunil Dutt were among the first guests to arrive. Nargis kept gushing about her son Sanjay, who was now all of three. Rajendra Kumar, who was now on a streak of consecutive 'jubilee' pictures, had accompanied them. Zoravar congratulated him for delivering what was the biggest success of the year, a picture called *Mere Mehboob*. This picture had taken the Muslim social genre to its zenith. Zoravar made a mental note to explore doing one of these films himself. He had become a fan of the genre and to see him feature in ghazals and qawwalis would be a welcome change for his audiences. It was funny, really, the dichotomy of fame, standing here at this club while a band played jazz, to celebrate people who took to the qawwali for success. Part of the reason Zoravar had chosen this club to host the party was that he was aware that Raj Kapoor, in particular, could be seen partying here practically every night. But tonight was the one night he did not show up, despite a personal hand-written invite from Zoravar.

A Hawaiian jazz band was performing, and a French troupe was to do the cabaret. Zoravar was about to cut the cake when tongues began to wag. A white Mercedes screeched to a halt and in a few minutes, the smell of powerful ittar filled the club. Even the band had stopped playing briefly. Parwaan had arrived, carrying a rather garish bouquet.

After handing it to Zoravar, Parwaan had a single drink and exited the party, post which the guests relaxed again. A special stage had been built for Bir's entry, and he made his way to the stage while the band played a Salsa song to enhance the dramatic effect. Bir was to make his entry atop a giant swing that had been made for him, accompanied by Luscious Lola & Corrina, the cabaret stalwarts who had been specially flown down from Calcutta. Bir, wearing a white tuxedo with a black bow tie, looked awkward and conscious. Zoravar noticed this but chose to ignore negative thoughts about his brother. As the swing descended, the applause was unanimous, and everyone welcomed Bir to the world of movies.

Just then, a handsome young actor who went by the screen name of Dharmendra arrived. He was one of the few actors like Zoravar who stuck to a single name onscreen. He had even told Zoravar that he had dropped his surname as an ode to the older actor. There had been rumours about Dharam and Meena Kumari and their alleged affair, but Zoravar had refrained from asking Dharam any questions about that. Meena had been invited to the party too, but she had not shown up this evening, despite the lure of alcohol. Zoravar noticed that the burly, incredibly good-looking actor largely stuck to the bar by himself pretty much the entire evening, looking ferocious and attractive at the same time.

The backyard of the bungalow had been converted into the office of Apsara Talkies Pvt Ltd. Zoravar had been a bit worried initially about the nameplate that now stood proudly at the back entrance of their house. He had confided in Santosh, 'I hate the word Limited. Especially when it is enjoined as a part of the identity of my firm.'

She had stifled a yawn. 'Well, this is what gives you legitimacy. All respectable entities are now using the word.'

He nodded but did not respond. Santosh, meanwhile, was thinking about how ambitious her husband had become. Initially, the ambition was healthy, because it was satiating his own hunger. Now it was only to prove other people smaller than him, or to compete with them. It was a professional hazard for anyone who chose this profession.

Santosh had found God recently. She had become increasingly influenced by the church and found solace in the Bible. She went for mass almost every Sunday. A largely agnostic Zoravar did not stop her from following this newfound ritual, but she knew deep down that he disapproved.

Weeks had become months, and they were still unable to find the right story to launch Bir. Zoravar had gotten entrenched in *Noor-e-Khuda*, the Muslim social that he was starring in. He had tried to get K. Asif and Mehboob Khan to helm the picture but both had turned it down. Zoravar then figured it was time to get in touch with Ismat Chughtai. The deal fell apart when she brought up the need to produce the film through her company Filmina, which had successfully produced *Sone Ki Chidiya*, starring Nutan and Talat Mehmood. She had also produced and directed *Lala Rukh*, starring Mehmood, and won laurels for handling a sensitive romantic story. A Muslim social, as long as it was liberal, was something that interested her. She would be involved in the production, and she would be happy to sign Zoravar as the leading man for what would be a beacon of the portrayal of a family saga. Zoravar had to decline. He wanted to establish his production company, and when he instead offered to sign her as a writer and director, she turned it down.

He then contacted his old friend Ezekiel, who had not been actively involved in films for a while now. He had moved to the hill station of Lonavala and was growing onions at a farm where he lived. When Zoravar drove down to meet him, he saw an ageing and borderline frustrated man who tended to onions all day and drank all night. He left Lonavala with a heavy heart. In any case, it seemed like a bad idea from the onset to offer a Jewish man a Muslim social.

Makkhan was passing Regal, and he looked up at the hand-painted poster of the picture that everyone seemed to be talking about. It starred a handsome Scot called Sean Connery, and he played a character in it called James Bond. The film was titled *Dr No*, based on a bestselling novel by Ian Fleming. Flashes of the war with China, the previous year and the gun-toting image of a man wearing a suit concocted a heady visual in his mind. This was it. They would launch Bir in a plagiarized version of *Dr No* and introduce him as an Indian spy in a suit who saves the world and teaches China a lesson, all at the same time.

Zoravar loved the idea. Bir loved the idea. Even Zohra, Zehra and Amandeep loved the idea. Santosh was familiar with Ian Fleming and even suggested other novels by the same author that according to her had better plots. Zoravar held a grand Mahurat at Filmyug Studios. Saraswath Mukherjee and his partners had been embroiled in an ugly fracas, and he had eventually decided to part ways with Film Lok. Saraswath had started his own independent studio and named it Filmyug Studios. Along with Bir, this spy film would to launch three new heroines, who would serve as his love interests in the picture. The film was titled *Secret Agent X*, and Premnath agreed to act as the negative lead. They were to start filming the picture in Goa and the setting was that of the freedom movement during the Portuguese rule from four hundred years ago. Colossal sets inspired directly from *Dr No* were erected simultaneously across different studios. All the initial expense was funded by Zoravar, and the mahurat was a ploy to invite distributors to cough up advance money and purchase territories of a picture that was promising to be the next big thing at the box office. They had offered Vijay Anand a chance to direct the picture, but he was immersed in a movie called *Guide* that would star his brother Dev. They had then approached B.R. Chopra, who also turned it down as he preferred to make a film with Zoravar instead. They had finally zeroed down on Maqbool to helm the project, the man who had delivered *Sipahi* for Zoravar and made him iconic. Maqbool too fell in love with the idea of helming India's first spy picture.

Distributors from across the country showed up to bless Zoravar, Bir and Apsara Talkies, but not a single territory was sold that day. They even attended the cocktail party at the banquet in the Taj Mahal hotel that evening, but every time Zoravar veered towards a business conversation, they politely walked away to the bar or changed the topic, more interested in what Zoravar was going to be starring in.

The filming began with the shooting of the climax scene, where an expensive part of the villain's lair gets blown to pieces. The action master was a brawny chap called Master Thiru – a renowned technician from Madras. The decision to bring him on had been to address the fact that the picture needed a fresh perspective on the action and a spectacle of this size needed a new approach.

On the first day of the shoot, the action masters from Madras got the rigging of the explosion wrong and due to a camera malfunction, the entire set was blown up.

The set that had taken almost a month to build would have to be re-built, and that came with additional expenditure – all of it from Zoravar's pocket.

As the shooting of his brother's debut film progressed, Zoravar also got busy with the planning of *Noor-e-Khuda*. It was eventually decided that he would also helm the film as a director, and this would be the first film in which he would direct himself. He had hired the actor-turned-writer Siraz Khan to write the script, but the man had had to leave the film when his wife Fatima announced that she was pregnant with their first child. An acting offer had also come his way, and after doing initial writing on *Noor-e-Khuda*, they parted ways amicably. Zoravar wrote the remainder of the film himself. He needed money to bankroll the project, and with most of his money invested in *Secret Agent X*, he had no option but to borrow, and he turned, reluctantly, to Parwaan and Pasha.

Noor-e-Khuda was set a few decades ago in Awadh. Zoravar was to essay the role of a fading nawab who eventually loses his mind after his wife refuses to forgive him for his infidelity. He wanders the streets as a mad fakir. Zoravar would be re-united with Sushma in the picture.

On the mahurat shot of *Noor-e-Khuda,* he had invited his father to give the first clap on the second picture that Apsara Talkies was producing simultaneously. The setting was that of a large, decaying mahal with fading green walls. Just as Zoravar finished the day's shoot, he received the news that Poornima and Bir had lost their first child, minutes after he was born.

Bir had stalled the last leg of the shoot of *Secret Agent X*. He wanted to be with Poornima, who had sunk into depression. There had been a pall of gloom in the house, and days turned into weeks. It was initially turning out cheaper to continue paying the rental for the sets than to break them down and re-erect them, but so much time had passed that the film was already looking like a flop on paper. Eventually, when Bir was convinced to resume shooting his portions and finish the project, he seemed lackadaisical and disinterested.

Zoravar had immersed himself in *Noor-e-Khuda* and was finding directing to be a quagmire of epic proportions.

'Actors have it so easy. You come, do your make up, say your lines and leave. Without bothering about anything else. Here I act and then I direct, where I am bothered with the casting of a junior artiste, and then I have to sit and negotiate their prices. This has been most exhausting,' he told Pasha one day when they were drinking as prominent courtesans from Peela House performed before them.

'Oh, yes! Zoravar, I can imagine,' Pasha said.

'Chutiya, what can you imagine? What the f*** do you know about movie-making?'

'Enough to know that if you don't return the money to Parwaan, this will not end well. The interest is almost as high as the amount of money you have borrowed now. I am glad he does not know that you are cutting corners on *Noor-e-Khuda* and funnelling all the borrowed money onto *Secret Agent X*.'

'I have recently watched rushes of *Secret Agent X*. The action is of a quality that has never been witnessed on the Indian screen before. This is the *Mugal-e-Azam* of action films. You just wait and watch,' Zoravar said with a confidence he did not feel.

3

Secret Agent X was still a few days away from completion, and the action and canvas were phenomenal, barring a few scenes that seemed dated due to the amount of time the film had taken to complete. Zoravar ordered the director to re-shoot some of the portions that looked dated, and those sets had to be re- created and the scenes were re-written for them to be relevant. In the meanwhile, Dharmendra had established himself as a macho man who excelled in action films. There was another actor on the block who also kept a solo name – Jeetendra – and he too was working on a spy film. It was titled *Farz* and had spy games with China as an integral part of the plot.

Noor-e-Khuda was being geared for a release, and everyone who watched the trial screening came out in tears at the remarkable ending.

When it finally came released, it opened to packed houses. The picture was declared a huge success instantly, and it picked up even in belts such as Bombay and the posh parts of Delhi. It was the ending that had worked, even with audiences with a certain refinement.

A month later, *Secret Agent X* was finally up for release as well. The posters and publicity material, for which Zoravar had paid from his own pocket, had been received well, and could be seen all over Bombay. The money that had flown in from *Noor-e-Khuda* had helped bolster the effort.

27 May 1964 was a Wednesday, the day Zoravar had chosen to premiere *Secret Agent X* for the entire film industry and members of the press, two days before its intended release. Expensive invites in the shape of guns had gone out to everyone. The show was supposed to begin at 6 p.m. and a party would follow at the Taj Mahal Hotel. It was around 3 p.m. that day when the news broke. Prime Minister Nehru had been declared dead. India went into mourning, and the last thing people wanted was to watch was an action-filled, raunchy movie with a new leading man in it!

Zoravar had lost four of the five cars he owned and did not receive a penny for them. Dwarka Das and Arvind

Shah were among the moneylenders he owed money to. When they had been incessant about getting their money back, in a drunken rage Zoravar had walked down the staircase and handed over two keys each to both of them.

'Adjust your money against these cars. If their value is more than what I owe you, good for you. If it is less than what I owe you, come back in a few months, but leave me alone right now,' he had sneered.

He had also mortgaged his bungalow to pay off the interest to Parwaan. The verdict had been clear. Even if the movie hadn't released on the weekend of Nehru's death, it was still destined to be a disaster at the box office. The shoddy camerawork, the synthetic sets and, most importantly, the immensely irritating lead actor 'who felt like an allergy', as one critic wrote, were enough to deliver the biggest box office failure in a long time. The songs had been disliked, and eventually, after three weeks of running, it went off theatres. The cinema owners were dejected and had made huge losses. Bir had taken to spending most of his time in his room with Poornima.

The only solution Zoravar now had was to sign as many pictures as he could to make up for the losses that had piled up. His first priority was to unmortgage the house. It had his mother's name on it, after all. Zoravar, despite having delivered a huge success in *Noor-e- Khuda*, could no longer be picky about the films he signed. Makkhan brought him offers, and if the stories were half decent, Zoravar signed them, albeit for amounts that were a tad bit above his market price. Unfortunately, that also resulted in a lot of starstruck producers who paid him signing amounts, used up his time and then shut the pictures halfway due to lack of funds. This caused further delays between his next movie and his last release, *Nood-e-Khuda*. He knew he would have been at the peak of his career had he not sunk all his money in trying to launch two films at the same time. To make matters worse, Raj Kapoor produced and directed a picture called *Sangam*, which became the highest-grossing movie of 1964. It was an unrequited love triangle, a space that Zoravar owned, and for the first time, he felt his monopoly being broken. Rajendra Kumar was signed to play the second hero and not Zoravar. That caused him further heartburn. Out of all the pictures he had signed, only two saw the light of day, one of them was another Muslim social, a shadow of *Noor-e-Khuda* titled *Mezbaan*. As expected, it flopped. Another picture titled *Baagh*, a love story about a couple resisting their families went on to earn a respectable figure and did not lose money.

The trade was beginning to wonder at the choices Zoravar was making in his career. He started going to producers to ask them for work. He met directors and scouted for new talent he could bank on. He was fortunate that he found support and signed at least three more pictures. The signing amounts from all those movies went into repaying his debts, though he was still far away from being completely free of it.

Surprisingly, the only person who did not press Zoravar about returning his money was Parwaan. Every time Zoravar went to meet him, Parwaan would say, 'Bhai, you figure out your other creditors first. I am here only, and so are you. We'll adjust in the next project.'

Zoravar was beginning to worry about the negative things being said about Parwaan in the press and the notoriety he had begun to gain because of his involvement in nefarious activities. All these years, Parwaan's activities had been private, but now, with him getting press coverage, it was getting difficult to continue associating with him. Zoravar shuddered at the thought that he may have to collaborate with the man on another project to make up for the debt he owed him. He would rather pay off the money and then slowly and surely cut off ties.

Zoravar shunned his ego and finally relented. He called on Guru Dutt for a meeting. He was sure that a picture with Guru Dutt at the helm would be the best thing for his career and boost his sagging fortune. His image of an unrequited lover, blending with the melancholic depth of Dutt's writing and direction, would make him reach the pinnacle he had been chasing. When he rang Dutt's residence, no one picked up. Zoravar tried again and again, but there was still no answer. Frustrated, he decided that he'd take the bull by the horns, and just show up the next day at Dutt's residence.

Guru Dutt stayed at Pedder Road, in a rented apartment, which was close from Zoravar's bungalow.

Zoravar woke up early and took a long time to get ready. He had not even drunk whisky the previous evening. He was confident about pulling off a coup. He and Guru Dutt together would be a huge announcement. It would also put a blanket to the colossal disaster of *Secret Agent X*, which was going down in history as the single-biggest financial and critical disaster of all time.

He sat in the only car he had left, and as Makkhan drove them to the apartment, he felt his energy surging. As they got closer to the posh Ark Royal building, they saw a small crowd gathered near it. As Zoravar got down, a boy came running to him and started screaming his name in excitement. Zoravar politely signed an autograph before moving away from him, worried that the child would spoil the well-ironed creases of his shirt. Makkhan had dropped him off and driven away to look for parking. When Zoravar entered the lobby of the apartment building, he saw the familiar faces of technicians he recognized from movie sets. One of them came forward to meet him.

'We cannot believe it, sir! Guru is dead. Just like that! Suicide, apparently!' he said to a stunned Zoravar.

PART VIII

Aaj Phir Jeene Ki Tamanna Hai ...

1

Another year of making movies went by and it was time for another award function. Barring the financial losses he had incurred from a couple of years ago, from which he was still recovering, Zoravar had had a decent year at the box office. He was nominated for Best Actor as well as Best Director for *Noor-e-Khuda*. He lost out on both counts: Raj Kapoor took home the direction trophy for *Sangam*, and Dilip Kumar won for his performance in Sashadhar Mukherjee's *Leader*, which Zoravar had opined was the most boring picture he had seen and its below average box office collections had confirmed his opinion.

Losing out on the awards in both categories was a double blow for him, and he did not attend the afterparty. He drove home rather sombrely with Santosh by his side. He lit a cigarette and rolled down the window as they drove down an empty street. 'At least they should have given me something this year. Over the years now, I have been nominated seven times. Every time I go home empty-handed. The kids are growing up. What do I tell them?' Zoravar said.

Santosh chuckled. 'You are the only parent in the world who worries about what he will say to his children. Stop being so hard on yourself. You'll get it next year,' she said.

Zoravar was shooting for a multi-starrer picture titled *Khandaan*, where he played one of three brothers leading the film. He had agreed to be a part of a multi-starrer despite his self- imposed rule of only acting in projects that had him as the solo lead. This was because, after the success of *Sangam*, ensembles and multi-starrer projects were in vogue. BR Chopra's younger brother, Yash Chopra, was almost ready to release the picture he had directed, called *Waqt*, which had a massive star cast. There was also Manoj Kumar, who was headlining a picture titled *Gumnaam*, about a group of people stuck on an island with a murderer who begins killing them off one by one. That picture had several well-known actors as well. The advantage of doing multi-starrers for an actor of his stature was the fact that it allowed him to be paid well. Negotiations were easier as actors hated sharing screen with other actors, and the producers did not mind coughing up top dollar due to the hype they could create with so many leading names sharing the same poster. It was like an extravaganza for the audience. Also, if the film failed, the brunt of the failure would get divided rather than affect just the leads. Multi-starrers were also generally fun to do. The sets were like one gigantic picnic, and, post shooting, there would be raucous parties. Each outdoor schedule was like a paid holiday and a memorable one at that. Zoravar had figured out a trick to stand out among others while sharing the same frame. He would gauge the performance of the other actors while enacting the scene, and if he felt they were performing well, he would intentionally forget his lines or fumble an action or miss his mark. After multiple takes, the other actors would lose their energy and the director his patience. That is when Zoravar would deliver an unrestrained performance with all the energy he had conserved till now. By then the director, tired, would call 'OK' and move on to the next take.

When *Khandaan* came out, it set the cash registers ringing and received a lot of love from everyone barring one critic, who questioned how three leading men who looked as different from each other as chalk and cheese could convincingly play real brothers onscreen?

1965 was in its second month when Zoravar and Santosh were readying themselves to attend the premiere of Vijay Anand's *Guide*. The soundtrack was a marvellous one, and the picture came with tremendous hype. After the screening had ended, the audience sat still in stunned silence. People simply got up and left their seats, and began trickling out of the auditorium. The leading man, Dev Anand, and his director brother, Vijay, were standing at the exit in great anticipation to gauge the reactions of the fraternity. People just shook their hands, and some embraced them, but there was not a single word exchanged. Zoravar shook hands with Dev and smiled at Vijay sympathetically. As he sat in the car and they drove, he told Santosh excitedly, 'Finally, they've mucked it up. This picture is too long, too boring and too nuanced. It is not going to run at all. Let us celebrate!'

She was lost in thought, and it seemed as if she had not heard a word he said. Zoravar repeated himself, and she finally turned to look at him, confusion on her face.

'What do you mean? It is a masterpiece. The best I have watched in a long time. I am stunned beyond belief.'

The two of them did not speak a word for the rest of the drive back home.

When R.K. Narayan, the author of the book the movie was based on, called it 'The Misguided Guide', Zoravar drank more whisky than he usually did, for once out of jubilation rather than anxiety.

It was a beautiful rainy day in Bombay, and Santosh had arranged for a barbecue to be set up in their garden, taking a cue from the images of American families she saw in magazines and from her visit to New York. She had become famous for throwing the warmest holi and diwali parties at their house, though she rarely befriended people from the fraternity. She was far more content in her library than making small talk at parties. Even Bir came out of his room for this one, and his face looked thinner and his cheeks sunken. There were broad dark circles below his bloodshot eyes, and his hair was thinning. He hadn't shaved in days and looked like a hermit. Zoravar walked up to him. 'Clean up your act. Once an actor, always an actor. Let's make another picture together. It is time for our banner to be active yet again. Apsara Talkies needs another production, and it is going to star you. And this time, I will direct the picture,' he said.

'This is not agreeable to us,' chimed Poornima, who, unlike her husband, looked more radiant than ever. 'If you direct Bir, he will be side-lined, and all the focus will be on you,' she said

'Fine. We will get an able director, of Bir's choice, and work on something,' Zoravar said.

'Sounds like a plan. You must announce it as soon as possible,' she said.

Throughout the entire conversation, Bir had been entirely silent.

Makkhan came running into the room. 'Turn on the radio. They've made an announcement. It seems we are at war with Pakistan.'

Various stories are born out of the trenches of war, and Zoravar's *Jung* was one of them. Patriotic fervour had hit the nation once again, and there were strong pro-nationalist sentiments all across. With an ongoing war, jingoistic nationalism was back in vogue. A bunch of war movies were announced and various were in production. In January 1966, the war with Pakistan, had come to a halt, owing to a ceasefire treaty signed in Tashkent by Ayub Khan, the President of Pakistan and his Indian counterpart, Lal Bahadur Shastri, who had died under mysterious circumstances the very next day. Before he died, Prime Minister Lal Bahadur Shastri had spent some time with actor Manoj Kumar, and the latter's directorial debut was inspired by Shastri's popular 'Jai Jawaan Jai Kisaan' slogan.

For *Jung*, the director Zoravar had chosen was Jayanti Kumar, a newcomer who had worked on Chetan Anand's *Haqeeqat*, a war-film with the Indo-China war serving as a backdrop, which had done miraculous business at the box office, establishing Dharmendra as a top star. It had also won the National Award for Best Film. Zoravar figured the next step for him to win the National Award or any award would be to work on a war film with overt patriotic sentiments and yet play the guy who always gets handed the tragic end of the stick. He had been advised against backing a new director for a picture of this scale, but he had hired a director smaller in stature than him so he could control most of the film.

As days passed, Jayanti found the film far too ambitious for his liking and any crew member would swear that Zoravar had ghost directed the film entirely.

When the picture came out, it became among the highest-grossing movies of the year, and Jayanti won accolades and the award for the Best Director at multiple film guilds. Zoravar had been nominated for Best Actor, but lost out to Dev Anand, who swept every acting award for *Guide*. When Jayant won the trophy for Best Director, he gave a speech on how difficult the shooting process had been for him but was thankful for a star like Zoravar to have had faith in him. The applause had been resounding, and Zoravar had clapped with such feigned enthusiasm he was worried for a second that the pretence would show through. He could not believe that someone else won an award for something that was his, for something that had eluded him for so long. It was the ultimate twist of fate.

2

Zohra and Zehra both got married, and the former moved to Texas with her engineer husband. Zehra moved to a remote part of the British countryside. Zoravar bore all the expenses for the weddings, and Zehra drove out of the mansion during the bidaai in a Mercedes car, which had to be sent by ship to Great Britain. His youngest brother, Amandeep, was gearing up for a career in the movies. Zoravar took his opinions seriously, and his prediction of how most pictures would turn out was bang on. He asked Amandeep one evening,

'Would you be interested in directing a picture?' Amandeep replied on cue, as if he had been waiting for a long time for the question to be asked. 'My script is almost ready. It is about a blind man who falls in love with a handicapped girl,' he said.

Bir was narrated the idea and agreed to do the picture. This time, Zoravar had decided to keep the costs low. A small shooting schedule began in a humble set that was erected in Rajkamal Studio, and the first all-colour film to be produced by Apsara Talkies was in motion. The film had ironically been titled *Rang*. Zoravar had only scheduled thirty days to finish the picture. He had ordered Amandeep to complete the film in the said time, and there would not be a single penny more for him than already budgeted for.

On the twenty-fifth day of the shooting schedule, Zoravar came home to a party that was being held in the garden of his bungalow. Amandeep had finished the film ahead of schedule and with lesser money than was allotted to him.

As 1967, the first year of India under its first woman Prime Minister, Indira Gandhi, was coming to an end, Zoravar had a look at the numbers of the highest-grossing pictures of the year. At the prime position was his own film, *Jung*, and the other nine films that followed starred Dharmendra, Manoj Kumar or Sunil Dutt. He found himself in a precarious situation. He wondered if the era of Dev Anand, Raj Kapoor and Dilip Kumar was coming to a close. He was technically not from their generation as they were his seniors, and the likes of Sunil Dutt, Rajendra Kumar and Dharmendra were his juniors, as they had made their debuts after he was already an established movie star. He did not know whether to count himself in the ranks of stars whose time was up or whose time was coming. He was almost as big a draw as the older stars, and perception wise, he was still far more established than the newer lot.

When Zoravar watched *Rang*, the third film produced under the banner of Apsara Talkies, in the mini-theatre he had built for himself and his family in the garage of his bungalow, he was unable to stop the tears from streaming down his face. Not only had Amandeep shown great sensitivity as a director in handling the emotions of the film's characters, he had also made a visually stunning picture despite the low budget. Even Bir had seemed bearable in the picture. He hugged Amandeep after the film ended. 'This is a picture I am going to be very proud of, regardless of whether it does well at the box office or not. Even Mother would be very proud,' he said to his youngest brother.

'What does "regardless of whether it does well at the box office or not" mean?' Aman asked, mocking his elder brother by doing an exaggerated mimicry of that baritone.

'What I mean is that it's a bit of an arthouse film. It is great, of course, but will people in smaller centres get it?' Zoravar explained.

When the picture opened, all it managed was a single matinee show in the bigger theatres. The poster had proudly proclaimed 'Zoravar Presents' and the font was bigger and bolder than the title of the picture itself. When the reviews came out on Sunday, they were the best any film associated with Zoravar had ever received. They called *Rang* a 'cinematic masterpiece', and some said that the 1960s were indeed turning out to be the best decade in India's movie history. Even new directors such as Raj Khosla and Yash Chopra had proved to be strong voices, and veterans such as Raj Kapoor continued to shine with their directorial brilliance. There were filmmakers such as K. Asif, Mehboob Khan and Kamal Amrohi who were making pictures as well. This was an unprecedented gold rush, especially when Amandeep, the debutante director, showed as much flourish and craft towards his art. The only negative comments the film had drawn were about Bir. Even people who raved about the film had ripped him apart. It did not help when a magazine printed the headline 'Why didn't Zoravar act in this picture instead?'

Thanks to great word of mouth, the film picked up, and contrary to Zoravar's opinion, it actually ran in and the so-called mass centres more than it did in urban pockets. The film raked in approximately 300 per cent of its cost, and Zoravar, who had distributed the picture thanks to nobody else showing interest in it, kept all the spoils of war that came in from the movie. Every single person involved in the project benefitted from it, except for Bir. Many in the trade felt the picture was overrated, like they always did once a film became successful, and it was the music that had actually done the trick.

Zoravar did not want to lose out on this lucky streak and immediately announced a new picture in which he would star alongside Bir, which would be directed by Amandeep. A little film called *Love In Tokyo* had released and gone on to become one of the sleeper hits of the year. It was shot in Tokyo, and an insipid screenplay had been trumped by the exotic and unseen locations onscreen. Zoravar would mount a picture under the Apsara Talkies banner now, that would be shot in the Paris. A love triangle involving two brothers, real and reel in this case, set against the backdrop of the most romantic city in the world. It was mostly a rehash of his earlier films, and Amandeep had warned against it, since he believed that the tide was turning towards more sombre stories.

Zoravar gave Amandeep six times the budget of his earlier movie to make this one, and he decided he had to sign at least four more films, the money from which would come handy in bankrolling this new venture. Amandeep had turned it down, convinced it was a bad idea. After days of cajoling, he had agreed to come back on board when Zoravar told him he would be given a free hand entirely and no creative interference in any aspect of the making would be entertained.

Sathyanarayan too was back in Zoravar's life. He had made more successful pictures in Madras since *Prithviraj-Sanyutka* and wanted to try his hand at another Hindi movie. He narrated a story to Zoravar about a fictional revolutionary who is half-'Madrasi' and half- North Indian. Zoravar liked the idea and was not the least bit fazed that their last outing together had been a failure. On the first day of the shooting, Zoravar had a sudden bout of nervousness and wondered if signing the movie had been the wrong choice. Would he be able to play a Madrasi? Despite the external visage of magnetic aura and confidence that is attributed to success, most times there is a storm brewing internally. And that storm was brewing within Zoravar now. He decided to divert his attention by glancing at the newspaper – one of the rare times he did. There was an upcoming leader, a former cartoonist, Balasaheb Thackeray who was making waves and becoming immensely popular, rising up the ranks with his 'sons of the soil' stance, and Zoravar immediately decided to change the title of his film to Mitti Ke Sapoot to cash in on the fervour. The decision helped assuage some of his nervousness.

3

Zoravar was invited to attend of an All India Talent Contest that was co-organized by the guild of United Producers and India's leading film magazine, *Filmfare*. The panel of judges included G.P. Sippy, B.R. Chopra and Shakti Samanta among other prominent producers. The winner was a rather handsome young man who went by the name of Rajesh Khanna. He had beaten well over ten thousand contestants across India to win this coveted prize. Since all the major stars of the day had their own production companies, it had created a paucity of leading men for other independent producers to work with. Out of frustration, the producers had decided that they would introduce new acting talent every year, and each one of them would sign the said actor to do a film with their respective banners, thereby introducing more stars. Rajesh Khanna was signed by each and every one of the producers on the bench, and it was Chetan Anand who got to launch the boy in a film titled *Aakhri Khat*, which went on to become India's official entry to the Oscar awards.

Rajesh Khanna, who was now fondly known as Kaka, a Punjabi term of endearment, delivered ten back-to-back successes and become India's new sweetheart. There was nobody before him who had seen such frenzy. He had to stop leaving his house for his mere presence in public places created chaos. He began to frequently collaborate with Kishore Kumar and R.D. Burman, and the trio became synonymous with legendary music scores and sentimental romantic films. Kaka had dwarfed all his contemporaries and seniors alike. There had been very few instances of fans writing letters to their favourite stars in their own blood, and this became a regular thing for Kaka.

Zoravar had heard that every morning at his residence, four prominent filmmakers who wanted to schedule the rest of his day would wait for him to wake up, while their sets and crew would be on standby. He would emerge in his silk night suits and get a shave done as they discussed the scenes of the day with him. Once he had decided the time shifts for each one of the makers, he would have a leisurely bath and then show up on sets to finish his work for the day. Whisky and soirees would follow every single evening at his residence. He came from a wealthy family, so he had no real hunger for more wealth. He once told Zoravar in chaste Punjabi, 'I used to struggle in a sportscar. What can these producers give me?'

Zoravar would look at him and marvel at the comfort with which he could dictate his terms, no matter how impractical. Even after almost two decades in the business with a successful filmography, a bungalow in Napean Sea road, and having built an empire, Zoravar still felt like an outsider.

In the middle of 1970, Zoravar's elder son, Dilawar, returned after completing his education at The Lawrence School, Sanawar.

Dilawar had turned out to be a good-looking young man with a well-toned body. He had his father's height and his mother's dreamy eyes. He had grown his hair to the collar and spoke about The Beatles and Elvis, people Zoravar had absolutely no interest in or inclination towards. He spoke of Hollywood films and of that strikingly handsome actor Clint Eastwood or that rogue James Cagney. When Zoravar asked him if he had watched any Hindi films off late, he shrugged his shoulders in arrogance and walked back to his room. Zoravar's younger son Tarsem had been sent to The Doon School.

Amandeep was finally ready to direct his next film. His last outing, which had been titled *A French Evening*, had been bulldozed at the box office, prompting him to go on a rather long sabbatical. Bir had taken its failure the hardest. Poornima and he had taken to spirituality and found solace in a Guru who went by the name of Rajneesh. They started wearing Maroon robes and were so devoted to the cause that their first child, a daughter, was born in the commune and they wanted to bring her up there. Zoravar had been wary about his brother following someone he himself saw as an eccentric and strange man, but his son Dilawar had found it 'swell' for his uncle to be so 'groovy'.

With time, Zoravar's anxieties had worsened, and he was prescribed meditation, but he preferred Scotch instead. He once told Santosh, 'No great work is born from a calm mind. The most path-breaking work from the greatest artistes have come when they have been on the brink of insanity, including me. If the soul is not dishevelled, it is not going to instruct the mind to do any great work.' He had turned red from the tirade.

'Why does your work-life go well only when your personal life is going badly and vice versa? Is that a rule?' Santosh had asked, smiling fondly.

Papa ji, on the other hand, had become a former shadow of himself and kept mostly to his room, reading the Granth Sahib every day and reminiscing to his grandchildren about the days he had spent in Lahore with his beautiful wife.

Raj Kapoor finally released his long-in-the-making *Mera Naam Joker*. Zoravar was curious about the movie because Raj's son, Rishi, was going to be making his acting debut in it. If he or the picture succeeded, he could start working on a story that would also launch his good-looking son Dilawar. Like Raj, he would direct and produce the movie himself. If Rishi could make is debut at sixteen, so could Zoravar's seventeen-year-old.

Mera Naam Joker released and was immediately met with a reception that few movies in history have received. It sank like the Titanic. It had two intervals, a ton of cameos from every conceivable star you could think of, except Zoravar, who had turned down the offer. He had politely told Raj, 'I only do films when cast in the lead'.

When he saw the movie, Zoravar thought that the only good thing about it had been Rishi Kapoor. The losses from *Mera Naam Joker* had been so dire that it was being said that Raj Kapoor had sold even the last piece of clothing he had left.

Zoravar had called to comfort him, to tell him that he was there if Raj ever needed anything.

'The show must go on. And who knows about producing a disaster better than you?' Raj had said in a drunken slur before hanging up.

On the other hand, *Johnny Mera Naam,* starring Dev had become the flavour of the season. It ran for weeks. Dev had hit back at everyone who thought he did not have it left in him, by delivering the highest-grossing film of his career thus far.

Zoravar had been nominated, this time for Best Supporting Actor for *Khandaan*, and he realized that as one got older, the categories of nominations changed regardless of the screen time in the said picture. He was caught unaware and aghast when Raj Kapoor won the Best Director for *Mera Naam Joker*. He had scoffed when he had read the nomination list and seen the man's name, but him actually *winning* the award was something Zoravar had not expected. The best actor award went to Rajesh Khanna, and Zoravar went home to the whisky bottle, skipping yet another post-awards celebration bash.

Another dream that had eluded Zoravar was that of owning an entire studio. There was R.K. Studios in Chembur, there was Filmyug, Mehboob Khan owned Mehboob Studios in Bandra, Kamal Amrohi owned Kamalistan. It was high time Apsara Talkies had its own shooting floors. Zoravar had been searching for large tracts of land on which he could make this dream come true. He was invited to look at a studio in suburban Bombay. He realised that he was vising the same studio he had come to Bombay for –Firdaus Talkies, formerly owned by the Mogul of the silent era, Cawasjee.

Now, he had the choice of buying the man's dilapidated studio, save for one floor that was mostly used for the small, devotional genre and regional language films. As he explored the vast space, he thought about how much it would cost to re-do the entire thing. There were posters of some of the great silent movies such as *Shakuntala* and *Bhakta Vidur*, remnants of the reason he was in the business today. These were some of the earliest pictures India had ever produced. *What a joy that must been, and what a legacy to leave behind,* Zoravar thought as he walked the corridors of the place.

Though Zoravar had the feeling that even the mildest of wind would cause the structure to collapse, he made up his mind to make them an offer. He would take the loan he needed, even mortgage his wife's jewellery, if it meant getting the property. It was time to be studio head, and what was better than owning the first movie studio that was ever built.

'How much is this place going to cost, Desai?' he asked the estate agent.

'The owners want to sell, but only if the price is right,' the man said self-importantly.

Zoravar leaned against a grimy wall. 'If the price is right, you can get a man to move out of his ancestral home before he has even had his morning tea. This is my lifelong dream we are talking about. Stop f****** around and get me the damn place,' he barked.

As he turned around and began walking out of the studio, a familiar scent hit his nostrils. A scent that reminded him of the old days. Off late, Zoravar had taken to reminiscing about his past life, the one he never spoke about. Pasha was the only other person who knew everything, but even the two of them never spoke about the old days.

Just as he turned a corner, he saw her in front of him, for the second time in his life. She was dressed as an ethereal goddess. The oval face, the aquiline nose and those large almond-shaped eyes, none of it hidden despite the loud face paint and the long red tikka that was streaked across her forehead.

She looked at him, her eyes widening in recognition. He had the same scar, and he had aged gracefully. He looked even more handsome now, if that was possible. As a gust of wind rattled a nearby window, Zoravar was transported to the days he had never spoken about for a long, long time. To that evening when a woman had made love to him for the first time.

Naseema! The spy and the prostitute. What was she doing in the middle of a movie studio in Bombay, dressed like an Indian goddess?

The temple was being guarded as hordes of people from the village wanted to kill the woman sheltered inside. She was, after all, a grave sinner, and women who have sold their bodies for a living do not belong in the temple. When the patriarch of the village, a moustachioed Sarpanch, broke open the temple and was about to stab the woman inside, the idol of Amba Maata miraculously came to life to protect the woman. The Maata then slayed the Sarpanch and stood atop him with her trident firmly stuck inside his chest, as she gave the villagers a sermon about how it was a cardinal sin to judge women, and that all women were a form of the very idols they prayed to.

The villagers embraced the crying woman with open arms and took her back into the village.

When the director said, 'Cut and pack up!' it was time to go home. The unit of the tiny regional film crew that was shooting the devotional picture had been overawed to have such a gigantic movie star in their midst. Zoravar noticed how everything on the set was of lower quality, from the costumes to the food that was being served.

Naseema, who was playing the reel life version of the goddess, travelled back with Zoravar in his White Mercedes Benz. He was now smoking 555 State Express cigarettes, finally finding a premium brand he could make peace with.

She told him everything. How she had fled from the desert on a horse she'd stolen; how her uncle had sold her to the brothel; and how the Intelligence Bureau had their own nexus with the madam of the house. She had been asked to be their informant and spy with the promise of freedom in return. She had then escaped, and tried to find respectable work, and when she had failedto do so, she went on to become a tawaif, in one of the kothas of Lucknow. It was there that she had become the muse of a major playwright, who then made her his mistress. He was an eccentric megalomaniac but tarried with some writers who were writing plays in Bombay.

She had somehow managed to escape his clutches and flee to Bombay with the help of a friend of his, who had helped her get her work in minor roles on the stage circuit. Because she danced well, some assistant director noticed her and gave her a break as a background dancer in small films, and she got by financially. She wanted to become an actress, but she was in her late-thirties, no age for an actress, and she had resorted to playing supporting roles in regional and low-budget pictures. She told him about how she'd seen his face on the posters of his movies and admitted that she often watched them. Zoravar marvelled at her story, and somehow, his own struggles seemed to pale in front of hers.

'Fate is the only reason I am where I am, and you are where you are,' he said to her.

'Being a man is the reason you are where you. Women do not have that luxury, in this business or otherwise!' she replied.

He dropped her to her tiny home in a poor part of Bandra, and took down the number of the landlord, the only person with a telephone in the entire colony. He promised to ring her up. And he did.

4

It was not a secret anymore. They had initially met in clandestine hotel rooms on the outskirts of Bombay. But the tabloids had caught on. Was Zoravar really having a serious affair outside of his marriage?

At home, things remain unchanged, although he noticed that Santosh barely spoke to him nowadays. Before this, the topic of his infidelities had never come up. She had turned a blind eye to all the rumours, despite the way his heroines looked at him when they came home to dinner. Thus far, he too had behaved like he had been faithful to her all this time. Now, Zoravar was recommending Naseema to almost every producer and director he met. He even got her cast opposite him as the lead actress. He paid tabloid writers to spread rumours about how Naseema was charging more money than actresses senior to her, in the bid to up her stock. He even set up a film offer for her, which he then made her turn down. 'Those who can be seen saying no have more value in this business,' he told her.

The movie she turned down would not be a loss for her anyway. It was opposite a lanky actor who had featured in far too many flops by now, and clearly had no future in cinema. Zoravar spread the word that Naseema was a doyen from regional theatre and created a perception around her of a veteran actress who could trump everybody.

'Are you ashamed that I was a whore?' she asked him once. He had looked at her confidently. 'We are all whores. Aren't we all?'

Zoravar had got the shooting location of the picture starring Naseema and him shifted to Ooty, to take the tabloid heat off. Staying away from Santosh would be better at this point too. He did not want to be spending the day with Naseema and then going back home to Santosh. A hotel always made it less personal.

But the truth was, it was personal. He loved every single thing about Naseema, and the whole thing was about much more than just physical attraction. He could not get over the tiniest expressions she made when she spoke. He could not get over the way her hair curled and rested on her forehead. He could not get over her slender fingers and those long nails which often caressed his bare back. He could not get over those tiny ears. He felt for her in a way he had for no other woman before.

The truth was, he had fallen in love with Naseema all over again. He wanted to be with her for the rest of his life, and Santosh knew it. 'A woman always knows,' she told Zoravar.

This entire situation was taking a toll on her and pushed her even deeper into her faith. She started attending church almost every day.

He should have cared more, but the only feeling he had towards Santosh now was guilt.

Moving out of the house had been a hard thing to do. Papa ji had made it very clear that Santosh would continue to live in the house. It was Zoravar who would have to move out.

Zoravar had held Santosh's hand for a long time before leaving the house, and the two of them did not exchange a word. Tears rolled down his face, but she refused to show any emotion. She had promised herself she would not cry. It was not worth it. Even when he got up to say goodbye, she had maintained her stoic face and not given away anything. As Zoravar walked out, the last thing he saw was the gleam of the cross she wore around her neck.

He told himself that at least he had managed to maintained a healthy relationship with his son Dilawar, who was now a handsome and strapping lad, towering even above Zoravar. He was training to be an actor, and Amandeep was constantly mentoring him. Together, they were even thinking about radical ideas for the film that would launch him, especially because of the freshness that Raj Kapoor's *Bobby*, starring his son Rishi and a new superstar Dimple Kapadia, had brought to the business. The movie had been a gamechanger, and the genre was a fresh start in Hindi films.

Zoravar had bought a large terrace flat in Bandra, near the sea, in Naseema's name. They had had a court wedding, with only Pasha and Parwaan there to act as signatories. Even Makkhan had apologized and refused to attend.

5

The spectacle frames were so big that they almost covered his entire face. And the fair politician with a heavy accent hated giving speeches. He preferred doing work rather than talking about it, but he had been advised to 'always show himself to the masses; connect with them'. He was aware of how his critics made fun of his speech pattern and shrill voice. Hindi was not even his first language.

It had been barely a few days since his mother had declared emergency in the country, and despite their machinery doing everything to squash it, the backlash had been severe. His friend and aide had set up a meeting with Zoravar. 'Get film stars on your side. If they support the emergency, the nation will too.' Zoravar had flown from Bombay to meet him. That he looked even better in person than he did on screen were the politician's first thoughts when they met.

'Hi,' Zoravar said as they shook hands. 'Sorry, but I have to fly back in the evening itself. It is a particularly busy time for me. Too much work,' he added and smiled.

The other man re-adjusted his dark frames. 'And they say the country is going to the dogs.'

Both men laughed at the rancid joke. 'Well it would be of great help if you could say some good things about our government,' the politician said.

Zoravar was genuinely amused. 'And why do you think it will help? I have stayed away from politics my entire life. I know nothing about it.'

'Well, zero is a good number to begin with.' The politician and his cronies laughed again.

'The only brush I have ever had with politics was when I visited Russia as a part of a delegation,' said Zoravar.

'Oh! Those Commies! I don't trust them.'

The man once again readjusted his spectacles. 'Speak with our men in Bombay, whoever you are comfortable with – maybe that writer, if you want. And I think when we go into polls' – he corrected himself – '*if* we go into polls, at some point in the near future, I can get you a ticket to fight for the elections for the party. You are half-Muslim, you are also married to one. It will help bolster our image. It is a myth that we are anti-minority.' He paused. 'The nasbandi drive,' he said in a Western accent, 'is not targeted towards a single community. It is for everybody. Including him,' he pointed to an old pot-bellied kurta-clad man, who laughed at the joke. His cronies followed.

Zoravar feigned miled. 'As far as my religion is concerned, I am just a drunk, who happens to be an actor,' said.

Zoravar had reached out to and requested the master director Raj Khosla to meet him. Known for creating iconic characters and making stylized, path breaking pictures, a film with him could rejuvenate Zoravar's image. The two had been drinking at the Flora restaurant on Worli Seaface for the better part of the evening, when a younger man, joined them. He wore big glasses and was simply introduced to Zoravar as Khosla's protègè. Khosla had been basking in the success of his latest picture, Prem Kahani. It starred Rajesh Khanna, Mumtaz, Shashi Kapoor and Vinod Khanna. Khosla said 'After Kuchhe Dhaage and Mera Gaon Mera Desh which gets so much love and respect for its feared dacoit villain, Jabbar Singh, it is time to create another iconic character.'

Zoravar swirled the ice in his Johnny Red. 'So, what do you have in mind?'

'Well, I want to make a film that is fictional yet real with an anti hero at the core. There was a feared dacoit once, someone the British had gone nuts after. His name was Sultana. I want to adapt his life-story for the screen. You could play him, Zoravar. Have you ever heard of him?'

When he had come home in his usual drunken stupor that evening, he found Naseema writing a letter. Early on in their relationship, she had mentioned something about a son born out of wedlock from her time as the mistress of the playwright she had fled from. Her son had been sent away for education to a school at a hill station, and his father had refused to give up his custody despite refusing to give him his name. Naseema rarely mentioned her only child, and Zoravar never asked. He thought of his own son Dilawar, who had also received his education from a school in a hill station! Dilawar often came to visit his father at the new house but maintained an ice-cold stance towards Naseema, who despite her best efforts could not get Zoravar's first- born to warm up to her. Zoravar informed Naseema, slurring, about how he had been offered to play the role of Sultana and her face had turned ashen.

'You know what,' he lisped as he made another stiff drink, 'I think I am going to accept the offer. It will be a big-budget extravaganza, and who will be more adept at playing Sultana than me?' Naseema disagreed completely but knew better than to argue with her husband, especially when he was under the influence. She resolved to find another way to talk him out of it. She did not need him to be visiting the darkest places of his life ever again. Not when everything was going as blissfully as it could.

On India's 28th Independence Day in 1975, Ramesh Sippy's *Sholay*, starring Dharmendra and Hema Malini, Sanjeev Kumar, Amitabh Bachchan and Jaya Badhuri, had released. The critics panned the film, but the morning release reports from all the screenings confirmed that the film was all set to go a long way.

Zoravar was to speak at a rally and publicly announce his support for the Emergency. He was using a flag hoisting ceremony as a ruse and had invited lots of people from the press. He had heard that Dev Anand was in talks to launch his own political party as well, as he fiercely criticized the Emergency, and there were murmurs that his films were going to be banned by the government.

Zoravar did not possess a single political bone in his body. He missed Santosh and was sure she would have guided him well, but he had made his choice. When he shared his ambitions with Naseema, she had been appalled at the very idea.

'If I get a ticket just by supporting the emergency, what is the harm in it? My hair is dyed; even my chest hair is dyed. I am not getting any younger, and it is a matter of time before Dilawar becomes the leading man. This is a great way for me to continue being in the limelight,' he had said to her defensively.

He had even convinced himself that the emergency had been the best thing to happen to India since Independence. He was to give his first speech supporting the emergency in the Muslim-dominated neighbourhood of Bombay Central.

Haji Parwaan and Pasha had been his go-to guys to bolster crowd support. They didn't care about the politics, as much as wanting to impress their movie star friend. And getting crowds for them took far less than threatening, considering they practically, albeit unofficially, ran the entire area thanks to their nefarious operations that had now grown in leaps and bounds. People in large numbers turned up at the rally, and the journalists present were speculating as to what this was going to be about. Zoravar stood at the podium, wearing a Nehru jacket that he had specially got stitched from Akbar at Kachins. He adjusted his dark shades and turned to smile at Naseema, who was sitting behind him. He had just begun speaking when the first bullet hit his chest. The second bullet came at him immediately after and punctured his stomach. Zoravar fell on his knees, and blood spurted from his mouth. As he slumped down, he heard Naseema scream. Visuals from different stages of his life started playing in his mind, like a showreel from a rickety projector. He was wondering if he had died – or was his mind playing tricks? From the corner of his eye, he saw a man in a police uniform. He wasn't sure if he was hallucinating, and he fought hard to retain consciousness. Finally, he saw the face of the devil, one he would never forget. What on earth was Brij Bhushan Rai doing at Zoravar's first political rally? Or was his mind making him encounter his greatest fear? He turned behind to call for Naseema, but no words came out from his mouth.

And then for the fourth time in his life, everything went black, and this time, Zoravar feared it would be the last.

TO BE CONTINUED …
IN
BOLLYWOOD SAGA #2

Author's Note

As far back as I can remember, I have loved the movies. Most of what I know about historical events, philosophy, the arts or even human emotions, has come from an insatiable appetite for movies. Maybe it was the fact that I was a single child in a generation where the concept was a bit rare. I turned to stories as my companions from a very early age. Almost everybody who knows me, knows about my obsession with the movies and how my life centres around them, and that nothing, frankly, is dearer to me, and getting an opportunity to work in the film industry and make a career in it has been a dream come true.

So, when the incredible team at HarperCollins India gave me a chance to work on a series of novels steeped in the history of the Hindi film industry, with a fictional superstar at its core, it was my chance to bring to life all that I had heard and learnt and knew about the industry. I have spent hours with other film trivia buffs, mulling over what Dev Anand would have been like off camera, or how Dilip Kumar would have stubbed his cigarette, or what Suraiya would do when at home, and a lot of those bits in the book have been borne out of conversations with film historians and artistes from the Golden era of Hindi movies.

A lot of what is in this novel is fiction, but some real incidents and moments serve as a backdrop to bring an entertaining experience to the readers. Some of those details have been tweaked for dramatic purposes and I hope that this liberty I've taken will be forgiven. This is a love letter to the movies from its biggest fanboy, and there is nothing but worship and romance within me for the real matinee gods and geniuses mentioned in the story.

The movie theatre is my temple, and it has been cathartic to bring alive the glories of Hindi cinema through this book.

I hope that it brings its readers as much joy as it has brought me, and allows them, as it has me, to relive the incredible and awe-inspiring moments that have been associated with one of our greatest national obsession – The Movies.

Maharsh Shah
Mumbai, November 2020

Acknowledgements

It is not true, what they say about writing being an utterly lonely job. Saying that takes away the credit from the people who help shape the novel and give it its final form. I have immense gratitude towards Arcopol Chaudhuri of HarperCollins India, who introduced me to the world of publishing. You don't have to know him well enough to know that he has a kind heart, and that must count as a superpower, considering the times we live in. I have to also thank my friend Chirag Nihalani, who egged me on to focus on this idea and was the first person in the world to show faith in the concept and instil confidence in me to write it, because he felt it had immense potential. I must also thank every single member of HarperCollins India who helped make this book happen – Ananth Padmanabhan, Diya Kar, Rahul Dixit,

Akriti Tyagi, Shabnam Srivastava, Bonita Shimray, Amit Malhotra and the man behind the cover artwork, Wasim Helal. As a commissioning executive on the studio side, I know how often storytellers forget about the immense contribution we actually make to their material. So big kudos, guys! And keep up the good show! I have to thank my wife, Sneha, who lived through my erratic mood swings over months of writing and patiently looked after our new-born daughter, Ira, never once asking me to compromise on my sleep or writing, while I continued to write late into the night after an agonizingly long day making movies. If not for her constant coaxing and encouragement, I would have procrastinated the writing of this novel by another decade or so.

Lastly and most majorly, I have to thank a person I had never met before in my life: Swati Daftuar, Senior Commissioning Editor at HarperCollins India and the sole reason this novel exists in its current form. I am using an empirical cliché here (Zadie Smith's term), but it is true, and clichés used well always work! William Faulkner said, 'Get it down. Take chances. It may be bad, but it's the only way you can do anything really good.'

Swati took a chance on a new writer with no formal background in writing fiction whatsoever. She has shaped what was a long, torrid, incoherent ramble of an initial draft into the edible version that you now hold in your hand. Swati has to be particularly thanked for not giving up on me especially during the painstaking edits and for the immensely valuable suggestions that have only helped create a novelist out of a novice. I think she is the best editor a writer can ask for. This novel is as much hers, as mine, if not more.

I am a geek and a fanboy before I am anything else. I have helped other people tell their stories and been in awe of the multitudes of the storytellers I have devoured. It is the reader that makes a storyteller a writer, and that's why this final 'thank you' is a huge shoutout to the reader. I guess if you made it till here, you survived the book and hopefully liked it. After having read so many books by other writers, finally, somebody read mine. There is nothing that gives me more happiness than that, and I am secretly jumping up and down in glee. And for that, I bow to you.

About the Author

Maharsh Shah was born in 1984 (ironically, a year considered to be the best ever at the cinemas) and has worked extensively with major movie studios as part of their creative development and commissioning teams. He has been involved in the development and production of various mainstream Hindi feature films, apart from writing columns about pop culture and movie trivia in leading newspapers. He lives and works in Mumbai but would prefer to migrate to the hills and run a tavern-cum-bookstore instead.

This is his first novel.

He can be reached via Twitter: @maharshs